ORANGE GLORY
The Zoomins Must Die

John Klawitter

ORANGE GLORY
The Zoomins Must Die

DOUBE DRAGON

A DOUBLE DRAGON PAPERBACK

ISBN 978-1-78695-591-3

Double Dragon is an imprint of
Fiction4All

This Edition Published 2021
Fiction4All
www.fiction4all.com

CHAPTER ONE

The late 1950's and some years later

Jesus is talking again. "Pull the trigger, Kate," he says in that softly persuasive way of his. "Pull the trigger."

Kate is out of options. She is over two months pregnant, courtesy of her grandmother, more precisely, thanks to Grandma Lulubird Twillinger's crusty old lover, and now she has been held down and sexually assaulted again, this time by a brutal biker gang. The common opinion in those parts may be *the bitch should be used to it by now*, but the truth is, she isn't.

The work shed spins around her. She has lost too much blood. She staggers back against the big, red-painted gas tank. Granma Lu's crew uses it to fill the tractors and the orange tree picker-crane. Kate doesn't have the strength to crawl into town for help. And yes, Jesus, the man-the myth-the legend, is still standing right there. He is watching over her with his warmly encouraging smile and flowing robes, for all the good that does anybody. *He cannot possibly mean actually pull the trigger, can he? What, shoot herself? What trigger?*

But there is no gun. Then what does he mean? She puzzles it out. decides that the crazy fool Savior probably means do something, anything. She grimaces and pushes back against her pain. She picks up an empty beer bottle from the floor, and then another. She carefully fills them halfway with gasoline, wads dirty rags in the top. She gives each one a little shake, The cold liquid stings her fingers. The pickers store plenty of matches in the bathroom. Fuck Jesu Christi, she's going to have to do this one by herself, just like always.

Charley Birch touched the cute little blond girl's nose with the tip of his Rambo knife. He told himself he was not torturing her or anything like that; it was just to get a reaction. There was no response, of course, and he dutifully scribbled *No Reaction* on his note pad. No answer was an answer. It just was not the one he wanted. His mind was swarming with questions. He felt like a dull dunce in fifth grade. The girl had extraordinary pale skin and blue eyes. She was a porcelain doll, not really a human, at least not to him. Nothing made sense. The experiments were failures, all of them. Little dollie here was just one more example. Kill them all, the directive said, and he finally had to admit they were right. But if there was a way to kill them, he had yet to find it. The millisecond any of them realized they were in danger they went *thin* like this one. It wasn't right or precise, but thin was the only way he could describe it.

In a sudden fit of exasperation he jammed the Rambo blade through her left eye. It easily slid in and exited from the back of her skull, shiny steel appearing abruptly between her golden hair. But there was no reaction, no death-jerk, and no blood. And when he pulled the knife out, her skin moved back to its unwounded wholeness like water in a pond. The girl was there, right there in her flesh in front of him, silent as a statue. He could see her, feel her, stab her. And yet she wasn't there. The only way to explain it made no sense: Little dollie was half way in their dimension and half way somewhere else.

"I am in deep shit here," Charley muttered. He was talking to himself a lot these days. "I don't know how deep, but it is most certainly shit all the way."

Standing to one side, a man in military fatigues shifted uneasily. Charley knew it had nothing to do with the girl, who was simply test subject #7641f, the 'f' standing for female. The fellow was recruited from Argentina, an ex-German technician who could be trusted, in fact was trusted with a Z clearance. That was the one that meant if you even look funny at us, we kill you. It was lunch time, and the fellow was hungry.

"Send her to the island," Charley said. He gave a brief nod at the motionless blond doll. "Get her started on her way. Then you can head for the mess."

Charley made his own way past the enlisted men's mess hall to the executive's dining room. The food was marginally better, and they piped in music. Ike's man showed up for lunch as planned, eager to know where all their money was going. He wore a baggy blue suit and a pair of the thick tortoise shell plastic rim glasses, a bookish look that was the rage in DC because it hinted at intellectual pursuits, *here's a man who wore out his eyes reading weighty tomes.* Charley wrapped an arm around the man's thin shoulders and led him into the project projection room, where the unit cook had laid out a feast of ham-and-cheese sandwiches with crunchy pickles, a basket bicycled over from the local deli.

They sat on uncomfortable metal chairs pulled up to a folding metal table. Charley snapped his fingers and a young fellow wearing a short crew cut, summer fatigues and the rank of a corporal clicked the lights off and started a short silent film. It was crude black-and-white 35 millimeter footage. The projector clacked and an image of a heavily bearded man appeared on the screen. He was wearing nothing but a pair of white army white briefs and he]was standing motionless as a statue. They had other footage of women, young boys and cute little girls, but Charley had thought this out carefully. *Better to stay on point.*

"That a real person?" Ike's man asked with a note of disbelief. "That's a manikin, right?"

"No. That is a real person."

"He isn't moving."

"That's test subject #3228. They're all like that when they get in their state."

"What state is that?"

"Like that," Charley said, pointing at the screen. He did not want to have to say he didn't know.

The footage pulled back to reveal two soldiers with M-1 rifles. They pointed the rifles at the fellow wearing the white shorts. Ike's man gasped, but before he could protest, the soldiers fired point blank at the man.

"NO!" But nothing happened. Ike's man blew out a breath of relief. "Looks like they missed."

"No, they didn't miss," Charley said. "Watch now. We had a Mitchell Hi-Speed running at the same time.

The next footage was a close-up of the man's abdomen. The frame just showed the top of the white briefs he was wearing. Two bullets moved in slow motion toward fragile skin. They penetrated the man's body. The flesh made way and closed up behind the smoking projectiles like pale peach jello, a moment later making their exit from his back.

"What the hell just happened there?"

"Nothing. Bullets can't kill them. Or grenades. Or bayonets."

"In-CRED-ible! Our dream of the unstoppable warrior! The President must see this!"

Under ordinary circumstances, the reaction would have delighted Charley, but had other problems.

"I don't think we're ready for that.

"What?! This is fabulous! We've got Vietnam, Laos and Cambodia ready to tumble like dominos, and the Chi Coms have a million soldiers ready to take over the Philippines…and after that Hawaii and next thing you know, the California Coast."

"I know the urgency."

"Well then, what's the problem here?"

"We don't know exactly how this works…"

Charley let his words trail off into silence. He did not how to get past the fact that nobody on the project could explain what was happening – the test subjects had other characteristics that made them anything but ideal soldiers. If they did not want to do anything, they simply ignored the command. Give them a direct order they did not want to follow and they turned dumb as rocks. You could yell, curse, whip them, and the reaction was all the same.

Someone other than this bureaucratic pencil-pusher from DC might have been alerted by Charley's response. But Ike's man was an appointee, not a man of science.

"Nonsense! We've made our big breakthrough!"

Charley nodded, going along with the flow. *Feed the fool his treats, take the funding and run with it.* Maybe they could fix things, claw their way out of the shit pit. He ran the footage again.

"I call them 'zoomins' I don't think we can really look at them as ordinary human people any more. They look like humans, but they really are something else."

"And nobody can kill them?"

Charley nodded. He stared at the ice cubes floating in his tea glass.

"They are nearly impossible to kill. We hope to get one or two in at Ground Zero out in Nevada, but I'm pretty sure even that won't affect them."

Ike's man proved to be smarter than he looked.

"*Nearly* impossible?"

"Well…a couple of them have died. We're researching that."

Actually, *hundreds* of zoomins had gone missing, but their disappearances were random. And, as none of them had shown up, it was assumed they were dead.

"You're not sure why?"

"That's right," Charley said. "We're not sure why."

Of the eight thousand and some few hundred unsuspecting subjects from all over the world who had been quietly culled from the herd and folded into the project, only a few hundred had survived. Of these, several dozen were physically and mentally warped into something vaguely prehistoric. Ninety percent of the rest were like the blond dolly girl and the man in the white shorts, unkillable but also unreachable. It was as if they were floating in a dreamlike state in never-never land. They were no longer of this world, not in this dimension, not really.

"Regardless, your progress is outstanding! The Russians are outclassing us in the Cold War. We need this! How soon can we arrange a meeting with the White House?"

"Well, let's go to my office and look over the calendar."

They set up a firm date, and Charley would have had to do a big dog-and-pony show but the thin man in the baggy blue suit and the tortoise shell glasses's was driving his rented two-tone DeSoto sedan to the Orlando airport when it was struck by a garbage truck.

The name zoomins stuck. But in the years that followed Charley's meetings with the string of new men Ike sent to replace the thin man, the project had not figured out what made their remaining subjects tick.

Among the many unknowns they displayed was the real reason Charley called them Zoomins. He named them that because they had the ability to move with lightning speed. One moment a subject would be right there, standing in front of him, and then they would zoom out of sight, and then reappear somewhere else in the room, that is, if they chose to show up at all. Nobody could figure out how they did it. And it was a special ability the zoomins themselves were not able to control. *If they ever did gain mastery over that particular talent, look out!*

As costs mounted and there was no progress, enthusiasm dwindled. The goal of creating a team of super warriors was as far away as ever, and the people in Washington decided to cut their losses. After that, the project objectives transitioned to cleanup and containment. An ongoing attempt was made to capture the subjects and detain them on a remote island off the coast of California. As his punishment, Charley was put more or less in charge, in a position of responsibility-without-authority. Years passed and yet the few remaining zoomins were as difficult to corral as a herd of scorpions.

One of their most promising subjects, a young teenager named Kate Twillinger, was being triangulated for elimination. She was special to Charley, for he believed her to be a relative. He had no affection for the girl, just the vague irritation there was yet one more loose end to tie up. And this one was a more slippery knot than most. Charley had more experience than anyone left on the project, and he was absolutely certain they would not be able to *take her out*.

This was in late August, pushing toward September. Their mission was to drive to rural Central Florida, to the sleepy village named Orange Glory. Yes, Orange Glory, where the project had originally gotten its name.

It was rural country village, dozens of miles from the ocean one way and from the gulf the other, and isolated from Orlando by patches of suburban development that thinned away to miles of flat farmlands, citrus orchards and undeveloped low swamplands.

Avoiding the highways, they chugged along back roads in one of the project's troop carriers disguised as a garbage truck. Morning moved on to become a sultry afternoon. As they approached Orange Glory, moody nature warned of their approach; an uneasy silence settled over the town like a bad memory. Birds and the usual scatter of small wildlife slipped into quiet hiding. The sky overhead was a hypnotizing deep blue. A bank of towering white clouds hung over the southern horizon, creeping in so slowly it seemed stationary as a faraway snow-crested mountain.

At the local general store, a rusty dial on the paint-flaked red Coca-Cola barometer plummeted unnoticed into the red zone. Buck Owens wailed *The sun's gonna shine in my life once more*. An Orlando disk jockey interrupted with a static-impeded report warning of heavy rain moving up from the Keys. Oh yes, hurricane weather, but this was Florida and it was, after all, *the season of the wet*, so nobody was paying any real attention.

At this time the old Twillinger home still stood, having endured for decades in the harsh tropical climate. It was set down square in the middle of Twill Grove, the generations-old family owned orange grove. The original settler, Great-Great-Grandaddy Eban Twillinger had chased off the devil-thieving itinerant Seminoles who were camping on his property and had personally planted the first little citrus saplings he'd stolen from a local Catholic priest's property after the holy padre died of old age or something else. Eban's first wife used to bring baskets of food to the wandering redskins, but, after the devils stole the wife and his first-born daughter and sold them as white whores in the Caribbean slave trade, his practice became *get out Ol' Betsy and shoot on sight,* although his attitude righted itself considerably when his new wife turned out to be a whole lot softer and more cuddly than the old one.

A tattered ghost of forgotten dreams, this house itself had been built in the 1880's by Eban's son, Great-Granddaddy Hubber Twillinger. Those were the flush days as Hubber sold off about two square miles of property, including the entire present day town of Orange Glory. Daddy Eban had got there first, not counting the devil-thief Indian savages, so of course all of it was his by right. The home Hubber built was splendid for its time and place, but the years and the humid, buggy climate had worn it down some considerable. By the time the project had scheduled Kate for elimination, it was a shabby two story, paint-peeling, broken-lace Victorian octogenarian, as out of place in that rural area of shacks and trailers as an aging church chapel in honkytonk pork town city.

Worse, the old homestead house suffered the indignity of a brace of what the locals referred to as *them damn gov'ment 'lectrical intrusions.* These wires draped uncomfortably close over the front porch. The encroachment of the electrical wires was an old story, though it had not spread beyond local legend, and that for reasons as vague and undecipherable as *that damn gov'ment bid'ness.*

Back in the day, the Twillingers had fought hard that nothing of that sort should cross their property. But nobody in memory had ever won out against *gov'ment bid'ness*, so there they remained, *galdanged* heavy strings of wires on their strutting steel legs, all the way from the coal burning Itchimoli power plant, thick-buzzing interfering metal ropes that swung down low without so much as an *excuse me* before snapping on east in the general direction of Orlando.

Any hour of the night or day, the wires overhead might think to give off a brief high-pitched hum. This time when it happened, Granny Lulubird Twillinger snapped without warning. Granny Lu had been inside the summer kitchen, hunched over the old Formica topped table. She'd been busily sipping her cold coffee and digesting the obits from a two week old Sunday Sentinel. But then she jerked upright and pitched her heavy coffee mug across the room at her granddaughter Kate.

The mug-fling was unpremeditated, or it might have struck the intended target, the soft side of Kate's skull above her ear. To the original Orange Glory Project way of thinking, this would have been an absurd waste of resources, but of course it would have solved their current mission to eliminate her. The suppressed documents showed Mrs Lulubird Twillinger always had been as unpredictable as they come, not that any of that mattered once the entire adventure was tagged, bagged and burned so no trace remained of what it was, how it got out of control, or what it did to the world.

August, in the summer of 1964, about the time when the first cracks began to appear in the known universe. Few of the agency's *cogni scenti* suspected anything so astoundingly absurd might trace back to Charley's project. In those days, nobody was trying to connect the dots; nobody had any idea of the changes to come. The world was complicated enough, what with the devious communist menace, the godless love bead children, the black people's discontent and Elvis running around in full hip gyration like some lewd tight-pants clown.

It was no secret in town, either, that Granny Lu liked slapping her granddaughter around; let's just call it her own private exploration into the unknown. Granny had tried to explain her seemingly cruel behavior to her friends; her fond hope, she said, was that maybe a couple of hard knocks on the kid would bear interesting fruit of the whacko-bird tree, that is, bring out some of the witchy unpredictability that had been so much a part of her own daughter, Crazy Tillie's, unpredictable persona. Tillie was Matilda Twillinger, Granny Lu's own daughter and Kate's mother, and she had been quite mad even before she went missing with the numbers and the passwords to the Twillinger off-shore accounts locked up tight as a drum. *Where had the Twillinger genes run so amuck?* Grandma Lu swore it couldn't be her fault. *No way! Could not be!*

Other than the rock solid conviction it had to be Crazy Tillie's failure, withered and dried up old Granny Lu wasn't exactly sure why she herself was so hell-bent on smacking her granddaughter upside the head. Them damn *gov'ment wires* would get to buzzing overhead and the old lady find herself at the end of her patience and the only thing to do was smack the annoying little whelp.

Maybe the truth of it was the way the old woman from time to time confessed at church prayer meetings: It was demonic pure evil Satan – or more likely, demons disguised as outer space aliens who had imprinted bad notions in her brain. *But no, that had to be just crazy talk, there warn't no such thing as aliens from outer space, was there?*

Clatching over coffee and butter rolls with her pal Berta Mae, Lu took comfort in the belief none of it was her fault.

"I dearly believe that girl expresses things normal folk do not.

"Like what, Lulubird?"

"She com-municates with the poison swamp lilys and talks with the pythons – I done seen her do it!"

Bertha Mae crossed herself over her massive bosom.

"Lord of mercy! My own sweet Mamma tol' me she once seen your daughter talkin' with the pictures in the family scrapbook like they was right there in the flesh." Her voice dropped to a whisper. "Folks in town whisper Tillie would lie down in the warm dust between the orange trees and ask a favor or two of the saints and beasts of burden."

"That shame is on my own family name."

"Now Lulubird, you know that ain't your fault. None of it."

"Well, I tell you, if I catch the little bitch in any of them odd wonderments, I'll praise the Lord for small favors."

"Why be that?"

"I catch her in perverted notions and she'll be in a brown straight jacket and a padded cell faster than she can blink."

Bertha Mae nodded sympathetically. The whole town knew that then Granny could then petition the state of Florida and hopefully find a way to unlock the family trust, until then as out of reach as the last juicers high on the tree because of Tillie's devious cunning.

Everybody in Orange Glory Junction could see it bothered Granny Lu no end that Kate was still alive, though the kid looked barely a teenager and from the drift of things was not destined for a long or fruitful life.

"Lord knows, Bertha Mae, I done my best to get rid of the problem. Twixt the two of us, I once tried to pawn the kid off to a Jamaican crop duster who claimed to was descended of the same sex slave traders who done whisked away my ancestors."

"That would have solve your problems right there."

"Yes, it would have. But that damn skinny little teen bitch slipped off into one of her secret swampy places and did not come out of hiding until the islander's rotten wing old biplane took off for Georgia."

Granny Lu wasn't about to reveal it even to her best pal, but she had once tried a little arsenic powder, left over from spraying the trees. But that day Kate said she wasn't hungry, even though she angrily warned the kinky redhead that was all she was getting to eat until come tomorrow. It was a sour experience and a sore memory. After Granny Lu realized her ploy had failed, them damn wires started buzzing overhead and she got onto a fit of temper and threw the oat meal out the back door and it killed two of her dogs who fought nearly to the death over it before it killed them.

Kate's naturally curly hair was bowl-clipped almost short as a boy's, the strawberry blond by-product of an angry semi-annual ritual, the scissors snipping like shark bites, Granny Lulubird's claw-like hands, arthritic with the plucking of countless Florida oranges, hip-hopping about the young girl's face without regard for eyes or nose, her high-pitched, rackety old voice warning, "You don't want to get mite-fleas, girly-girl!"

Kate survived through the long seasons and dangerous times by practicing invisibility. She grew alert, and clever at slipping out of range. But this time, in the afternoon of the day in late August of 1964, she was too slow, and when Granny's favored cracked ceramic mug glanced off her shoulder before it shattered against the wall, somebody had to pay.

Kate nearly made it to the back screen door before Grams lurched from her chair and caught her a good one on the side of her head with the heavy end of her knob-gnarled cane. *Not her head! Not again!*

At that moment the kitchen timer dinged, alerting Granny Lu it was nearly time to take the citrus pies out of the oven. Granny was distracted from her crazed desire to beat Kate's brains out long enough to reach for the shelf over the sink and screw another ten minutes on the timer.

Kate, lying helpless on the floor, focused on the stubby white finger on the timer. She heard the steady beat of the seconds, loud as a hammer in her ear. And then there was a pause when she seemed to blank out and she heard and saw nothing. And then – impossibly – the ticking increased and Granny's movements seemed to slow down until she was barely moving at all. This was a gift from the angels, as Granny had been moving in to deliver a killing blow. Regardless where it came from, Kate snapped to her feet and bounded out the door before her astounded grandmother could move a muscle.

"Oh no," Granny Lu moaned, settling back down at the table with her head between her hands. "That little bitch done learned to twitch like her momma."

Just as an aside, you should know that, up to that time the very heart of the Orange Glory project had demanded cranial impact to their subject's heads on as regular a basis as might be instigated, with a schedule matched as closely as possible to the electro-magnetic treatments from the power lines and the spray of particles from the big grey box that the power and light representatives had assured the local yokels were step-down transformers. *Mental transforming*, more obfuscation, you see, the truth wrapped in a convenient code word. The military, as you probably know, loves riddles and word games. But that is the other side of the story, unimportant for the moment, and, as Granny's furious outbursts had never been controllable, aside from this narrative all future military historians would have to go by might be a series of unverifiable local events and their unintended consequences.

Regardless, Kate was moving too fast for her own good. The door frame loomed up and smacked her on her left ear and she tasted blood in the back of her mouth. She darted out the rusty old screen door and skittered from the back of the house like a dizzy colt, wearing only her underwear. She thought nobody would see her. That, of course, was a mistake, but understandable in her panic, and young supra-humans are far from perfect. Due to ill-luck, fate, the predetermined course of the universe or the next spin of the cosmic prayer-wheel, the army was watching.

An army specialist with the rank of Private First Class was the first to spot her blurred image. He was the driver, little more than a low class vehicle-handler trained to get behind the steering wheel of medium-to-heavy weight trucks. He had been cleared to drive the MGT387, a ten wheeled vehicle disguised to look like a big garbage truck because it was a part of the Orange Glory project. He was short and had a round, generally blank face, bristly blond crew cut hair and the embarrassing habit of idly reaching his right hand down to readjust his balls in public.

His name was Fritz Harper, and he was promoted to driver because he had failed at every other task they gave him. They stamped a clearance code at the top of his file because if he became an embarrassment, which was likely because of his surly disposition and presumed low I.Q., it would be easier to dispose of him. As it turned out, he did screw up a lot and they did keep track of all that, but sometimes a demotion or reassignment is just easier than burn-body & bury, and, beyond that, the actual truth they were all trying to ignore was they had tried to kill him a dozen times and nothing had worked, and that, of course, meant either that their specialists were not all that accomplished or, unthinkably, Fritz was actually one of the supra-humans. This last notion was the least likely, they believed, because Fritzy-boy was so damn stupid he was one step removed from Neanderthal, while the zoomins were quietly, frighteningly superior in dozens of unexpected ways.

This couldn't have been more than a few seconds after Granny Lu had flung her coffee mug at Kate, on that muggy afternoon with the crystal blue sky and sno-cone clouds moving up from the south. Fritz, short at five foot seven with his chunky worker bee body and stiff blond buzz cut fortified with a max load of Brill Cream, was driving the militarized garbage truck through the actual swampy little backwash town in Central Florida that had given the project its name, Operation Orange Glory.

Charley Birch was there, too. Charley, who had personally fronted the project in its glory days, now saddled with the dishonor of dismantling it. He tried his best to ignore Fritz as he looked out through the grey one way glass, both of them morosely eyeing the endless groomed rows of citrus trees as they stood at attention like parade soldiers. Charley Birch, nearsighted, middle aged, balding and pot-bellied, gone to seed as he'd slipped out of the service and turned civilian in a quietly desperate attempt to escape at least some few of the consequences of his failure.

Charley picked at his McDonald's scrambled eggs and pan cakes from Orlando, now rewarmed a second time in the MGT's portable toaster oven. A third passenger was jammed in the close interior of the vehicle. General Filbert Redelak had invited himself along. He was a prissy, thin-lipped twin star from the agency. The General was clearly not impressed with any of their preparations for the subject elimination, and, after the latest bits of messy mischief involving the missing squadron of fighter planes and the unfortunate mess on board the Philadelphia Experiment, Charley was sure the General had shown up to shut him down again, only for good this time. *Jesus H. Christ, the Philadelphia Experiment! Though there were some similarities in the disastrous results, Charley had nothing to do with that, and he could prove it!*

The fourth man onboard was a sniper, a specialist named Ollie Krell. Ollie was a thin Nordic with cancerous, pockmarked yellowish skin stretched over a skull head of a face. Charley Birch had asked he come along simply to prove the point that even a top kill specialist couldn't take down a zoomin.

"How did this craziness start in the first place?" the General asked in his whispery-thin voice. He had finished his own sausage-and-eggs meal and was slurping the last of a giant Diet Lime Coke.

Charley tried to toss it off to post-war innocence, pretty much the way he always did. "Well, you know, we had the girly troopers doing the DC bars and they ran into some very interesting dudes from the USSR who didn't know how to keep their mouths shut while their trousers were down around their ankles."

But Redelak knew Charley too well to hum along with that old tune.

"Birch, quit blathering; get to the heart of it. Anybody who has read the files knows it started in Chicagoland."

The General's quiet but holier-than-thou act annoyed Charley no end. In referring to the specially designed particle accelerators in their grey metal boxes, General Redeldak thought he was cutting to the chase, but to Charley he was acting more like an accountant than an agency man. Hadn't he even read the confidential grade briefings?

"Sure, looking back it is easy to dismiss Sexual Intercept as some sort of spy game of little consequence, but what you dismiss as a rude exchange of fluids for info was once at the heart of our intelligence gathering. That was the late 1950's, not all that long ago…"

"Right, except 'heart' is the wrong organ."

"You can snigger and sneer all you want, but the information we got proved conclusively the Russians were making big progress developing superhuman intelligence."

"Right. Conclusively," the General's tone showed his disbelief. "Only somewhere along the way they lost it again."

Charley's face reddened and his tight lips betrayed his anger, "You blame me, but I had the go ahead for Orange Glory from the highest levels. Nobody can pin this on me."

"I'm not forgetting and nobody's blaming you, Mister Birch."

"They better not try."

Charley knew how hollow his words sounded, but he had no choice other than to hopelessly argue his case. "The Ruskies had been, so the story went, creating wonders through an exotic blend of chemicals, electro-magnetic brain cell warping on levels assumed to be sub-atomic, and the fairly rough physical damaging and re-healing of those cells. Charley and his defected Russian assistant had thought to do them one better with their heavy grey box accelerators.

"Comic book stuff," Redelak sniffed.

"Yes, but theoretically possible."

"You never did have more than a vague notion what you were doing."

Charley shrugged,"That's what research is."

"And you still don't to this day."

Charley went silent, turning his gaze to watch the orchards, ponds and undeveloped swamplands drift by. Truth was, the General didn't know the half of it. The bright boys had built their first particle accelerators outside the old German town of Batavia in Northern Illinois, Codeword Chicagoland, and Charley had managed to get any number of his experimental subjects into the particle showers, not in a direct line with the protons themselves – they found out soon enough that killed about 99% of them right away – but in what they calculated as an extremely narrow effective range during the mille-seconds after particle impact when the fundamental recreation of the universe was taking place. In that tiny moment of opportunity, some very strange things happened. Wonderful, terrible, exciting things. Nobody knew much about any of that, and they still didn't. Dark matter, hell – it was a dark subject, and over the next decade the Orange Glory project had blossomed like some unknown and unknowable poisonous night flower until anybody in the agency with even a half-assed clearance was aware it existed. And yet here was a tight assed know-nothing Two Star General sticking it to him, Charley Birch, like it was entirely his singular personal fault.

"Your curiosity got a little out of hand, didn't it, Mr. Birch."

That was more a judgment and a condemnation than a question, and Charley had to fight to keep a lid on his temper. *How like the army to go looking for people to stick with the blame!*

Charley felt he had to admit to a little something to keep the bigger disaster out of the discussion,

"Well, a little at some point in time, but we have been able to put things back on track."

In truth, things had gone terribly out of control, and when they had, Charley had started the first lie, that the abnormalities cropping up in his test subjects were minor aberrations and nothing they could not handle. That had probably been a mistake. They should have simply clean-slated all the Zoomins before it was too late. The good old burn-body & bury solution.

"We told you to clean up your mess, and you didn't. You defied direct orders."

"No!"

"Oh, yes, Charley Birch."

"Well, I-I did hesitate, but that was because I couldn't figure out how to get rid of them. They become not strictly human, you know that. But it starts gradual. It's a learning process."

"What do you mean?"

Charley couldn't believe it. Hadn't this fool read anything? "They get to a state where you can't simply kill them. You can't. We can't. I can't. Maybe nobody can."

"So you bottle them up and fly them off-shore where it is costing us half the national debt to contain them."

Charley shrugged, pointing to the distance where the top floor of an old Victorian house was poking its eaves over a green quilted blanket of orange trees.

"There. Right there. That's the Twillinger place."

"And there she is!" Fritz yelled with a bob of his round melon head as he took one hand off the wheel to point. In the next second he slammed on the brakes and the truck skidded to a stop.

"Gift from God!"

"Shut up, Fritz," grim faced Ollie Krell muttered as he fiddled with the scope on his rifle. Krell hadn't said anything all morning. In fact, he hadn't spoken a word for three days, some sort of offshoot Buddhist program he was working on for self-improvement.

"Kate Twillinger. Confirmed."

Charley caught a fleeting glimpse of a slim girl darting through the orange grove. He couldn't shake off his sense of foreboding. No way this could turn out well.

Ollie Krell squinted into his riflescope and shook his head. The target wavered in his vision, watery and indistinct as she moved through the foliage in the grove.

"Where? Where is she?" the General was shouting like an excited schoolboy, clearly thinking they would clear up their assignment with one quick shot.

"Right there! Running from the house!"

"But she's just a skinny teenager!"

By now Charley was beside himself, "Jesus Christ, shoot her!"

But the General was now on a new tangent. "I don't see what is so dangerous about her, Mister Birch. Are we now exterminating little girls?"

The Two Star held up one hand, indicating the grim faced shooter was to wait. That was a relief to Ollie Krell, who had unaccountably lost his target in the scope sight, something that had never happened in all his experience shooting men, women, cows and dogs in World War II and Korea.

Fritz started the truck lurching forward in low gear, barely managing to keep Kate in sight as she hurried away from the house.

Charley spoke through clenched teeth, "She-is-no-longer-human."

The General shrugged, "What's wrong with that? Monkeys and cows and dogs aren't human, either."

"She-is-better," Charley said.

"How better?"

"Beyond you and me."

"And there's something wrong with that?"

"Ask your children's children."

"What? Why?"

"They'll be her pets."

"Bullshit! She's just a little teener bitch."

Ollie Krell was disgusted, "I could have offed her a dozen times already. That's what you wanted to find out, wasn't it?"

"But you didn't," Charley said with a grim tone that implied he couldn't.

The General sighed and nodded his go ahead.

"Well, Charley-boy, let's just see what the hell you're talking about. Okay, now we're into snuffing out little girls. I've changed my mind. Go ahead, take the subject down, Specialist."

There was a slight delay, as the firing angle had changed. This forced Ollie Krell to move further back in the vehicle and crank down another small window. So it was a few more precious moments before he again had Kate swimming in his sight, but that was when Fritz unexpectedly slammed his foot on the brakes. The scope gave Krell a nasty rap near the big scar on his forehead and the GT387 skidded to an abrupt halt.

"God damn it, Fritz!" Ollie shouted, rubbing his bruised eye socket.

But the stubby little driver had already hopped out of the truck and was jogging up to a man wearing undershorts held up by red suspenders and a faded fireman's shirt. The village idiot had parked an aging fire truck in the middle of the road.

"Damn, get out of the way, you stupid backwoods hick! We got a bad batch of contaminated garbage here!"

The local man didn't seem impressed. "All garbage is contaminated, and who you calling a hick, you pumpkin headed lame-brain?"

Clearly the local wasn't impressed with Fritz, outfitted as he was in his fake garbage man uniform.

Fritz's diseased garbage ploy was so totally bogus as to be obvious, but that was what the operations manual said to do and these were dumb locals anyway, what did they know? Still, by the time Fritz got the local lame-brain scooted out of the way, Kate had disappeared.

"Shades of Nam," General Redelak muttered. "I tell you we have to kill them all."

"Except," Charley insisted, "zoomins are unkillable."

“There is no such word in my dictionary,” the General said.

“Or mine,” Krell added, but with less conviction.

“Supra-humans, then,” Charley sniped back at them. He suspected the General had conducted his war from a boardroom and had never been anywhere near Southeast Asia, “You can’t even kill one dinky little girl. How do you propose we kill them all?”

“A few of the big busters, laid on their island resort in the middle of the night. We claim it’s a big meteorite. Boo-hoo, too bad, a few dozen unknown victims turned to cinder and ashes. Problem solved.”

Fritz, who had returned from his encounter with the local fireman, took it in their conversation from his driver’s seat, but he said nothing. Yes, he’d heard rumors of bleak and barren Santa Barbella, where the agency kept their subjects. *Kill them all*, the General had said. That sounded like a direct order to Fritz, and this was an order from the top. To his way of thinking, there was no deadline on such orders. They were in effect until they were countermanded.

Charley angrily shook his head, not bothering to point out that something had yet again interfered the moment their shooter had raised his rifle to take out Kate Twillinger. Was it simply bad timing? No, no, and no. Charley was certain it was something else, though exactly what that something else was, he couldn’t even begin to imagine. Something bad, though, he was sure.

“We’re late,” the General said, eyeing his watch.

“For what? Pork sandwiches and grits?”

That caught Fritz’s attention, and he grinned, showing a mouth full of pointy yellow teeth. “I could go for some of that.”

“No,” Redelak said, idly dusting the gold stars on his left shoulder with the soft cloth towel he’d been using to clean his Ray Ban aviator sunglasses. “I’ve got meetings. You’ve had your little show, Charley, and we learned nothing. We give it up for now.”

Fritz threw a careless salute to anybody who cared and started up the truck’s big twin-diesel engines. In a half hour they had bumped their way back along the unimproved oil coated gravel roads, finally hitting an asphalt two lane and then the expressway.

The cloud bank was now towering in the near distance, the white anvil tops of thunderheads showing a violent promise; but these were grown military men and veterans of the Floridian climate, trained to ignore the unpredictable vagrancies of the weather. What was more, they had plans and important procedures to perform. They paid the clouds no mind and proceeded without undue haste until they pulled off the expressway to stop in a quite suburb north of Orlando city proper.

“You get out here,” General Redelak told Charley. He waved to an inconspicuous brick building that was set back by rolling green lawns about an eighth of a mile from iron gates. “Your new home. Don't worry; we already moved your personal belongings."

"You, too, Fritz," the kill specialist added.

"But I'm driving," Fritz protested.

"No more," the General's lips grew even thinner. "You're assigned to guard dog Mister Charley Glory-boy here."

Grim Ollie Krell screwed a silencer on his short barreled pistol as he scooted Fritz and moved over to take his place in the driver's seat. Charley waved off the show of force.

"Violence is not the answer."

"It pays the bills," Ollie shrugged.

"Come on, Fritzie," Charley said, as if he was calling a pet dog, and the stubby little corporal doubled over and jumped out of a small side door.

"Yeah, Fritzie-boy, get out," Krell added.

Fritz put an unhappy face on his round melon head, looking like he wanted to say something else, but the silencer trumped any ideas he might have been forming in that slow brain of his. He showed his disapproval by pursing his plump lips and silently made his way out the door after Charley.

Standing on the roadside, Charley Birch breathed a sigh of relief. He had been sure they were going to kill him, had been certain a bullet was coming his way ever since they figured out he was lying about that disintegrating universe business. *As if they could have come up with anything better!* And, as is always the case with really believable fraud, there was an element of truth to the entire business; because of Orange Glory, everything of reality, as current-day humanity knew it, was a bit frayed about the edges. Unless space and time settled back down, life was never going to be the same for anybody.

CHAPTER TWO

26 August 1964

This was a Thursday, the same for everybody in sunny Florida. One of those ordinary sun loving Floridians was an interesting fellow named Jimmy Jinx Warner. Jimmy was occupying the exact space his presence needed at the Opa-locka airport as he stood next to his silvery T-6 Texan looking up at the most amazing blue sky he'd ever seen. He stood there, silent as if posing for one of those War Bond Posters, a hero with a carefully clipped beard, the very replica of a legend in his stressed leather copy of a WWII flight jacket with the acrylic painting of the pin up babe on back, the sexpot waving as she rode a bomb down into Jerryland, the both of them, Jimmy Jinx and the blond bomber babe hopefully gazing into the heavens as rain spattered their faces. Rain out of a clear blue sky! That had to be some sort of sign from heaven.

Jimmy had gotten up late after a mid-week binge, having hit the old sauce a tad too hard the night before. The leading edge of a weather front had pummeled his apartment building, and, alerted by the loud drumming on his roof overhead, Jimmy had climbed into his Hillman Minx and headed out through the spattering rain to see to his aircraft.

As he drove across the airfield the wind was fluttering and dying down, even as the last rain was still moving in a heavy sheet across the tarmac. His faithful Texan looked okay, stout as ever, dripping but tied down and with the blocks tight under her wheels. No big deal and no use getting soaked over nothing. Jimmy sighed, resigned to head on back home to pour himself another bout of alcohol inspired forgetfulness. But, as luck or cosmic fate would have it, in the next minute or so, while he was still looking skyward, the clouds moved to the north and the rain came to an end. He was right under the eye of the weather disturbance weather historians would later refer to as 'the mighty unpredictable Hurricane Cleo.' It was the center of mighty Cleo, at that moment moving right over Opa-locka. The sun came out and the sky turned into an intensely beckoning blue disk high over an encircling wall of towering grey-black clouds. Just trying to imagine what it might be like up there was a glorious temptation. In no time at all, Jimmy pulled the blocks away from the wheels and had the Texan fired up and ready to go.

Jimmy Jinx Warner had always had a way with a certain type of casual lady that he might meet in hotel lounges or at those little *tiki-moderne* poolside bars featuring howling Pacific island monsters with paint stripes on their faces that in turn were carved out of giant bamboo stalks, or perhaps soft pine shaped and varnished to look like thick tropical shoots. Jimmy would smile in his warm and friendly way and with his soft drawl he would tell the ladies stories about when he had been a pilot in WWII, though not much of that was strictly true, not really. He had been a youngish carnival barnstormer in the late 1930's, selling rides in a beat up old threadbare fabric-winged

Jenny, adventures that enabled farm kids in their overhauls to cop a feel in the sky before bedding down for an innocent bout of hot and juicy sex in the haystacks back at the barn and the hard life that followed, bringing up the brats and attending the wishes of their unexpectedly altered life partners.

Truth was, during the war itself, Jimmy had hidden out from aerial combat action with a gig he stumbled into, winging dope and other contraband for a crappy little air service down in Venezuela where as luck would have it he came across a huge pile of cash in a moldy duffle bag. He hustled back to the States right after Truman dropped the bomb on Hiroshima, and his clever investments in the post-war stock market had done him right until, by 1960, he was retired and living along the Florida coast near Miami.

The Sunshine State was at that time socially unsettled; it was a crowded, swampy lowland full of alligators, squinty-faced cracker rednecks, crazed old snowbirds, enterprising Cuban refugees and the weary and wary remnants of long suffering rural Indian and black populations that for one reason or another had been unable to migrate up north. Everybody was jostling for beachfront property, a hit of white lightning or at least a tip on the fleetest mutt at the Sanford greyhound racetrack in Orlando.

Jimmy had settled in to his quiet afterlife, watched his investments bulge, sipped plenty of rum cokes and manhattans, and enjoyed a bit of recreation flying on the side. The flying was the best part of it. Back then, about once a month he would rent a Piper Cub. He felt home-free and easy when he was up in the air, and he told himself it was what made everything else bearable, though any casual observer might come to the conclusion there was not much that was undesirable in his life.

Well, there was the boredom. When everything else is going well, there is bound to be something. Once, in the late 1950's, after a particularly restless fit of doing nothing, Jimmy went to an air show where he ended up buying a T-6 Texan, a single engine little zipper that had been built to train novice pilots from all over the States to fly in Europe and the Pacific fronts. It had a cruise speed around 145 miles an hour and a ceiling something over 20,000, though Jimmy couldn't be certain about that one, the altimeter being a little on the blinkola.

He rented space for his sturdy little bird at the Opa-locka airport a few miles south of the sprouting condos and dark watering holes of Miami, and life, if not great, was at least much more entertaining than before. Jimmy took to island hopping around the Caribbean in his silvery tight-ass Texan. His favorite stop off watering holes turned out to be Bermuda, Puerto Rico and Jamaica where he knew ladies who appreciated what he had to offer in the way of trinkets and beads. An astute believer in paranormal events will recognize these locations as being in or near that vague quasi-geographic area known as the Bermuda Triangle, though this proximity may have been merely coincidental to the unusual and perhaps paranormal events that later befell Jimmy Jinks Warner.

In any event, one day toward the end of August in 1964 Jimmy was sipping a tall rum drink in his study with the Bermuda blue walls and pastel yellow ceiling while the Beatles song lyrics *It's been a hard day's night/ And I've been working like a dog* poured from his cheap tomato colored plastic radio, and that was when an announcer cut in on the thumping rock and roll with the breathless report that a tropical cyclone system named Cleo was lumbering in on Cuba, erratically but somewhat doggedly meandering up from the south. Deep in his rum-induced haze, Jimmy wondered why this should be news enough to break away from such a hot diggity song, though this particular weather disturbance was of some mild interest to him as the storm would run through his favored Jamaica, and after that its projected course had it on track to continue north directly across Cuba and on up the spine of Florida. Jimmy had dabbled in hurricane chasing a time or two, and it gave him a nice rush. He always played it safe, generally managed to stay out of real trouble, and always was left feeling refreshed from the buffet and push of the wind tossing his stout Texan about like an autumn leaf. So here was a gift from the gods, this fairly big storm slamming in from the south, and holy cow, maybe he would have a fling at it.

About this time, Jimmy was affecting a full beard that, with his curly brown hair and kind eyes, some few of his pastime ladies said reminded them of Jesus, maybe if the Savior had lived past the crucifixion and was going a little grey around the edges. This amused the Jinxter-man, as Mavis Manymoney, one of his sweet island ladies called him, and he'd taken to wearing Birkenstock sandals, without the socks, of course. He had even tried a robe a time or two for Halloween parties, a beige cotton thing he bought from a costume shop. He liked the rush of impersonating The Holy Savior almost better than smoking good ganji, it was a part he could get lost in, the gentle smile, blessing with his right hand, two fingers up, imagining he himself had mogrified the fine French merlot in his glass from water. It was a pleasure to go along with the notion he was in a passion play or moving down the aisle on Palm Sunday, playing the Original Superstar himself sitting on a donkey whilst the Lord Lovin' Jerusalem folks waved palm fronds at him. But now Jimmy Jinx was setting the joys of religious impersonation aside, for the thought of riding Texan up there into Cleo was almighty appealing.

He lost interest over the next day when the winds slowed down to 70 over Cuba. However, they did pick up again when Cleo got back out over open water, and she was an estimated Cat 2 with 110 mile per hour winds by the time she hit the Florida Keys.

And now here he was out at Opa-locka, climbing into the cockpit of his Texan, itching to get up into that intense atmospheric moment and maybe do a few loop-de-loops right in the eye of a hurricane. And then he was pulling the canopy over his head. By God, he was going to do it! The engine coughed to life, and wasn't that as if it was all a part of God's plan! There was no conversation from the control tower, but the runway was deserted, and so Jimmy Jinks Warner taxied on out there and took off into the wild blue and was never seen or heard from again. At least, not in the regular sense, the way common, ordinary humans view these things in the course of their everyday lives.

CHAPTER THREE

A bit later that same day

Outside the ancient wooden frame of the Twillinger house the late afternoon air was thick and moist as a soggy, warm blanket. Eerie St. Elmo's fire ran along the low hanging electrical wires and enveloped rows of the power company's nearby metal globes in a misty plasma of cold blue flame. The overhead wires looped low and the sullen wall of clouds now dominated the sky to the south, still snow white on top, but showing dark underbellies. The dull grey metal box attached to the wires was silent, patiently waiting for something or somebody else it might transform in its mysterious and quasi-magical way.

Kate ran along a dusty path through the family orange grove, moving easily between the familiar rows of citrus trees. When she felt she could not run any more, she plopped her rump down on the soft soil with her back against the mossy black trunk of one of the ancient orange trees. She rubbed one forearm against her bleeding temple and listened to the pounding in her chest as it slowed and her breathing came back to something like normal. The lowest branches bowed down to nearly touch the ground, and she felt protected, as if she was in her own leafy tent. *What had happened back in the kitchen? How had she escaped Granny Lu's gnarled wooden cane, upraised as it had been for the final killing blow?* She remembered the tick of the cooking timer slowing, almost as if time itself had slowed until the seconds nearly stopped. She remembered that Granny, too, had stopped her forward motion, everything slowing down so Kate could make her escape. But wait – everything in the room but Kate had slowed down! How did that work? Did she will it? Had she been able to do that?

A grey coyote approached, padding quietly closer until it poked its head under the branches to look at her. The settling sun cast a weak pallor and a restless breeze rustled through the trees.

"Dangerous stuff," the coyote said. "Timers don't last long in the neutral zone."

"I have no idea what you're talking about," Kate whispered. "Go away."

"Just trying to help." The coyote took a hesitant step back, but even as he did so he grinned. It was clear he wasn't going anywhere without another shot at whatever he was up to.

"Your mother used to talk to me."

"And Granny told the strangers and they put her away and blessed her with chemical remedies and electrical shock treatments. It is not a secret."

"Sure, don't listen to me. You are smarter than your mother."

Kate mournfully shook her head. "I wish so, but I'm not…"

Even though they spoke in hushed whispers, their conversation was interrupted by a gruff man's voice, speaking out from his own nearby tent of tree branches. "Who you talking to over there, little sister sweet treat?"

The voice came from a burly Hells Angel wearing a three day old stubble of beard. His name was Killer, and he was the leader of a swarm of bikers that mostly just drank beer and drove aimlessly around scaring the locals in Alabama, Georgia and Florida. Killer sat with his back against his own tree trunk. He was as hidden by the low hanging branches, as was Kate, with only her bare legs and his biker boots and dirty jeans short shorts sticking out into the heavy afternoon air. His leather jacket told the same gruff fable popular at the time: *Kill them all and let God sort it out*, a slogan originally from the Korean War or maybe the Peloponnesian, later to be adopted by the American veterans of the Southeast Asia scuffle.

"N-nobody," Kate told the burly fellow. "I'm just talking to myself."

The biker sighed and got to his feet. He shuffled over to her tree, awkward in his heavy Marlin Brando biker boots, and ducked his head between the branches, taking the place of the coyote, who had gone off to only God knows somewhere.

"Jesus, kid, what happened to the side of your head?"

"Grandma Lulubird smacked me."

She peered up at the man. He was in his mid-30's, scruffy, angular and tanned, and smoking a hand-rolled toke. She was not frightened or even surprised. The far end of the family orchard where the pond was located ran along the two lane blacktop and was a common hangout for hikers, bikers, Seminoles off the Big Cypress reservation and an assorted bunch of beatniks, adventurers and

Henry David Thoreau wanna-bees on the run from the varied strictures of society.

"Where is your motorbike?"

"Down by the pond. I'm Killer. Who are you?"

"Kate Twillinger. We live here. Are there any more like you?"

"Why? You gonna call the cops on us, young Miss Twillinger?"

"No. Of course not. Are they swimming in the pond?"

Killer shrugged, "I suppose. Biking around these parts this time of year is a dirty business. Bugs in your teeth and all."

Kate jumped to her feet. "They should not swim in there! We have to warn them!"

"Don't be alarmed, little lady. They ain't gonna mess it up none."

She looked from him to the distant pond, from where could be heard the distant sounds of playful thrashing around, the biker gang freshening up..

"That is not it at all! Harvey Goldfine will kill somebody!"

"Who?"

"Grandma's alligator. He is hungry enough."

"How do you know that?

"I sometimes feed him one or two of Granny's range chickens, but she is running low on birds. Blaming me for that, too…"

Your alligator is named Goldfine?"

"No time to explain. Come on!"

The biker took a last drag of his toke, reluctantly flipped it into a pile of brush and followed after Kate, more out of curiosity than any real concern. It only took a minute, but by the time they arrived at the pond the scene at the water's edge had changed from horseplay to shock and awe. A half dozen naked bikers stood around, nervously stamping their feet and staring bug-eyed at exactly nothing. The surface of the pond was dark and oily-looking. On closer inspection it could be seen to be roiling a little, something going on way down under there. A few bubbles broke the surface, then nothing more..

Kate pushed her way through the crowd of bikers until she stood at the edge of the pond. She yelled, and her voice was strangely powerful, unnatural in the way that it boomed out of such a little waif of a girl.

"Harvey! You mud-sucking bastard lizard! Let go of him right now! He-is-my-friend!"

There followed an odd, not quite normal moment. Blame it on the elements blame it on nature, blame it on acoustics, if you will. The wind was picking up, and there was a distinct mutter, a low rumble of thunder from the clouds piling in from the south and now churning overhead in a nasty grey snarl.

For a few seconds nothing happened underneath the pond water, and then there was a flurry of wild splashing and a frightened young man surfaced, gulped in a huge gasp of air and then frantically paddled the few yards to shore.

"Don't go back in there," Kate warned, and without waiting for an answer she turned and walked away from the pond. The wind was now definitely on the rise and lightning crackled in the low clouds. Without bothering for dusk, the evening darkness was upon them. Fat rain drops danced on the smooth face of the water.

"Hey, don't go, sweet thing," the biker nearest her said as he grabbed her arm.

"Let her go," Killer growled, backhanding the fellow. "And get some clothes on. All of you. We're so out of here."

He draped his leather jacket with the horned red devil's head around Kate's thin shoulders. "This little lady just saved dork-brain's life."

There were a few grumbling protests, but just then the pond scene was interrupted by a distant voice yelling from the house. They saw an angry old lady jumping up and down and pointing to the brush pile, now a small blaze that had fast little flame runners licking at the piles of dried leaves and old brush. The old gal began whacking at the flames with a short-handled coal shovel, but did not seem to be having any success. The breeze had stiffened and it was a bad time to have a fire loose if only because it had been a dry summer and in lowlands like this that could be a bad thing.

Killer shrugged, "I guess I could have started that. Maybe the rain will put it out." He didn't look like he was going to lose any sleep over it. "That the lady what whacked you in the head?"

"Yes. That is Granny Lulubird."

"She better get out of there." A grin lit Killer's face. He fancied himself to be a dude in the classic Brando image; he liked action and he was not inclined to sort out good from evil except in a random subjective way that felt right at the moment. He took a closer look. "Oh, oh. Looks like that fire maybe is headed for the house." Killer was right about that; the gusting wind had started the tall brush blazing next to the old wooden shingles.

"We have got to do something!" Kate cried.

"I wouldn't if I were you. If you go back there, don't you think she'll whack you again?"

"She will kill me..." Kate whispered, seeming to talk to herself.

"Think so?"

"Oh yes. I can see the newsflash on our local station."

"That might make for interesting watching."

"Yes, but I'd be dead," Kate nodded unhappily.

"Yeah, I guess you would. Stay here. I'll take care of it."

Killer walked slowly away, heading in the direction of the house. He moved with slow, confident strides like he was taking out the garbage or ambling over to smack a few dock workers in the head. Even from a distance it could be seen that a flicker of hungry flames was already licking at the back porch steps of the Twillinger home. Killer looked back one time to glare at his band of not-so-merry men, "She's like your sister—understand?"

The biker's voices rose in a chorus, claiming that to a man they did understand.

That said, biker boys will be biker boys, and they still were only half dressed. They waited prudently until Killer disappeared down the row of trees before closing in on Kate.

Jimmy Jinks Warner was singing, "Up in the wild blue yonder/ flying high...into the sky!", singing the same phrase over and over again until he switched to the next part, "We live in fame/ We die in flame! Nothing can stop the Army - Air - Corps!"

He'd already completed two or three curving loops around Cleo's eye with the thought that, with his hangover and headache and the ringing in his ears, this little adventure might not have been a great idea after all. But when he banked that last time and took a look for the airport runway down below, he saw that the south wall of the hurricane had drifted north beyond the Opa-locka landing strip and so now he would have to dip through the edge of the eye to set his Texan back down in a cross-wind wind landing. Tricky, but he'd done a thousand similar maneuvers in his South American flying days, and so he was not all that concerned about his chances. And maybe that was a mistake, though there was noone to say whether the events that followed were a blessed miracle or an unmitigated disaster.

Jimmy chose the north face of the encircling cloud bank and cut into the grey goop at about 2000 feet. His first surprise came as his little plane was grabbed and up-drafted as if it was being squeezed in the firm clutch of a giant's fist being raised in some sort of victory gesture. And the giant didn't let go. In the grip of a relentless elevator, Jimmy Jinx and his Texan shot up, up, up, until he was panting for air.

A second remarkable sight, lightning was everywhere, up, down, all around him. There were streaks and balls and blinding electrical flashes, and the continuing crash of thunder was a bewildering drum roll in his ears. And then one single ball of energy pulsed like a glowing plasma directly in front of him in the cockpit. It wavered back and forth as if uncertain what to do next. Jimmy went completely still, hands off the wheel, staring at the strange and unknown phenomena. One second, two seconds, three seconds, and then it streaked for him like an arrow of pure energy, striking him directly in the face and lighting him up like a bulb on a Christmas tree. No, it wasn't just him, the entire airplane glowed with a strange electrical force. His eyes opened wide and his face took on an expression of wonder.

"So this is what it is!" Jimmy said, his voice carrying a tone of quiet wonder.

And then he was falling, no, floating. The buffeting was diminished, no longer important. He felt he was a part of everything that existed. Or maybe nothing existed, nothing was real, and that was okay, too. He knew God's problems and the ambitions of ants, the secrets of Zoroaster and where Inca gold was buried. He knew everything, all the answers to all the questions ever asked by any living creature. He knew, but none of it mattered. Reality itself, the very fabric of his trusty Texan, of his hands held before him, everything wavered and was distorted as if it was coming apart like sand washed by waves at the beach. And perhaps what saved him, he wasn't afraid. He was unbelievably calm and happier than ever before in his life.

That was the day Jimmy Jinks Warner's T-6 Texan disappeared without a trace. If the guy in the Opa-locka control tower who was coming back after taking a dump in the bathroom hadn't seen his departure, they would never have had even a single clue as to what had happened. A few months later Jimmy's Hillman Minx was sold at some flea-bag auction and the proceeds given to charity. After the appropriate time, his known assets were accepted by the state of Florida according to law and the application of the appropriate procedures. From time to time one of the ladies he frequented genuinely missed him, at least, sort of, a little bit. Juanita, Carlita and Rosa would all remember their sweet Jinxer as the gentle man with nice eyes and a beard that reminded them of the playing card size pictures of Jesus they had received with their 1st Communion prayer books.

Meanwhile\in the orange grove, by the time Killer ambled back from the Twillinger house, rain was pouring from a blackened sky. Four of his bikers were holding Kate down, spread eagled in the mud by the bank of the pond. He had to knock them senseless to get their attention and pull them off of her.

This was an ugly scene; Killer lost his Hollywood Bad Boy cool and turned into a raging wild man, yelling and punching everyone he could reach.

"She saves Rodder's life and you idiots rape her?!"

But there isn't much else he could do. His boys were fast workers and the sex rave was nearly over by the time he got there.

Kate slowly staggered to her feet, found her muddy panties and pulled them on. Her breasts ached and her vagina and lower abdomen were aflame with pain, everything inside her burned, raw and damaged perhaps beyond human repair. A bloody stain at her crotch widened and a red rill appeared and made a slow way down her inner thighs. As lightning flashed all around them, the friendly grey coyote reappeared at her side.

"This way," the coyote said, giving a cunning nod in the direction away from the gathering. "Follow me."

Though she was outdoors and nowhere near, in some unexpected way Kate felt rather than heard the tick of Granny's old white porcelain kitchen timer as it started to slow down. She saw Killer was busy pounding on his men so she left with the coyote, moving after him into the gathering gloom. That took Killer by surprise; one moment the sorry little girl was right there in front of him, and then he must have taken his attention off her or blinked or something, because in the next moment she was gone.

The rain was now sweeping through the rows of orange trees in drapes so thick it was hard to see clearly. Killer decided that had to be it, she'd slipped away in the heavy rainfall. He looked in a sort of innocent wonder at the wild scene around him. Just when he was sure wet and wild nature would come to the rescue of the Twillinger house and put out the fire, a ragged, white hot blast of lightning struck the steel tower nearest to it. Blue-white energy raced down the wires and exploded in an angry orange ball of flame directly over the old wooden structure. Fueled by Granny T's big metal heating oil storage container, the old wooden Victorian roared into fiery life. It swiftly became an angry inferno, a bright beacon glowing in the night sky.

Killer heard the wail of a fire siren sounding in the distance. That could spell real trouble for his kind. They often were blamed for bad things not their doing. He yelled at his biker band, "Come on, you idiots! Time to fire up and blow on out of here! Fire and blow, men – fire and blow!"

Motorbike engines coughed to life and the band of Biker Boys roared through the night rain, heading away from the grove. As a pair of outdated fire trucks raced past them going the other way, the bikers accelerated down the narrow two lane blacktop through the heavy downpour, heading for the Eatonville loop and the Beeline Highway.

Although it might well have been an event entirely unrelated to the fiery happenings at Orange Glory, two months later Killer and his squad of merry tattoo clad dope addicts were camping out somewhat surreptitiously on the Darling National

Wildlife Refuge west of Ft. Meyers Beach. They were happily partying in the classic Born To Be Wild tradition, watching in stoned wonder as the full moon rose over a bay near Fort Meyers. That was when a huge wave, not entirely unlike a tsunami, rose out of the silent waters and came rushing at them like a moving wall of black angel fury topped with frothy moonlight. What a mess! Killer, who managed to survive, took six months for his broken limbs to mend and then caught a fishing boat for Haiti where he had heard they needed missionaries to pass out t-shirts and bottled water.

The morning after Cleo roared and spattered through their neighborhood, all that remained of the old Victorian Twillinger house was a square-shaped patch of soggy blackened bits of timber, looking sadly out of place in the shining sunlight. The rows of orange trees, sparkled fresh and clean as a color lithograph on the end of a wooden box, the trees geometrically stretched away in neat and customary directions as if nothing had happened. But the old Twillinger house was gone forever.

Later that day, Granny Lulubird's freshly cooked body was found in the root cellar, her crisp-skin arms hugging one of those fireproof porta-safes with the key still in it. The wooden cellar door was so burned away no one interested in doing anything about it noticed the coat hanger twisted around its metal hasp in a way that looked as if someone might have wired it shut from the outside.

The pudgy little policeman who found the body turned the key to open the dandy little porta-safe and took the gold coins and the stack of $20 bills for himself. He was in a hurry, and he left the costume jewelry and Granny Lulubird's dead husband's WWII bronze star and a gold colored ring with an orange-pink stone that had belonged to Kate's mother.

"Goddamn rosy quartz," the cop said, tossing it back in the box. He was sure a gem stone like that had to be too big to be anything but carnival wax junk. But then it is said that even experienced pawn brokers have confused pink diamonds for wax costume jewelry.

In the middle of the following afternoon some workers from the power and electric company came out and picked up the heavy grey metal box and the round metal objects that had been staked around the old Twillinger place. That made sense to the locals; after all, as there was no longer a house with any people living under the high tension wires, there was no need for whatever those little globes were supposed to do to protect them. And a few weeks later, the wires and the steel poles themselves were removed. That made sense, too, with the scrap price of copper wire being what it was.

CHAPTER FOUR
that night

The night of the big blow, while Cleo was still knocking things about in Orange Glory Junction and flames from the house were lighting up the night sky, about all Kate remembered clearly was she had said goodbye to the sly and perhaps friendly coyote and then had curled up in one of the narrow bunks in the tar-roof tin shed at the far south end of the orange grove. She hugged the burning area below her stomach, hoping the pressure of her hands might stop the bleeding. Dizzy as she was, she was sure she had lost a lot of blood. She had lost blood before from the various cuts and slashes Granny Lu had bestowed on her, but this seemed worse, particularly the hallucinations. The shed was deserted, the pickers not due to arrive for another two weeks. She looked up to see a robed man sitting on the bunk across from her. Upon closer inspection he seemed to be hovering a few feet above the grimy mattress. He was holding his thumping, glowing heart in his hands. The Sacred Heart, of course.

"Ukk, please. Put that thing away," she groaned, waving him off with one hand.

"As you wish," he said in a comforting, mellow voice. The heart, which was surrounded with a crown of thorns, dissolved to nothing as if it had never been there.

The newcomer looked something like the statue of Jesus she'd seen at the First Episcopalian church in Orlando. But not quite.

"You look older. Grey around the ears."

"Just a little touch-up may be in order," he agreed, and at the suggestion his hair effortlessly morphed into a more youthful curly brown perfection.

"That's some big bruise on your forehead," Jesus said.

"Well, Granny Lu meant to kill me."

"She must have packed some punch, your grandma."

"How do you know about her?"

This Jesus apparition hesitated, looking as if he was picking his way through his own thoughts like a traveler in uncharted lands. "I guess because you think I'm the son of God that I have to know everything…but that's apparently not actually true…"

Kate sat up and looked at him. "The word 'packed' is past tense."

"Yes, it is," he agreed. "Nobody lasts forever."

Kate frowned at him, the aching pain between her legs forgotten for the moment, "She is really gone?"

Granny Lu had been such a constant danger it was hard to believe.

The bearded fellow nodded, "From this earthly plane, as Shakespeare might have said."

"Well, if you're God and everything, why didn't you do something to help her?"

"I'm not sure. I don't think it's my style. If I had to interfere in everything I'd never have any peace."

"So you never help anybody?"

"I didn't say that. More like, I get to be selective. At least I hope so."

"What's that mean?"

"I don't help everybody who thinks they need it. I get to decide."

"Based on what?"

That sent the being who looked like Jesus on another round of mulling. "Well…you know. Virtue. Common decency. Consequences. Murphy's Law. Lots of stuff."

"And Granny wasn't virtuous enough?"

"That should be obvious."

"What about me? Why did you let them have their way with me? Or didn't you care about me getting pierced by a bunch of wicked dicks? Or are you so prudish you don't talk about such things?"

The being who had been Jimmy Jinx felt himself sliding into the role. It wasn't something forced on him; it was the natural way of things as they now were, "Don't be silly, Kate. Didn't you ever read the new testaments? Mary-Mag and me and the rocking times in old Jerusalem?"

"What's your excuse, then?"

"Maybe I'm saving up for when you really need me."

"Oh, yeah, that makes sense. I get knocked on the head and raped and savaged and everything and you're saving for later."

He effortlessly floated over to sit on an upside down wooden crate, smoking what looked to be a twin of the fat toke Killer had been inhaling. Kate was thinking he didn't walk, he more like *cruised.* The Savior's brown hair and short beard were slightly curled, and he wore a tan robe, Birkenstock sandals and a light blue baseball cap set rakishly homey-style on his head. Kate felt too sick to react to most of it, but the hat was too weird to let slide by.

"I can't believe it. The Almighty Savior wearing a UCLA hat?"

"No, it isn't a UCLA hat," he corrected her. "It's from La Celeste. Same colors, though. La Celeste. Uruguayan soccer. World cup two times, 1930 and 1950." He blew a little puff of blue-grey smoke in her direction. "Uruguay is the smallest country ever to win a world soccer championship. And they did it twice. Amazing, no?"

When she didn't answer, an empathetic look flowed from his classic bearded features. Jimmy Jinx could feel himself definitely getting into the love bead thing, "Sorry. I find I've become calloused over the years. Too much suffering, I try to remember the 'h' in humanity stands for 'humor', but it gets to be a stretch."

"You going to jump my bones, too?"

"Stop talking crazy."

"What, I'm not good enough?"

"Of course you are. But you really don't want that, do you?"

She eyed him and sat up. Her vagina throbbed and was sticky wet with blood. She shook her head. "I guess not."

"You're pregnant, you know…"

"Am not!"

“Not the Hells Angels. Nasty Old Gund.”

“That creepy old man doesn’t have a live sperm left!”

Old Gunderson was Granny’s off-and-on sleep-pal. He managed a motel down the road from their orchard. He’d forced his way with Kate a time or six. Once, when Granny caught her pinned down under the flabby old man, she’d blamed Kate and come after her with a heavy old wooden potato masher.

“Well, apparently he does have a little life left in his balls,” Jesus said. “Or did.”

“I’ll kill myself!”

“Cut the hysterics. Just chew a little of that weed over there.” The Savior tossed Kate a kindly if somewhat aloof smile and nodded to a wild vine crawling up near the front of the shed. She limped over to inspect it. It was a dark leafed vine with purple flowers and dark little berries.

“Not the berries. Just the leaves. I don’t know why you need me to tell you; you’re the swamp rat, you already know these things.”

“Do not!” she muttered. But she did as he directed and for the next hour was so sick she hoped she actually would die. The Christ sat there, just an ordinary robed fellow having a relaxing smoke. When one toke was finished, he’d roll and light another from fixings that appeared out of thin air.

When he saw she was watching, he conjured a winkling little halo over his head, to keep up appearances, he said. After a time her shakes went away and she started to feel a little better, probably from the second hand smoke as much as anything. She lay down on one of the worker's narrow bunk beds and he put a grimy blanket over her. The ancient cloth was dirty and smelled of motor oil and old orange peel, and she found it familiar and comforting.

"Get some shut-eye now. Everything will be okay. I'll take care of the rest."

"No rest for the wicked," she murmured as she drifted off.

"That's why the son of God's work is never done."

His voice seemed to come from far away. She watched through heavy lidded eyes as he snubbed out his last smoke in a little red can filled with sand that was hung on a bare wall stud for the purpose. He bent over to pick up a few beer bottles that smelled of gasoline and then straightened back up with a yawn, politely covering his hand over his mouth. Then he floated gracefully out the open shed opening and away from her down a long row of orange trees. Her eyelids were heavy and in another moment she was asleep. In her dreams Granny's kitchen timer slowed down until it stopped and she raced around committing monstrous acts of vengeance she'd only dreamed of in real life.

Kate woke to an acrid, burning smell. She couldn't have been sleeping long. Perhaps a few minutes; certainly not an hour. The eastern clouds were stained red-orange with pre-dawn light. No, wait—it was still pelting rain outside. But now there were two fierce but separate and distinct fires, defying the storm as they flared angrily up into the low sky. Her mental balance felt tilted as she tried to take it in and make sense of what she was seeing. It was clear that now both Granny's house and Old Gund's Sunny Days Motel were blazing like signal bonfires in the night.

The bursts of rain were still coming and going, but the downpour was having little effect on the old Twillinger house. The firemen had hosed down what was left of the wood frame Victorian for some time, mostly for something to stay busy while they drank beers and passed around a bottle of rum, but then they gave up entirely on firefighting. Even as volunteers, they could see the job was hopeless. The men were winding up their hoses and singing "Mammas don't let your babies grow up to be firemen…" They had a nearly empty case of Budweiser and were throwing their empties into the still sputtering fire.

Kate, seeing what they were about, ran for the house.

"Get away from there, child!"

One of the men grabbed her arm.

"More than a child," he grinned approvingly as he eyed the budding breasts pressing against her thin wet t-shirt. She pushed mentally, the timer in her head slowed marginally and she easily squiggled out of his grasp. *Why, she wondered, couldn't she do that bit of useful magic all the time?* From somewhere she heard the echo of her pal coyote's voice singing nonsensical gibberish,

You can, you can, you can, you can/ Because of the wonderful thing that you am!

But the drunken firemen pulled her back to reality, "All dirty and scratched and banged up."

"Sooty sex. A fire fighter's wet dream."

"Jail bait," warned a scraggly-bearded fellow who had done time in the county lockup for his actions in a moderately similar circumstance, though that messy business hadn't been entirely his fault as he'd been grieving at the time for his wife Shirley who had run off with Leonard, the local mail truck man, who had been a half-breed Seminole, to boot, worse the shame.

"And the beer's mostly gone." The fire chief's volunteer assistant shook his head. He had a millstone of a wife and a squalling baby, to boot, and, as if that wasn't enough of a heat retardant, he needed to hang on to his assistant manager's position at Taco Billie's, where he stole enough cold burritos and wilted tacos to hardly ever have to visit the grocery store.

"Come on, let's go home."

The men reluctantly got to their feet and stretched the kinks out. After a few minutes of shuffling around and loading their gear, they unsuccessfully tried to paw the inexplicitly slippery young girl a little more. After a handful of nothing they piled onto their trucks, and started up the diesel engines.

"But the house…" Kate said.

"It ain't going nowhere, child."

"Granny Lu might still be in there!"

"If that be so, she ain't going nowheres, neither."

And that last prediction proved to be true. It was late afternoon of the next day before the last flames flickered out and the embers cooled enough to reveal the barbequed remains of Granny Lulubird and, a half mile away, those of Old Gund, deathly quiet in his own narrow twin size bed. Everything was charred so badly that the local experts did not spot the clues that Gund might have been tied down prior to ignition. The idea never came up, though in the days that followed, the chief of police had his suspicions. But nobody paid him much attention, as it was the dang fellow's job to suspect everybody of everything, just a man going about his business.

It was a few days later over at the Orange Glory cop station building. Things had pretty much dried out by then from Hurricane Cleo, though it was still a subject of considerable conversation and even more unspoken speculation. Police chief "Big Bug" Jack Harmony was talking over the recent wild flock of weird and unaccounted-for happenings that had taken place in their neck of the woods as he chewed the fat with his longtime friend and associate, Fire Chief "Hot Pants" Lloyd Peabody.

"Lenny Skittles found a squirrel he swears can play the violin, *pissy catta,* of course."

"Pissy what?"

"Furry little fucker plucks the strings with his paws. Lenny says he can play Bach."

"You get him to bang out a tune for you?"

"Nope. I wouldn't know Bach from Ballyhoo Biggins.

"Who?"

"Never mind. Anyway, Lenny says the squirrel got away. I shooed Lenny on out of my place – you know I don't like to conduct business at home, and besides, he's crazy, you know that for gospel – but not ten seconds later, the Parsons twins come breezing in without a knock or a howdy and there's me standing in my stained old Bugs Bunny shorts."

"You got bunny shorts?"

"Will you stop interrupting my story?"

"Well, sure, if you'd just get on with it. What did they want?"

"They swore their dog Puggy could bark-talk, whatever that is."

"You hear it?"

"I most certainly did. Sounded like pure howl to me."

"I hear tell that Ben Tucker's body done bolted off a slab at the Eternal Rest Funeral home and walked out the door?"

"Lord almighty, maybe Ben wasn't dead! That right there is one of my biggest fears, waking up in the coffin."

"Three stab wounds in the heart. And full of formaldehyde, toes to the crest of his brow – I'd say he was dead enough."

"Talk about a dead man walking!"

"Yep. From the looks of it, Old Ben done shuffled hisself a half mile in the direction of the

Glory Days liquor store before pitching over stone cold dead again for the second time and this time probably not never ever coming back. Found him floating face down in a roadside ditch.

"Almost made it to that last six pack, did he?"

"Probably just some kids funning around with a corpse," Big Bug said. "That's what I'm deciding, at least on the report."

"Think you'll ever catch them?"

"Probably not. Was me, I wouldn't fess up to that one."

By this time, Cleo had moved on to the northeast, gathered a new store of energy out over the Atlantic and then back-tracked west to dump a load of misery and destruction on Georgia and the Carolinas. But in Orange Glory, the wind and lightning and blazing fires were over, and cleanup was well under way. The two men were entirely willing to put a few small and unconfirmed incidents of musically inclined animals and rumors of the thirsty walking dead behind them.

Orange Glory's two most responsible officials, Big Bug and Hot Pants shared a combined office. It was a squat Quonset hut that the police chief was happy to share with the fire chief because of their simpatico natures. Now, on the morning after, they were verbally pitchforking over recent odd events. As they discussed these unusual matters, each from the point of view of their official individual responsibilities, the two chiefs poured warm beers into big plastic tea glasses filled with cold ice cubes. They had brought a new stockpile of winning collector's brews back from the recent

Best Florida Beer Championships in Tampa. Every year they undertook an official expedition, motoring a few hundred miles on over there to taste and test and come back with a fire truck piled high with cases of their personal favorites.

The Bugger, who had gotten his nickname for placing microphones in the bedroom of his house trailer and catching his ex-wife in a liaison with Jimmy Hinson, a fast talking steel building salesman from Orlando, was short and squat and wore his gold plated cop badge pinned to suspenders over a big display of hairy bare chest. He carefully poured a lukewarm bottle of Swamp Head into a frosty mug filled with ice cubes he had hammered into splinters, chatter-lip cold just the way he liked it. His companion Hot Pants got his name when he caught fire and set his own trousers blazing in his heroic efforts to put out an unexpectedly spectacular display of Roman Candles, M-40's and Rose Pinwheels at a local fireworks stand. He was drinking a dark ale named Black Water, though with ordinary un-hammered cubes that he preferred because they did not dilute the alcohol quite so fast.

Police Chief Big Bug was upset enough that he spilled a bit of his liquid gold.

Hot pants gave him a critical look, "What's eating at you, Bug?"

"It ain't the walking dead. I been hearing lots of rumors about Filbert."

"Your man Filbert? What about him?"

"I got it on good account that Filbert done stolen a wad of money from the open safe they found over at Granny Lu's place."

"Who told you that?"

"Confidential source that I can't reveal. I didn't think much of it, but then Filbert comes back from Orlando with a big bass boat. Now you know he don't make that kind of money."

The fire chief nodded, "You got to do something about that."

"I already sent him packing. But the damn thief went off all grinning his denials. And that has me raising my suspicions as to how much he actually got away with."

At this, Chief Hot Pants patted and rubbed his head where the heavy fireman's hat, his badge of honor, was at least one cause of his premature baldness. "Well, I'm hoping everything is done with and over now. Been nothing but trouble out at the Twillinger place. I blame it on them dang-fab electrical wires."

"Huh. You figure that's it?"

Big Bug gave him a skeptical glance.

Lloyd Hot Pants took a swig of tepid Mountain Dew straight from the can and a bite of a glazed donut to freshen his palate for more of the frosty suds,

"Sure. Power company rammed that project through the county over forty years ago and it's been trouble for me ever since. I calculate we had twice as many fires to say nothing of the spike in domestic proturbances. My theory is, them wires cause fires seven ways from Sunday. Spooky sparkling, I calls it. And that has led to family dis-restivity as displayed in that entire Twillinger clan."

The police chief puckered up his face, his mind clearly in the deep thought mode.

"Spooky sparkling? That's a real thing?"

"You ever seen swamp glow, you wouldn't ask that."

"I seen it," the Bugger nodded.

"More than that, Bug. We been having strange and unexplained combustings for years now."

"Well, I do know that at one point in there last night the flames from Granny Twill's place was going all sparky and unpredictable."

"Me, too. That's why I stayed in the truck, let them crazy-ass volunteers toast their own testicles."

"You'd think they would figure that one out."

"Yeah, you would, but they never do." Hot Pants grinned, "I see any problem in an emergency, I delegate. I wave 'em into the fray; I get busy on the cell phone with important stuff. You should try it. Domestic violence, skinheads, drunken rednecks, any problem with the smell of danger whatsoever, send your troopers in. That there is the secret to the longevity of my survival. "

Big Bug nodded, "Well, sure, lesson number one. I was in the army too, you know."

"Yep. I know, Bug."

The puckered expression on the police chief's face intensified, "You serious about them electrical wires, I mean, from a professional blaze-snuffer's point of view?"

Chief Hot Pants held his beer glass to his forehead. "If you was ever out there on a muggy August night when them wires start popping and buzzing, you wouldn't be asking. There was always something not right about it, running volts like that through hell and high water."

"I hear that's why they put them little metal cone things around the Twillinger place. Supposed to deflect the electro-magnovites or what the hell ever."

"Who told you that."

"Geek in a suit."

"Who?"

"Fellah named Britches or Birches or something like that, I can't rightly remember. Came out from the power company."

"You know that for sure?"

"Well, hell, no, but why else would anybody come all the way out here and be telling me about such stuff? They put these here small metal cones up in the orchard. Britches said it would keep the electric badness away from the house. Little bitty metal balls on steel fence posts they drove in the ground with a tamper. Where it was too swampy they had to use, like, tripods, and that dark grey metal box thing they actually laid in concrete. I don't for the life of me see how those things could have helped much. We're talking serious volts hanging right over her head. Granny Lu should have moved."

"She was never going to sell, and I believe they knew it."

"Crazy as a loon."

"You got that right. That old bitch told everybody who would listen her house was set right on a corner of the Bermuda Triangle! Imagine that, and us over a fifty miles from the Atlantic, as the gull flies."

"Where you think the other two corners are?"

"Stands to reason, one of them has to be Bermuda."

"Nuttier than a fruitcake, that one."

"Yeah, but she could hump like a happy bunny."

The two raised their tea glasses and drained them exactly together in their studied ritual.

"Well, here's to happy endings," Big Bug Jack said.

"Amen to that, bro. Amen to that."

CHAPTER FIVE

after the big blow

Early entry, presumably from a scrap of Charley Birch's handwritten diary extracted by the cleaners in the early 1970's from an inconspicuous hole in the wallboard at a retirement home north of Orlando where he was confined. Apparently he'd been keeping private notes for over a quarter of a century:

April Fools Day, 1952 – Unfaithful bitch Tillie has disappeared again, this time I think for good. Not bitch...witch, more likely. Trust nobody – that was my motto and still is. Not my fault, really, that I fell for a crazy lady who never could be true to me. I'm convinced she pulled some sort of magic wool over my eyes. Times there were back then under her spell, I would nearly forget my duty to country, to the OG Project, to the important things in my life. Happened nearly whenever I was around her spells. Worse, she's left our rat bastard son with me. I guess it was those big round soft pleading eyes, made me forget her steel will and that trapdoor mind. Me, the guy who never wanted kids, the guy who felt the earth was already overpopulated, and I end up with a son! At least he'll be fodder for the project. One thing I don't get, that kid is supposed to be older but he looks like a teenager, not that it matters one way or the other. I've already had some of our guys install the wiring. Kid's got no option but mogrify or get off the pot. Sure, he's my own son, but no remorse, I'm not going to go soft at this late date. Show no mercy. Off the bastard, one and all!

In his last days at the retirement home, Charley Birch was pretty sure he was dying. He thought he could tell by the declining quality of the food; they didn't give good rations to the fellows on their way out, or maybe it was just that his taste buds were going south along with the rest of him. He'd been at the Eastside Winterhaven Rest Home for a long time, stuck in the scrubby suburban swamplands twenty miles north-northwest of Orlando, near as he could tell. When they first dumped him here, they said it was just temporary; but even back then he could read the signs for what they were. A jail by any other name is still a prison. And what the hell, in spite of everything, he'd managed to outlast most of his enemies and now he was nearly seventy five, all wrinkled and arthritic and constipated. Nobody wants to live forever, the saying went, and now he could see why.

They were afraid he'd talk about Orange Glory, of course, scared shitless he would turn into a blabbery old man and spill his beans. That was what this was about. He knew too damn much. The goddamn agency was so predictable, and in the end it was all so hopeless. It was such a load of crap in the first place. The absolute truth was, after they'd poured all that money down the rat hole, decades of research zapping all those people and still nobody knew much of anything about any of it except they had slipped in deep *merde* of some sort or other. What the hell were the zoomins, anyway? The few military left on the project were floundering around like flies trapped in an outdoor shit-house, looking for the tiny crescent moon cut in the old wood door that just might be an escape. An electronic crapper, more's the irony, of their own making, and one that, chances are, didn't have a crescent moon. And so they were left with an unstable keg of cosmic dynamite that could detonate at any moment, taking the known universe with it. Or something like that.

An orderly poked his head in through the door to Charley's private room, "Your son's here to see you."

"Which one? The lawyer or the no-good rat bastard?"

"You only have one son, sir."

Charley sighed and nodded.

"That would be him, then."

The old man couldn't help but notice the orderly was carrying, probably a .9mm Sig Sauer. He couldn't resist a little verbal jab,

"They let you carry those things loaded these days, sonny-boy?"

The orderly grinned. He wasn't afraid of the crusty old fellow, even though the scuttlebutt said he had been a general-equivalent, though quasi-civilian, so you never knew exactly. The orderly patted the firearm on his hip.

"Yep. And one in the chamber."

"Don't shoot yourself in the ass on your way out. I would have said dick, but it's too small and you're probably not that good a shot."

It was only army talk, real man banter. Still, as the orderly left, he was no longer smiling.

Less than a minute later, Carter Flinn entered Charley's room. Charley noted once again that his son never walked or strutted or hurried, he moved with a grace and a disturbing presence of mind that seemed to lull everyone he met into underestimating him. And although he was now much older, he still looked too young to have earned his law degree or to have passed the tough New York bar exam. His full name was Carter Flinn-Birch, though he'd dropped the Birch years before, ungrateful little rat bastard that he was.

"I never should have had kids," Charley muttered. "Why the hell wouldn't Tillie have an abortion?"

"Dad. I'm not Tilly's son, and probably not yours, and I'm busy. I left Manhattan to see you. What do you want?"

"Same as always. Kill your sister, get on with your life."

"No. I won't kill anybody. It's not what lawyers do. And she's not my sister. I saw the DNA tests. Incidentally, you're actually not my biological dad, either. Anything else?"

"This is the last time I'm asking you, Carter."

"Good." The son, who had barely had time to set down his brief case and settle into a bedside chair, now rose and flicked some imaginary dust from his grey pinstripe suit, clearly intending to leave.

"Wait…Christ, sit down, Carter. I know you think I'm vile and heartless, but…well, my intentions have always been on the side of good. We all were trying to do the right thing. In a way, we still are."

"Right. For *patre et familias.* Kill all the gooks. Throw the women and children in the ditch."

Charley felt a burst of old rage, "That's right, God damn it, if they mean the downfall of humanity! I'll take that to my grave!"

The old man's rant was interrupted as his throat tightened and he bent over in a fit of coughing. Carter handed him a glass of water, but still it was some time before Charley settled down again.

The old man caught his breath and started a litany in a low but firm voice, "Many virgins eat my juicy sperm under nasty pressure."

"Dad, that's gross."

"Yes, but it is also currently incorrect. The right anagram should be, 'precious juicy sperm'…"

"I don't get what you're driving at."

Charley waved a weary hand, swatting away imaginary flies.

"Mercury… Venus… Earth… Mars… Phaeton… Jupiter… Saturn… Uranus... Neptune… Pluto…"

"Dad, you're losing it. There is no Phaeton."

"Yes, you're right. But there was last week."

Carter had already started to leave when the magnitude of his father's delusion stopped him in his tracks. Charley had always been devious and furtive, but this was a somewhat more overt step in the direction of crazy.

"You are telling me last week there was another planet in the solar system, a planet named Phaeton that nobody ever heard of and now it is no longer there."

"How would you know it never existed?"

'Well, that's obvious..." But on reflection it wasn't quite so, and the thought intrigued Carter as Charley knew it would. "What was it like, this Phaeton place?"

"Green. Some water, but not much. About the size of Mars."

"What happened to it?"

"Charley gave him a haunted look, "I don't know."

"And how do you know about Phaeton if nobody else ever heard of it?"

"We destroyed it."

"Who?"

"My Russian pal and I." Charley snapped his fingers, "Five hundred thousand Phaetonian immigrants gone just like that, just a little bit of fallout from Orange Glory.

Carter sat back down. "Now you're responsible for the death of an entire planet? I'd say you need some help, but that would be a monumental understatement. You are certainly beyond anything meds could do for you."

His dad looked twitchy and irritable, more unsettled than his usual grumpy self.

"Yes. I am not sure of a lot of things that I used to take for granted."

Charley quieted down, a frail old man sunken into his thoughts, but then he started up again, "It was the goddamn Russians, started it all."

"Yes, the commies. I've heard all this before."

"No you haven't. A Ruskie defector, my old pal Vladimir Podofski. He was one of their blended scientists; his background was a combination of hard scientific disciplines and studies of the human brain."

"Yes, it was his fault. Dad, I know all this."

Carter's impatience brought out his venom, "You always were such a smart ass about everything. Ever since I sent you to those lily-lib colleges. Holier-than-thou, use a French toilet to rinse your butt. Jesus, why didn't I just have them off you?"

"Dad, I know – "

Did you know you have a daughter?"

There was a brief pause as Carter examined the possibilities.

"You're lying," he said finally. "Again."

"Too late for that," Charley said.

"Now you're saying the girl I have to kill is my daughter? Unbelievable!"

"Only biological. You don't have to think of her as your real daughter. Now here's your mission."

"First you dump a ton of lost planet crap on me, and now you're going to give me a mission?!"

Carter hadn't felt so off-balance since he was a teenager and his dad caught him jacking off in their four car garage in Alexandria.

"Listen up. Your daughter is crazy as a loon. And worse, she's dangerous. Something we did made her that way."

"We did?"

"The lab did. The army. Vladi. Me. It doesn't matter. You have to kill her. I'm dangerous, too, but you don't have to kill me. I'm too far gone for that."

"No. Why? What does she matter to you? And what's so dangerous about her?"

"If it makes any difference – and I do not think it does – everything that happened was an accident. At least, it wasn't intended. It took us by surprise."

"As usual, you're long on orders and short on specifics."

"The consequences were nothing we expected."

"Right. Death to the planet Phaeton. Maybe you better give me a few more hints about why you want me to shoot my own supposed offspring."

"You don't have to shoot her. Use a poison dart, some of that stuff from darkest Africa. It's the going rage around here. Or push her off a fishing skiff or something CIA like that."

"Why?"

"It all gets back to Vladimir Podofski. The Ruskies had had some encouraging results with electro-magnetic experiments on the human brain, alternating between doses of energy and chem-phiz shock treatments. Enhanced intelligence, maybe even the ability to move inanimate objects with the mind…though we were never able to prove any of that."

"But you went ahead anyway."

The old man shrugged, "The Cold War. We couldn't let the Soviet Bloc get ahead of us."

"So you experimented on people. My own father, though my saving grace is, not biological."

"What do you mean?"

"We don't look anything alike. And then there's the DNA."

Charley's frown deepened. He'd never had the courage to test Carter's DNA and he wasn't willing to believe his son's results.

"We acted for the good of freedom and democracy. I know you don't believe that, contaminated by pinko commie liberals as you are, but let me talk here. Time is short. Vladi and I found ways we believed were significantly reshaping and intensifying brainpower. But there were some bad side effects."

"What? They became normal again?"

"No. Some spazzed out and died. Some turned into idiots. Others into froth-mouthed animals. That would have been bad enough, but there was something worse. Something so inexplicable I do not understand it to this day."

"What, they became Democrats?"

Charley gave his son a sad grin, "Your warped sense of humor is the only thing that may save you. You're going to need it. What happened was, we couldn't kill them."

"Why? I don't believe it. You people kill everything."

"Some of them – not all, mind you – but some few of our subjects were no longer with us."

"Right. You made them into idiots."

"No. We made them into saints. We only found out about it when we tried to solve the problem."

"I don't know what any of this means."

"It means, among other things, they were capable of performing miracles. Well, sort of miracles. It wasn't like they were in control."

"And?"

"Once we saw how dangerous they were, we tried to eliminate the problem. But we couldn't."

Carter threw up his hands in disgust. "Layers and layers of depravity. You are like an onion of evil. You mean you couldn't murder them."

"Whatever. I am depressed to tell you the book of life turned out to read like some cheap, schmaltzy science fiction novel."

"You're not making any sense."

"Yes, but I'm not making it up! I don't understand it myself. Look at it this way; when you catch a big tuna you can actually see the color, the life, the whatever draining from it. But where does all that vital and indefinable whatever go? And don't give me that crap about we're all just batches of cells."

Carter gave him an unbelieving stare, "You are now going to make a case for existence of the human soul?"

"I'm not arguing here. I don't know."

The old man went on as if he was talking to himself, or perhaps continuing an unfinished argument with his Russian partner, "I'll tell you one thing, Carter: set reality free and you'll find the universe is a vengeful bitch. You don't want to dick around with Mother Nature.

"Dad, you don't know the difference between good and evil."

"I do now. We did a great evil, and now we're paying the price."

"Wait. Evil? You, of all people, are admitting you've done something wrong?"

The old man nodded sadly, "Against nature. Apparently there is a universal moral code after all. The devil discovers paradise, but naturally they won't let him in." Charley eyed his son, "Podofski had a streak of old Russian orthodox in him, and when he found out what we were trying to do and what the results were, he turned absolutely grey with fear."

"What did happen to your, ahh, so-called experiments?"

"We can't kill them so we keep them off-shore in isolation cells. Occasionally they drift away or maybe kill themselves or each other – at least, we think they do – so we were hoping the problem would go away. Still are, actually."

"Off-shore? Guantanamo Bay?"

"Somewhere else. Sometimes one of them drifts away, so we built a series of traps outside their prison cells."

"They can escape? How?"

"We don't know. Sometimes they walk through solid walls. Sometimes they disappear and show up somewhere else. This proves inconvenient when they reappear half stuck in a tree or a rock somewhere. That actually does kill them. At least, we think it does.

"Odd stuff, Dad. Unbelievable, actually, but with you, I'm used to it. Still, get this: I am not going to kill anybody. Is there anything else I can do for you?"

"Well, I'm dying, and you have to make a choice. If you can't kill your daughter, you have to convince her to go to the island keep."

"My daughter, the raving young lunatic that I never even knew existed before now?"

"Not a raver. An innocent, doesn't have any idea."

Carter shook his head, "Why should I?"

"She lives right here in Florida. Her name is Kate." The old man tossed a folder at his son. It was a careless flip of the wrist, the casual gesture of a man disposing of garbage. "Right here in Florida," he repeated, "where it all began."

"Why are you telling me this?"

"Just tying up loose ends. Don't believe me? Watch. I'm feeling a bit unstable, myself."

With that, an incredible happening took place; the old man's body began to float up from the bed, looking like nothing more than a cheese ball Las Vegas act. Carter's eyes widened and his jaw dropped as Charley floated up to the ceiling, where he pushed himself off of one wall and drifted over to one corner of the room directly above the crystal trophies and awards that glinted like spikes on his side table.

"What magic trick are you pulling?!"

"Watch this." The old man drifted up through the ceiling and then drifted back into view again. "My God, that feels strange. Goodbye, Carter. Wish you weren't so much of a pansy-wart."

Whatever the magic or miracle, the old man's body suddenly found gravity and dropped to impale itself on a sharp dagger of clear Lucite, fittingly, his National Security Agency award for excellence.

Carter rushed to his father's side, but there was nothing he could do.

"Pull the damn thing out of my back," Charley grunted through clenched teeth.

"Not so easy, is it, when it's you doing the dying."

Still, that sounded a little vengeful, so Carter did as he was told and carried his father back to the bed. An insane grin lit the old man's face as blood gushed from his wound.

"Killed your own father," he said. "Now you get to be a classic tragic figure – Oedipus Rex Carter Flinn-Birch."

Carter's mind was whirling with the vivid imagery of the odd floating trick, followed by Charley's sudden brief plunge to mortally wound himself, but he was certain it had to be some circus sideshow gag done with invisible wires and pulleys. It was a typical hyper-theatrical Charley Birch stunt, like the time he'd brought in a troop of hookers to deflower his son's high school graduating class *en mass*. His father wouldn't have been content to simply chew a poison pill or shoot himself.

"Christ, it hurts," Charley complained. And then he was dead.

Carter sat in the chair across from Charley's silent form, trying to think what might be best to do. He heard the steady tick-tick-tick of the cheap alarm clock on his father's bedside table. It seemed to slow for a few ticks, but Charley decided it was just his imagination. He tried to remember The Lord's Prayer, but couldn't get past, *Our Father who art in heaven.* He said it over and over, but nothing more came so he gave up on it. He had no idea what he might be praying for, anyway.

Finally he placed his father's hands together on the old man's shrunken chest as if they were folded in prayer. He didn't know exactly why he performed the gesture; perhaps it was his way of trying to tidy up some last little bit of what had been a very messy relationship. He gathered the folder and its papers from the floor and was about to toss them in the waste container when his careful nature overcame his disgust and his impatience to be out of the room and on his way. He placed the folder in his brief case, took a last look around, and then headed out the door.

The young-looking lawyer felt little surprise for the abruptness of his father's exit from the living, or for the fact that the ancient and devious old man had taken his own life. He was sure the theatrics had been some cleverly devised trick. Charley had sent him away to private boarding school practically from the time he was born, so there wasn't much of an emotional tug there. None, actually. He did not doubt for a moment that his father could have found a way to collect some of his sperm and impregnate some poor, unsuspecting girl for his pseudo-humanitarian experiments, so it was possible he could have a daughter somewhere out there. Not too likely, but possible.

Carter had decided early on that depraved Papa Charley had to be a renegade from the ordinary military chain of command and that his so-called operations were probably funded by some sub-rosa branch of intelligence like those one sees in the spy movies, and these latest scraps of evidence seemed to validate the little he knew about Charley's secret world. No sane, above-board organization would be involved in the sort of experiments Charley had described. A cold, shivery feeling washed over Carter; if Charley had been able to take his sperm and impregnate some unknown person, what other experiments might he have performed on his own son?

And then he had an even more disturbing thought. If ordinary humans couldn't kill these transmogrified people, how was it possible that other transmogrified people could kill their own kind? Or was that just a rumor? Charley had called them 'zoomins', the word spilling from his mouth in a derogatory way. If Charley detested them so much why had he enlisted his son's aid? Charley had plenty of his own contact with assassins, the so-called clean up men. Carter was thinking the odds as to his own survival were starting to dim. This could all have been arranged by his cunning old man. Were they even going to let him walk away from here?

As a young man living in strange circumstances, Carter had always been one to observe details, a great advantage in a lawyer: The Winterhaven Rest Home was somewhat an unusual place. Carter had noticed the firearm bulging under the orderly's white jacket, the nameplate on his breast SGT Fritz Harper. Something about that fellow smacked of Neanderthal, probably the low, sloped-back forehead and heavy jaw. Carter slipped the green folder in his briefcase and started down the hall. They didn't seem to have an on-duty nurse, but he suggested to Sergeant Harper, who was slumped in a chair behind the front desk, that someone might go take a look to see if his father, who was quietly at rest, would be needing anything.

"It's our busy time," Fritz told him, looking up from an ancient and well-thumbed Robert B. Spenser detective novel. "But we'll get around to it."

So they were going to allow him to leave after all. Carter climbed back in his rented Ford and headed for Orlando International. Charley's last words were to the effect that the universe was in danger of being shredded, and his son didn't have the foggiest notion of what that meant or what to do about it. Dissolution of corporations was more his bag.

Carter figured he would have plenty of time to read about his imaginary daughter on the trip back to New York City. His father had never told him more than half-truths about anything. Charley was a military man, sort of. Generals called his bulky and important mobile phone, which had a scrambler that made all incoming voices sound like they came from the same robot. He had a clearance above top secret. What would they call that? Hyper Secret? Ultra Secret?

Carter shook the scattered thoughts from his head and swung his car around a slow moving truck loaded with green limes, glad to be getting away from the land of swampy marshlands, theme parks, citrus groves and insane old men who could turn their own death into a carnival sideshow act.

The heavy truck looked like it was going to cut in front of him. There was no way to avoid it. But as the front wheels cut sharply in his direction there was a slick spot on the road and so instead of impacting Carter's rental the heavy truck spun out. Limes flew everywhere like giant green beetles. The grim faced driver of the truck cursed and slammed his hands on the wheel. His skull shaped head slammed into the steering wheel, and he saw stars for a moment. The roadside ditch was shallow and skull-head figured he could rock out of it and then catch up to the rental and slam it from the rear end. But the jolting exit off the road must have caused a wire to go loose because when he turned the key in the ignition, the engine wouldn't turn over.

CHAPTER SIX

on the flight back north

Two hours into his flight, Carter slipped the green folder back in his briefcase and sipped his weak American Airlines scotch-and-water. An old man sighed and sat down in the vacant seat next to him.

"That seat is taken," Carter said.

"Of course it is," the old man said. He looked exactly like a bust of Vladimir Ilyich Lenin that Carter had seen somewhere, probably in a National Geographic magazine on the wonders of the Russian revolution.

Carter fought down the cold shiver that ran through him. *Expect miracles,* Charley had said. "Vladimir Podofski, I presume?"

"The same."

"You look like – "

The man held up one hand. "I apologize, young Flinn-Birch, but after one goes through the veil it is all presumptive imagery. I mean specifically the only way to communicate is through the reconstruction of commonly shared visuals."

"Russian, professional, older fellow, Lenin equals my approximation of poor old Professor Podofski?"

"Yes, exactly. Forgive me, but I assure you, once you are dead you will have to communicate like this, if you're lucky enough to find anybody on the receiving end. Believe it or not, I no longer remember what the human version of me looked like."

Once he got past the idea he was talking to a ghost, Carter found himself more than a little interested, "Not even if I showed you a picture of yourself?"

"I don't think so. I have the vague notion that I was a great lover. But you, now, you are a cold cookie, not even afraid a little bit of me."

"And should I be?"

"Not of me, exactly, but maybe of what I know. Humans build a universe out of logic. Words are the fathers of our deeds. Were, in my case."

"You are as full of crap as my old man. What's the point, dead Russian guy?"

"The point is, Jesus broke all those rules. Water into wine, multiplication of loaves and fishes, dead Lazarus back to life."

"He interfered with the laws of nature."

"Yes, rude American boy. You can stop the sun, but there will be a payment for that. The universe as we know it cannot tolerate that sort of thing, wild experimentals, going out on one's own, making the rules as you go along."

"That why the Jews killed him?"

"It wasn't the Jews. It was Mother Nature, the natural order of things, she's the bitch what run him over and took him down, to use gutter rap talk. If not the crucifixion it would have been any of a dozen things. Run over by a chariot. A piano falling on his head like in a loony American Roadracer cartoon."

"Roadrunner. And they didn't have pianos back then."

The dead Russian shrugged, "A giant stone lyre, then…but that's not the heart of the problem. Jesus failed to respect the pace and beat of things, what you and I can think of as the gradualistic nature of the universe. Jesus did not heed the warnings, and, sadly, neither did your pops-man and I."

"Okay, the son of God miracled around a bit and in some way got nailed for it, but just what did you do that was so wrong?"

"Wild tinkering, hocus pocusing in the name of God and country – and we were ultimately betrayed by our own impetuosity."

"How? Just what did you do?"

"Squirrels eventually learned to fly and so became flying squirrels…but, for first ten thousand generations or so, the experimenters got themselves splatted on rocks far down below; imagine ten thousand splats before the survivors persistently manipulated reality in such a way that they could spread the fabric of their skin in an aerodynamically functional way."

"Okay. I guess I can understand that, but…?"

"All those generations of fuzzy little squirrels squashed like bugs on the rocks until their DNA finally figures it out. That is the natural order of things. That is how the universe tolerates evolution. Mere humans do not quell storms with their willpower. They do not ferment drinking water, cause the planet Phaeton to disappear or float over their deathbeds. And they certainly do not engineer the zoomins, a race of supra-beings, overnight. That sort of empty headed inventioneering frays the pattern of what is and how things can evolve into other things."

"Why are you telling me this craziness?"

"To convince you to do the right thing. The girl must be killed. She is the genie popped out of the bottle."

"Kill my own daughter to clean up the mess for you and my father?"

Vladimir shrugged. "For all of us. And she is not your daughter. Charley believed it was so, but in truth, she is mine. No miracle, just a little sleight of hand on my part, you know, messing with the vials."

Carter felt his head was spinning again. New lies were falling on the old ones like snowflakes on drifts that were already waist high.

"You were there, Vladi. You were in the thick of it. Tell me, did Daddy Dearest perform experiments on me, as well?"

"You have still more to learn. Charley was not your father."

Carter's head was spinning. With this sudden burst of new information he forgot the Russian hadn't answered his original question, *Did Charley perform experiments on him?*

"What? Not my father?! Then who was?"

"If I remember correctly it was Einstein's sperm and we managed an egg from Feynman's, Fermi's or Openheimer's daughter, somebody like that, I can't remember which, we did so many."

"Albert Einstein was my father?"

"Quite likely."

"You thought you were like gods."

"Like God, actually. What great times of optimism and enthusiasm! We were creating the new wonder…" His voice took on a tone of regret, "…Homo Superati…Homo Excellentius…We argued over hot tea about what we should name our new species…silly, I suppose, considering we finally agreed on Homo Zoominus"

"Why have you shown up here?"

A look of cunning awareness came over the Russian.

"Carter, you will learn to use what you do not know or you are a dead genie.

"How can I use something if I don't know it?"

"Instinct. Premonition. Blind guessing. I do not know."

"Finally the truth. You have no idea what you're talking about, and neither do I.

"You will be dead, like every human will be on earth, like everybody who ever existed on the planet Phaeton."

And with Podofski's mention of Phaeton, the same unknown but doomed planet Charley about which Charley had made unbelievable claims, a physical jolt ran through the passenger compartment and Carter woke to find he was fall through the sky at 26,000 feet, high above the clouds and tumbling through the thin, icy air without a seat, no thin walled tube around him, impossibly rocketing along with no visible airplane at all. He blinked and screamed, but the sound of his terror was torn from his lips by the wind.

There was another jolt and the frame of the aircraft grew thick and congealed out of nowhere and out of nothing to form itself around him, followed by the overhead compartments, the windows and the curved tan walls of the passenger compartment. He heard a disembodied voice saying, "I owed Albert that one. Next time you will have to save yourself."

A high wind wailed as the landing wheels swung down from the underside of the airplane. Carter, now wide awake, tried to brush his terror aside as the passenger plane began its descent over the Hudson River toward the runway at La Guardia Airport. Everything in the passenger cabin around him was perfectly as it should be to the last detail, including his empty scotch glass with the twisted lemon rind at the bottom. Still, things being what they were, whatever might have been of Vladimir Podofski was no longer in the seat beside him. Carter resolved that there never would be a 'next time'. He'd take a bus or walk if he had to, but he was never going to get on another airplane.

CHAPTER SEVEN
Time goes by

Ten years after his impromptu conversation with the ghost or spirit or memory of the dead Russian scientist – whatever it might have been – Carter Flinn arrived back in Orange Glory one hour and two minutes late for a state of Florida gathering that was intended to settle the financial and personal matters of Kate Twillinger once and for all.

He had gone out of his way to avoid meeting her, even though Charley had arranged for his firm to handle her family trust fund with him as administrator. Pouring over boxes of old paperwork, he had gleaned hints from the documents that Charley had been married, or at least in a relationship, with Kate's mother, Matilda "Tillie" Twillinger, and had handled her financial affairs. Old personal letters indicated that Tillie had implored him to leave his government responsibilities behind and run off to South America with her. Failing in this, she had married a super-rich Uruguayan suspected of dope running, and the two of them had boarded his yacht in Bermuda and motored in a southwesterly direction into the triangle, never to be seen again.

Carter knew well in advance about the meeting in Orange Glory, but it was a bit of a miracle he showed up at all. He had taken an ocean liner across the Atlantic and been to Chicago and Los Angeles via Amtrak, but he had not boarded a plane in a decade. In order to arrive in

Central Florida he had driven from New York down the length of the East Coast in his Bentley Sport. Since no one felt any consideration, affection, or traditional Southern Hospitality for the carpetbagger shyster from *Up North*, they had started the proceedings without him.

A motley assortment with varying degrees of interest gathered in the office of Mr. Reginald Keyes-Smythe, the portly gentleman himself a certified and in good standing member of the Florida bar association. These offices were located on one corner of the tattered Orange Glory village square, the green patch itself now functioning as the home of the Squeezers little league baseball team.

Reginald Keyes-Smythe (no one dared call him Reggie) was an old man with small, squinty eyes and a round pumpkin of a face that looked like it had been caught in a closing elevator door. Kate, of course, was there as the main topic, though from her disinterested gaze it seemed she might mentally not be there at all. Something strange about her; ten years had passed and she didn't look as if she'd aged more than a year or two at most. As a ward of the state, she had been passed from one temporary home to another, a cash deal that had little to do with family upbringing. She had been in a position to be raped a time or two by her foster parents or siblings, but she had proved annoyingly slippery, and the frightened humans had quickly passed her back to the authorities.

“This here be no ordinary child,” a State of Florida case worker drawled around a fat chaw of Wrigley’s Juicy Fruit gum. She jerked a thumb in Kate’s direction and droned from her notes as if she was talking into a recorder, which in fact she was. This was Bibbie Mae Bointon, and she sported a pouty makeup-free set of facial wrinkles accented by an oily head of straight, stringy black hair. Bibbie paid fearsome attention to whatever subject was at hand, and as she spoke, the muscles around her jaws made it seem like she was spitting and chewing at the same time, the question on every observer’s mind being *Would the big wad of gum stay in her mouth?*

“The subject never went to school.” Here Bibbie gave another twitch of disgust in Kate’s direction, the one she reserved for the ignorant and dimwitted. “This here Katherine Twillinger, under-aged minor, was non-schooled by her grandmother.”

“Non-schooled?” Keyes-Smythe’s wide face took on a puzzled lawyerly look.

“Her gran’mommy Lu locked her in the study in their house every day for eight hours except during the picking and packing months. Read or no food.”

“That sounds mighty harsh.”

“Lot you know about it, Hot Pants. No friends except for the pickers’ kids.”

“Picker’s kids?” Chief Hot Pants frowned. “I don’t like that.”

“Don’t matter what you don’t like,” Bibbie Mae shot at him from across the room, practically losing her gum in the effort. "Don't know why you're here in the first place, this bein' a State of Florida affair."

Things were about to get nasty, but just then Carter Flinn, his fancy English import car parked and cooling down outside, entered the room with quiet grace, brushed some imagined dust from a straight-backed oak wood chair and took his seat in the back of the room. He had not taken the bar in Florida and knew he was in enemy territory and would be better off to practice lawyerly invisibility.

Carter recognized Kate from her pictures in the green file folder that Charley had passed on to him over a decade ago, and from the trust fund that had been placed in his care. But it was puzzling. Sitting quietly in the room, up close she looked like a young teenager, sixteen or seventeenyears old at the most. She had to be at least twice that age just by the general facts in Charley's green folder. Her birth certificate and any papers suggesting her exact age were missing from the files, but before Charley died he had referred to her as a teenager. Even the family trust papers revealed nothing as to when she was born. Interestingly enough, her mother, Matilda's, birth was listed as 1895, and that could not be right, because she would most probably be too old to have a child in her fifties. Charley had referred to the mother as a witch, and how did the old saying go, *If witches rode broomsticks, time itself could hide.* But Carter himself, who was pushing forty, was routinely carded in bars and restaurants, so he was hardly one to question appearances.

The man Carter had always thought of as his father had been a devious and secretive fellow, and Charley could only guess how old he was. Charley hadn't aged that much over the years until right near the end when he seemed to fall apart all at once, so maybe Tillie had known some witchy business and maybe she'd passed it on to Charley. It was a fairly sure bet that if Charley had found the mythical fountain of youth, he would try it on himself. And Carter himself looking to be half his real age…well, it was just one more reason to suspect Charley had involved him in activities more unusual than kickball and fishing trips.

He found Kate fascinating and disturbingly attractive. He felt a momentary flush of shame, like he was some sort of cradle robber. Still, with her curly strawberry blond hair and sullen, pouty looks he couldn't help himself.

And then her head lifted and she was studying him, her light blue eyes resting on his face. Their gaze locked and something happened between them. It was electric, magic, impossible, unexpected, but undeniably real. He would swear in later years that one corner of her lips twitched with a little smile and she winked at him. Maybe that actually happened and maybe it did not, but something clicked deep inside him and he would never be the same again.

As for Kate herself, after that one look she shared with him, her personality scurried back into her shell. It was as if she had walled off the rest of the world and was living on some other planet, oblivious to every other person in the room. Her lips moved as if she was mouthing words to hidden presences in the room. Carter concentrated and found he could just barely make out what she was saying.

"They're talking about me like I'm not here."

He guessed she was confiding to a small faux bronze bust of Mark Twain that was sitting on top of Reginald Keyes-Smythe's cluttered roll top. Carter could relate, having grown up in his father's house of secrets. They always talked over his head, which was a mistake because he understood most of everything from very early on. Carter was the original alienated young person, the outsider, the perversely suspicious one who instinctively didn't like anybody, and yet here he found himself attracted to this odd and alienated girl, perhaps, he thought, because she was so like the young self he once was.

In spite of the barriers he automatically put up to stifle any personal feelings of emotion for anyone, he was feeling some sort of powerful bond, as if with one glance she lit some fire deep inside him that he'd forgotten or perhaps had never imagined existed. *What the hell was going on here?* And then she turned her gaze on him again and he felt the full penetrating force of those blue eyes penetrating into his soul, saw the curly reddish blond hair like a radiant blaze of glory around her perfectly shaped features and wondered why nobody else in the room saw what he did.

Kate Twillinger was beautiful, she was perfect, she was wonderful. And just like that Carter Flinn lost his heart forever.

Of course, he didn't know it at the time. It wasn't like there were violins or angels singing. He was in a musty old legal office, wrestling with matters of custody and inheritance. He struggled to drag his attention back to the proceedings. Ridiculous to think for a moment he could fall for an empty headed teenager.

"Little migrant worker bastard kids," the fire chief was saying, still talking about the picker's kids.

The Florida lawyer patted his big belly and nodded to the chief. "Here a few weeks, steal the tarnished silver right out from the drawers and *adios mu-cha-chos.*"

"The frickin' grandma beat her, Bibbie Mae spat out. "No surprise she ends up with her limited mental ambiguities."

"Capabilities," Kate corrected her.

"Whatever," Bibbie spitefully last-worded her.

"Beat her?" Carter asked, speaking up for the first time.

Keyes-Smythe gave him the cold eye, "You're that carpet bagging fodg-itator from the Big Apple, right?"

"Ahh, yes, Carter Flinn, esq."

His attention flicked to Kate, who was still in conversation with Mark Twain, and then back to Bibbie.

"What is this about physical abuse?"

"Regular Saturday night beatings, it says here,"

Bibbie Mae gave him a suspicious look and then squinted down at the paperwork in front of her.

"A church meeting sort of thing, whups a'side her head and such, for the good of her everlasting, ahh, soul. Religious method-ology started up just about the time we'd be getting them power surges, blowin' out fuses all over town.

"Them two circumstances hardly be related, Bibby Mae," the Fire Chief chided. "Conflagrations of the combustible sort is my bailiwick."

"What, Granny Lu whaling her dang little butt?" the police chief grinned. "Why that ain't no more than proper parenting.

"No, says here more like whups concentrating to the side of her head, to get her thinking proper in the ways of Christianity."

Punches to the head was a continuing thread running through the Orange Glory project. Carter stored the notion in his mental file. Something about it seemed familiar enough to make him even more uneasy than he already was.

Meanwhile, in a specialized military retirement home about 40 miles down the road, perpetual screw up and army misfit Fritz Harper was thinking he might have finally set his life on the right track. His stroke of good fortune had begun ten years before, when he was assigned to clean up Charley Birch's room. Mopping up dried blood wasn't exactly his specialty and so he was reading The Judas Goat, an old Robert B. Parker murder mystery involving Spencer, the American detective, going after a bunch of European terrorists. Fritz leaned back in Charley's old chair, the back of the chair gave way and Fritz found himself on the floor dizzily staring up at a thin stenographer's notepad taped to the underside of Charley's desk. Fritz ripped the notepad from its mooring and saw it was full of Charley's notes, handwritten in a crabby style so tiny as to be almost unreadable. It was just a list of names and numbers. He was about to throw it away when he saw his own name, and the few lines following that were to change his life.

Fritz Harper, #310270 – Incubation batch 32. Order to terminate countermanded by Podorfsky, who says he likes his 'aggressive' tendencies.

Fritz read and re-read the two lines. When he set down the notebook he saw his fingers were shaking. He stood and went to the bathroom to gaze at his own image in the small mirror over the sink. He was Fritz Harper, looked down on as a low-life military worker bee and only accepted because of his top secret classification, and that only given because they needed somebody to clean the toilets and take out the trash. He had been scuffed around by the military as long as he could remember, given the thankless job of shepherding and guarding Orange Glory experimental subjects for years, only to find out now that he was actually one of them, Fritz Harper, test tube experiment # 310270. *How could that be?* He hated them, every stinking last one with their superior airs and thinking they could talk to God and such. But Charley had also told him he believed *you had to be a zoomin to kill one of them.* Feelings and half-formed ideas began to merge in Fritz, and he thought he could see his future resolving itself right there before his eyes. He could become an assassin like Ollie the Sniper, only better. Much, much better. But wait, that would take training. It was going to be hard work. That evening he sent away for mail order karate lessons before he drove to the base, checked out his M1 rifle and jogged a mile and a half over to the firing range.

CHAPTER EIGHT
mulling Kate's future

Back in the lawyer's office, Carter realized the lawyer and the two local chiefs, one wearing a police badge and the other his fireman's boots, were staring in his direction.

"What?" he asked.

"We were talking amongst ourselves before you got here, that your purpose might be to steal this poor defenseless child from our custodianship and whisk her back up north with you."

"No such intentions. I am here against my will. Actually, at the demand of my deceased father, Charley Birch."

"I remember Charley Birch! Died maybe ten years ago, He come out here and was talking to me about the power lines and the grey boxes and such. I remember reading his obit. That damn son of a bitch never had no children! He was too mean!"

"If wishes were horses," Carter said with a sad shake of his head/

"…beggars would ride."

That was a murmured refrain from Kate, across the room/

"If turnips were watches," he said.

"I'd wear one by my side."

She didn't return the sudden startled glance he cast in her direction. A little rattled, he fished around in his briefcase until he found the document he was looking for and handed it to Keyes-Smythe.

"Charley Birch's last will and testament."

The fat Floridian took a brief glance at the document and began a sputtering protest, "But-but-but this says that daggum bastard Charley controls the entire Twillinger estate!"

"Controlled. Like your own man here said, Charley died some time ago."

It was a moment before the Florida lawyer could collect his thoughts.

"W-w-what are we supposed to do now? The estate! The citrus grove. That there property just lying there has to be over fifty prime acres!"

Carter shrugged, "Sell it for fair market value. You should have done so years ago. Rent it and grow bananas or mangos, I don't care. Money goes into the trust."

The Florida lawyer pursed his fat lips and his eyes narrowed. "The trust. A trust that you now claim to control."

"Always have controlled. Contest it if you want. There's enough money to crush you like a June Bug."

"And if we decide to play along?"

"Everything stays just as it is. The girl is in state school, right?"

"Institute," Bibbie corrected him.

"Whatever. I go back to the big Macintosh. Regular check payments head this way, just like always. You handle this end." Carter nodded in Kate's direction and the men in the room started jawing their options, leaving him and Kate out of it.

"Right here," Kate said to Mark Twain. "I'm right here."

"Maybe you're a figment of my imagination," the metal bust replied, "Like Huckleberry Finn or Tom Sawyer."

Carter overheard Kate's conversation, but no one else in the room paid any attention to her. His mind was spinning again because he thought he'd just heard a statue talking. Bibbie Mae had told them Kate had been hit in the head. Repeatedly, her insanity (if that was what it was) brought about by violence. Carter was remembering his own childhood, specifically the karate lessons his father had insisted he take, and the many kicks to the head he had endured. Charley had been furious when Carter decided on his own to quit. Charley had insisted he continue, but the teacher, a weird oriental with ideas of his own, had rebelled and unexpectedly left for parts unknown.

"I'm not sure we can in any way categorize her as mentally capable," Keyes-Smythe was saying, frowning at the papers on the desk in front of him.

"Well, that's not for you to say," Bibbie Mae dismissed his idea with a puff of breath that flapped her thin lips and nearly out-chucked her gum.

"It damn well is!" Keyes-Smythe flared, angry that his role in this entire business was now diminished to administration rather than control. This outburst brought on a fit of coughing and he wiped a few spots of bloody spit from his lips with a linen handkerchief that was already blotched with an irregular flower petal field of brown stains. "I am supposed to have the authority here!"

Carter gathered his wits and shook his head. "You have day-to-day responsibility to make sure the doled out proceeds of the Twillinger trust stay on track. That is an important responsibility. No matter what is decided here today, Kate is sole beneficiary. And the will, the trust, the funds themselves are not a Florida matter."

"Let's get back to the matter at hand," Bibbie Mae furiously chewed her gum. "Local folks at the institute school say Kate here talks to Jesus." The social worker pulled the big wad of gum from her ruby red lips in a string long enough to admire and then slurped it back. "That true, child? Do you talk to Jesus?"

"Oh, finally, you're talking to me?"

The sarcasm was not lost on Bibbie Mae, who replied with a thin smile, "Don't you sass me now, little Missy White Trash."

Keyes-Smythe looked in her direction, thinking it might be a very good thing, indeed, if the child proved to be addled about the wits, "Yes, dear girl, speak up. Tell us, do you talk to God? How about the saints?"

"All good people talk to the Lord Almighty Savior," Kate said. "It's called prayer."

"I mean directly to Jesus. One-on-one."

"That's what prayer is."

She turned her gaze on Carter Flinn, and the weight of her attention was like a minor earthquake on his emotions. Carter knew he would never be able to kill her with the small handgun he had brought along in his briefcase. And in that moment he knew so much more. Kate was not his daughter as that lying old Charley Birch had claimed. She was no relative at all, and yet they shared a kinship, something strange and powerful and unknown.

Now thoroughly rattled, Carter snapped shut his briefcase and abruptly got to his feet, ready to start back to his safe office high in a New York skyscraper.

"Sit down, son," Reginald Keyes-Smythe said. "We got a ways to go yet, and you might as well be witness to the forthrightness of our intentions."

"Simple child," the social worker snarled.

"I am not a child," Kate said.

Bibbie Mae angrily shook her head, pursing her lips and blowing out an exasperated breath that expelled the chewing gum from her mouth. The wad of gum arced in an unfortunate trajectory to land like a giant pink amoeba on the light grey woolen fabric of Carter Flinn's carefully pressed suit pants. Before anyone could say a word she snatched it with her fingers and popped it back in her mouth.

Keyes-Smythe ignored the chewing gum incident. His eyes narrowed as he considered his options. Maybe this outcome would not be too bad. He still could control the money flow from the north. That was more of a stalemate than a loss.

"What about a convent school?" Something about the idea amused the Florida lawyer. *That could be a match made in hell, a girl who claimed to talk with Jesus living with a pack of old maids who believed they were married to him!*

Carter Flinn was gazing down at the gummy wet spot on his trousers, seeming at a loss for any other solution as the disposal of Katherine Twillinger.

"Well, some sort of boarding school would solve your immediate problem, what to do until she makes it to twenty one."

"But I'm already way past thirty five," Kate muttered, too low for anyone but Carter to hear. "And I thought you were going to help." She gave him a momentary glare before turning away. She was feeling sad and furious and empty. Sad for her missing mom, and furious at these people who were settling her life as if she was a slave or a pet.

"I don't need any help from the state of Florida. I could go back to live in the tin shed, rebuild the house , run our orchard that for certain needs plenty of attention by this time."

"You ain't got the smarts for it, child," Bibbie Mae spat out.

"I'm as normal as the next person in this screwed up town!"

"Shush, girlie," Keyes-Smythe said. "You all go on and shush yourself down now."

Counting down to the last minutes of his morning shift at the East Side Winterhaven Rest Home, it was grumpy Detail Sergeant Bill Hilverson's bad luck to be in a great hurry to get to the Tuesday Noon Looper pole dancing competition at his favorite strip joint in Boomtown. He banged through the door into the room where Fritzy Dumb-As-A-Brick was supposed to be cleaning up, and unexpectedly caught the sharp leading edges of a multi-bladed shuriken in his neck. The spinning star cut into him like it was buzzing a celery stalk, only to catch on and bury itself in his neck bones. The chubby little Sergeant expelled one gurgling gasp of air through his severed windpipe as he saw showers of his own red blood spurt and spatter everywhere around the room. His eyes bulged and there was a last wild look of disbelieving horror on his face just before his shuddering body sank to the floor.

Fritz, who had been readying another star to fling at a pin up picture of some babe riding a bomb that somebody had tacked to the wall years ago, shook his head and muttered to nobody in particular, “Billy Boy, you have to have the worst timing since that iceberg hit the Titanic.”

Cleaning up the body wasn’t much of an extra chore. Fritz already had the mop and pail. He tidied up the room and rolled unlucky old Bill to the elevator and took him down to the crematorium in the basement. He wasn’t in any hurry. Something told him he had plenty of time to pick up his poison dart blow gun and drive north to that stupid little town of Orange Glory where he just might clean up that other mess that had been bothering him for a bunch of years.

CHAPTER NINE

what is to become of Kate

Carter was beginning to think he was never going to get out of Keyes-Smythe's claustrophobic little office. He felt something important was going on that he didn't understand, though he could not exactly say what the problem was or why he felt the way he did. He couldn't help himself; he kept exchanging glances with Kate, and there was something irresistible, wonderful, extraordinary about her. Sunlight streaming in through a dirty art nouveau stained glass window seemed to dance and twirl in a magical way among the dust motes in the air. In one sense everything was normal as it should be, and yet *his* senses were off the chart; the faces warping and looming in front of him just enough to give a dreamlike state to the meeting, and worse, he had a vague but somehow very real impression of some unknown danger that was looming in to destroy him forever. With the long history of odd events connected to his father and the Orange Glory project, he believed that in moments like these, nothing he saw could be trusted, nothing was as it should be. How could it be that back in his sterile white office in a forty-two story building high over Manhattan his life was so ordinary and here in this hick town in the Florida backwash it was suddenly so disconnected and unpredictable? He shook the cobwebs from his thoughts and tried to concentrate on the real here and now, even though these people were crazy.

Thinking to cling to some part of reality, he focused on the steady pendulum swing of the huge old grandfather clock behind Keyes-Smythe's cluttered desk. But the clock betrayed him, first speeding up like a racing car engine and then slowing to an unsteady heartbeat.

"So you can do it, too," a voice in his mind said. He looked across the room and saw Kate's intense gaze on him.

"D-do what?"

"Slip in and out of regular time," the voice said.

"I didn't know I was doing that." He was so rattled he wanted to jump out the nearest window and run for his life.

"Calm down, slick boy from the Big Apple. It is a blessing as well as a curse."

She seemed to be right about that. After a moment he looked around and everything, at least for the moment, was back to normal.

Carter nodded in the direction of his fat counterpart, the old Florida lawyer, "He doesn't know the first thing about you, does he?"

"No, he does not. None of them do."

"Honey-child," In real time, Keyes-Smythe was droning away in that patronizing, deep-sermon voice of his, "you are a minor until you're 18, and you don't get to even think the words 'estate' or 'inheritance' until you are 21. You can't take care of yourself and there's no one else." Keyes-Smythe gave her a humorless smile Carter figured he reserved for idiots and infants.

The grossly overweight old man pushed some papers in Kate's direction, looking at Chief Big Bug Jack while he spoke, "Her grandpa gave me power of attorney before he died."

The lawyer's monstrous moon face swam in Carter's vision. He knew the papers had to be wrong, but Carter himself was again feeling ill, like he was falling through space, frozen in time.

"That isn't grand pappy's signing," Kate said.

"How would you know?" Keyes-Smythe snapped at her. Carter saw the old man's teeth were round little barrels with gaps in between, perfect dentures for a creature with a pumpkin head.

"She was only four when he died," Chief Hot Pants nodded. "That there is the God's truth. How could she know?"

Carter looked around in dumbfounded bewilderment. Things were going badly out of sync again. The world was tumbling about his senses; the dark wooden paneled walls of the office were flowing like deep and dangerous water around him, the floor a wavering raft in a muddy stream, the fluorescent lights overhead a blinding lemon yellow sky. He did not dare open his mouth for fear he'd babble strange devil nonsense and speak in tongues. He had presented his papers; they were air-tight and shouldn't be contested. Maybe that was it. Maybe he was done. Maybe he could simply walk to his car, get back in and drive back to Manhattan. He was hoping he could take the three or four steps he needed to get out the door before he made a complete fool of himself.

But the Florida lawyer and his two *Chief buddies* formed a tight huddle that was blocking his way. Carter could feel the weight of their indecision as they studied the contested signatures on the old contracts. They were looking at each other and wondering what to do next. Carter turned to see if there was another way out of the room, but that was when he realized he had totally gone off the deep end into kookooville, for there was a bearded man in robes standing next to him.

"Holy crap, that had to be over a quarter century ago," Jesus muttered in the New York lawyer's ear, one hand on the nearest shoulder of Carter's fine dark woolen suit. "What do you think, lawyer-man? I guess they could have bleached out the originals."

"They couldn't do that to any good effect," Carter heard himself saying. "I have the originals back at my office."

Keyes-Smythe's wide face blanched at Carter's remark. He was looking past the bearded man as if he wasn't aware of his presence in the room.

Kate didn't remember seeing Jesu Christi come in, but he was here now, standing right next to her New York lawyer. While nobody else was looking, she saw the Savior rub his hand over the signatures on the paper, and the name Jerome Meyer Twillinger smudged as if it had been signed a half hour ago, which in fact it had.

Carter blinked and shook his head, the pain of a sudden full migraine blurring his senses. He reached for the edge of the nearby desk to steady himself..

“What the devil are you doing?” Keyes-Smythe glared at Carter and snatched the papers off his desk.

“Nothing,” Carter said. “Just had a little dizzy spell. Can I see those papers?”

“You just said you have your own copies.” The old lawyer hurriedly gathered up the pile of documents, sliding the one with the now-smudged and illegible signature in the middle of the pile. “We’re through in here.”

“Miracles do happen,” Jesus said, giving Carter’s shoulder a little shake as if to wake him to the real world of possibilities.

“Yes they do,” Kate replied.

“Get what you needed, Reginald?” Chief Hot Pants and Chief Big Bug both leaned over in a vain attempt to have their own look at the documents. Together they were so overweight there was very little room for Kate or Jesus. Actually, it was Kate and Carter, the Christ having murmured *My work here is done* and dissolving into thin air.

“That is one of his best tricks,” Kate said, staring directly at Carter, “Maybe better even than the wine-into-water gag.”

“W-w-what’s happening?” Carter managed to stutter.

By this time Keyes-Smythe had jammed the contracts in a desk drawer and slammed it shut.

“That’s not grandpa’s handwriting.” Kate insisted.

"It doesn't matter," Carter said, bringing his thoughts back to a real world he understood, that of legal abstractions. "Pumpkin head here probably moused the paper with his Xerox machine, but we have our own originals back at my office."

"Who are you calling 'pumpkin head?" Keyes-Smithe wanted to know.

"Maybe Granny Lu signed them?" Chief Hot Pants suggested hopefully. He grinned at Chief Big Bug. "She sure put her print on everything else around here, not even counting Old Gund."

"Orange Glory ain't that big a place," Chief Big Bug, who himself had found his way a time or two with the old Lu-bird, said by way of a gentle protest.

And wouldn't you know it, his old pal Chief Hot Pants took that opportunity to stick up for their God-awful town, "What, we got the general store, the post office in the general store, the Wild Goose Saloon and the taco stand. One stop sign at the corner of Tangerine and Lime Tree Way."

"Can't be no more than ten, fifteen male citizens in all," Keyes-Smythe agreed with a sober nod, his anger over the slight to the plumpness of his features fading.

Carter Flinn said nothing, clearly out of his element. He was weaving on his feet, the dizzy spell continuing. He stared at the bust of Mark Twain on a nearby bookshelf. Mark proved to be no help, either, winking at him and reciting, "There is nothing in the world like persuasive speech to fuddle the mental apparatus."

Kate looked from Carter to the bronze statue, “I don’t remember you saying that.”

That’s when the lawyer from New York City admitted to himself that nothing in his once-orderly life was ever going to be the same. Still, he could see he wasn’t alone, as pretty Kate was clearly sharing his madness. *Pretty Kate.* There was a lot going on in his mind. This was not good, because while he was on overload, everyone else in the room was oblivious to the fact of Jesus smudging the paperwork, and now the bronze talking bust of Mark Twain.

“Maybe she is just plain crazy,” Big Bug Jack suggested, tilting his head in Kate’s direction. “Staring off into nothing like that. Old Lulubird always swore she was *whacko-bird*, that there was the term I think she used.”

“Yeah, sure,” Keyes-Smythe gave a bitter little kick at one of the bear claw feet on the legs of his desk. “We declare insanity, the state of Florida gets everything.”

“State of New York,” Carter managed.

“Whatever,” Keyes-Smythe suffered another round of coughing into his handkerchief.

“Oh.” Bibbie Mae looked off in the direction Kate was staring. The case worker was now hard about trying to figure ways to rescue Lulubird’s granddaughter from the charge of insanity, not for Kate’s own good but because Bibbie had finally realized that might take her out of the State of Florida’s control. “Well, maybe her brain isn’t empty as a new vacuum cleaner bag. Maybe she’s just thinking, uh, intelligent thoughts about stuff like nature and poetry."

To Carter's consternation, Jesus had returned and was sitting next to the green shade lamp, right in front of the police and fire chiefs. While this made for a very crowded room, none of the others seemed to notice the Savior except Kate, who gave a mocking snort in his direction.

And, of course, the bust of one of America's premier literary wits also noticed. "Always do right," Mark advised.

"Why should I?" Jesus asked, the pleasant curiosity evident in his manner.

"It will gratify some people and astonish the rest."

"Didn't work out that way for me," Jesus shrugged.

"There's an exception to every rule," Twain glared, not liking to be upstaged.

"You might have mentioned that a little sooner, saved me a lot of trouble."

"Oh sure, blame the soothsayer," the little statue grumped from under his tarnished patina.

Carter wondered why the rest of the people in the room weren't gaping at the Savior's soccer hat, now swiveled brim-backwards on his head. The hat was covered with Sam The Olympic Eagle pins, Sam lifting weights, pole vaulting, throwing a spear, heroic world-class athletics for a little eagle chick.

"You like my hat?" Jesus asked him. "Very big collector's items," he said. "I've got coffee mug collectables, too."

Carter frowned, "Interesting, as the Olympics have not been held in Los Angeles since before World War II."

"Think future-past," the bearded man told him.

"What?"

"Get outside your life and beat in tune along with it, attribution freely given to Ortega y Gasset You see, the Olympics will be held in Los Angeles in 1984. Be there or be square."

"What?"

"What – what – what. You're starting to sound like a skipping 78 rpm record."

CHAPTER TEN

meanwhile across the street

Just how Fritz Harper, wannabe army exterminator extraordinaire, who was afraid of any height greater than a few inches, came to be carrying a blow gun and three poison darts dipped in deadly curare as he teetered one step away from a disastrous plunge off the sloping and dangerously weak tin roof of the Steady Eddy Burger & Taco Joint across Main Street from Keyes-Smythe's faux adobe office…well, that was a story in how the human mind can take crooked paths on the way to what passes for clear thinking. Two days before, Fritz had been on a Tri-County Transit (TCT) bus heading for a small clean up job in Kissimmee when the bus squealed to a stop and a hunched over old lady scrambled up the steps and came down the aisle like a fusty old crab. She was small as a pigmy with skin smooth and dark as polished ebony, and the sight of her reminded Fritz of an article in National Geographic magazine featuring an isolated and seemingly friendly band of little Congo or Amazon rain forest people with their deadly accurate blow guns that could bring down monkeys and rhinos and elephants. And that in turn reminded him he had a CIA friend who knew everything about poison because of a spate of recent KGB trickery in that area of elimination expertise, and so he went to see his friend and sure enough there was a potent boil-down from something his pal called the blacklegged dart frog and for $250 dollars and a gallon of cracker white lightning Fritz came away with a technologically advanced plastic blowgun, three darts, and the warning to keep the wax coating on the tips until he was ready to puff them in the right direction.

"You know it's not an exact science, right?" the poison guy asked.

"Deadly. You said deadly." Fritz pulled back the wad of money he was about to hand over.

"Well, sure, deadly, but it could take five seconds or five hours."

Fritz shrugged and handed over the money.

"Dead is dead," he said.

True, this expedition was a bit off the radar, but Fritz was chafing with frustration; he wasn't being allowed to live up to his potential, and he figured the General would be pleased if Kate Twillinger was taken off the playing board, no matter how she slipped over the great divide. So he signed up for three day's leave, rented a Ford Bronco from Rent-A-Wreck and headed for the distant rural burg of Orange Glory.

And now he found himself just one or two puffs away from a kill shot and the big promotion he figured would be his due. The problem was, the tin roof was crackly and the wind was up and the curtains in the open window to the lawyer's office kept swaying this way and that, making it difficult to blow off a clean shot. The girl was right there, in front of the window! Fritz was sure it was her; she looked as if she hadn't aged a day in ten years. But first the overweight fire chief and then in another moment when the target was clear the clunky police chief would move this way or that to block his shot.

Inside the office, Carter wasn't doing so well. He went to the window and pushed it further open as far as it would go, breathing deeply like a man who couldn't get enough oxygen.

Big Bug nudged Hot Pants, glancing in Carter's direction. "Big Apple carpetbagger seems like he's not firing on all his cylinders."

"We best be careful, maybe it's infectious."

"Contagious, you mean," the little bust of Mark Twain said.

"Don't tell me what I mean, Bug."

"I never said nothing."

Keyes-Smythe hoisted himself out of his chair. The portly southern lawyer sucked his yellow teeth. "Come on, everybody, get out of my office. I'll take over from here." He pointed one chubby finger at Bibbie Mae, "You make sure she gets to the boarding school. Some school. Any school" He swiveled his rotund frame around and pointed the same finger at the carpetbagger from New York City. "And you make sure the bills get paid."

Kate protested, "No! The tractor shed is still standing! I can live there, and all Mamma's books are there."

"Impossible, child." Bibbie Mae shook her head, "And no church boarding school, neither. It got to be a state run school." Bibbie was already on her feet, slipping her notes into her briefcase.

Kate may only have been half in the so-called real world, but even she could see she had no control over her future. These Florida officials were going to shove her in a box and throw away the key. Her own lawyer wasn't going to be any help at all. She had thought there might be a connection, that he might be somebody special, but now she could see he was a wuss, a timid little mouse. Sure, he could see Jesus and give time clocks a push or two, but beyond that he was no help at all, the poor fellow looked stun-gunned, like he'd just come through shock treatments.

She felt herself losing her grip. She cast a wild glance around Keyes-Smythe's office. No help anywhere. Nothing had changed in decades. The ancient lawyer had been grandpa's legal resource practically since before time began and dinosaurs ruled the earth, and, although she could see he was ill and not long for this earth, chances were he wasn't going to keel over in time to help her out of the current mess. The heavy oak furniture looked at least three times older than he was, and he was pushing eighty with those ugly crusty spots all over the inside of his lungs.

Kate glanced at the portraits on the wall, prints of Thomas Jefferson and Franklin Delano Roosevelt, an odd pair of presidents to Kate's way of thinking. Jefferson frowned down from the wall at her and he made a foreboding cluck, cluck, cluck sound with his tongue, nearly impossible considering he was oil paint on a canvas.

FDR gave him that arch, superior look of his.

"Kids are less responsible today than they were in our time. Or more, I'm not sure."

"You know nothing at all about my time, Franklin, sir. And less about the constitution of the

United States of America, which you cuffed about rather seriously during your overextended stay in the oval office."

"My presidential years were harsher than anything you lived through, Tommy-boy. I led our nation through the Great Depression and a World War."

"No, you caused the first and messed up the second."

"Why, you scoundrel!"

Kate shook her head. *Two dead presidents arguing over their history rating!*

"Young lady, are you paying attention?"

The ancient Mr. Keyes-Smythe, the police chief and the Fire Chief were eyeing her.

"What do you mean, sir?"

Chief Hot Pants started in on her, "The circumstances of those fires are…somewhat suspect."

"That was ten years ago!"

Chief Big Bug added, "There ain't no state of limitations on that."

"Statute of limitations," Jefferson murmured.

"Young lady, we've reviewed your testimony after the Cleo hurricane disaster. You wove a lurid tale of rape and pillage. Entirely unbelievable. Absurd. And there is extensive evidence that you appear to be something of a habitual liar."

"The firemen saw the bikers!"

"They saw some motor bike boys driving past, but that is hardly documented proof."

"I was raped!"

Keyes-Smythe looked to his police chief for assurance, "You were somewhat bloody and bruised in your, err, private parts, however…"

That was when Fritz, leaning on his elbows on the tin roof across Main Street saw his clear shot and puffed his first dart at Kate, aiming for the alluring curve of her fresh young left breast. Unfortunately, at that moment the manager of the Steady Eddy chose to yell, "Goddamned raccoons!" and hammer the roof of the joint with a greasy spatula, causing Fritz to lose his concentration and the dart errantly flying across the street to bounce off the faux adobe of the lawyer's office a few inches to the left of the open window.

Inside the lawyer's office, events were proceeding as if there were no darts, no poison frogs, and no little people in some far away rainforest who knew how to fell big game.

"Stop battering at the child!" Carter Flinn raised his voice for the first time, surprising everyone. "You are just blathering! No matter what, the trust remains intact."

"But you can't presume to take her back to New York with you."

"No, but if anything happens to this girl, the money goes to charity. All of it. And I don't think foisting her off as a ward of the state is a good idea."

"We can take you to court!"

"Welcome to New York. You'd better be satisfied with what you're getting. Were it my say, your fee would be cut in half right now." 'Carter shrugged, "But it isn't. Stick to the deal. You sell the orange ranch, the money goes into the trust, and we pay a private school for her room and board." That said, he looked over Keyes-Smythe's head, staring at the paintings on the wall as if anything the Florida lawyer might have to say to him didn't really matter.

"A trust?" Jefferson asked. Both he and FDR were frowning down at Carter with the full weight of their historical presences, except that Jefferson was working his teeth with an ivory pick.

"Stop that public tooth-cleansing," FDR said. "Unbecoming in a President of the United States."

"You're one to talk. Franklin, you couldn't even poop your pants without somebody carrying you to the outhouse, you worthless pinko lefty cripple."

FDR gave him a look of shocked outrage.

Carter thought full-fledged hostilities were going to break out on the wall. He didn't even have time to think how crazy he was as Keyes-Smythe interrupted to address Kate through his bloody handkerchief, "Kate, dear child, once you're settled, I'll send along Tillie's books."

The mention of the name caught the bickering presidents' attention.

"Who in God's name is Tillie?" Jefferson paused to scratch his hairline with his ornately embossed silver toothpick.

"Kate's mom, you tottering idiot. And don't take the name of the Lord in vain."

"We slapped it on our dollar bills. That's honor, not irreverence."

"A polecat by any other name still smells the same," Mark Twain chimed in from his perch on the desk.

"What about Kate's mom?" the New York barrister asked his Florida counterpart.

"You mean the strange, possessed lady who traveled the world on her mysterious husband's insurance money, that is, when she wasn't resting in a home for the maniacally depressed." Keyes-Smythe's voice slipped into a tone of oily confidentiality, "Tipsy Tillie, it seems, heard voices and could not be trusted with the care of her own daughter."

"Where is my mom?" Kate asked.

"Haven't heard," Keyes-Smythe replied through the linen covering his nose and mouth.

"Is she alive?"

"No way to know, honey-child. She didn't leave no tracks."

"But declared legally dead," the police chief chimed in. "That's all that counts, right?"

Jefferson looked over at FDR. "What are they talking about?"

"Hiding money from the government, you moron. Swiss banks. Bermuda. Aruba."

"Why would anyone want to hide money from We, The People?"

FDR pulled a golden cigarette holder from his vest, stuffed in a Lucky Strike and lit up. "Go figure," he said, the light dancing merrily in his eyes.

"Can I try one of those?"

"Not in your afterlife."

Keyes-Smythe gave Kate another of his calculating looks, "There is some theory that your precious mommy pushed your Daddy Warbucks off his sports fishing boat and into the Atlantic somewhere near that triangle ocean business. She ever talk to you about any of that?"

The old man was wearing suspenders to hold up his pants, which had grown so tight it was nearly impossible for him to slip a hand inside and adjust Mister Bigstick more comfortably in his Jockey shorts, if that was what he was doing. Kate raised her eyebrows, her hands and her shoulders like all three of the zen monkeys rolled into one. See nothing. Know nothing. Hear nothing. But from the cursing that had gone on at the orange ranch, she guessed even the persistent Granny Lu and her flock of carrion eating psychiatrists didn't know where the money went. To date, no one had been able to solve the mystery of the missing millions.

His gaze locked with Kate's impossibly light blue eyes, and as if by magic their internal clocks willed time to slow down until it halted. She took his hand and they walked through the frozen statues of the few people in the room. An old pickup truck was twenty feet away, bearing down as if to run them over, but it too was suspended out of time. Across the street, a mangy dog was a statue of itself, sniffing at a garbage can in front of the burger and taco establishment, and a butterfly was suspended in mid-air over the bright orange trumpets on a honeysuckle bush. Carter looked around him in amazement.

"Thank you for showing me how to do this."

"What, step out of time? You knew all along."

"But I didn't know I knew. I know a trick. I can teach you something."

"Oh, that old line."

"No, not that. Watch me."

A look of concentration came over Carter's lean face. Kate couldn't help thinking how very attractive he was. But her eyes widened as, in the next moment, his feet lifted off the dusty pavement and he casually stood before her, suspended a foot above the ground.

"I want to do that!"

"Wait, there's more."

He ducked down and grabbed his knees and did a gentle roll forward. Then he straightened and gently settled back to the ground.

"Teach me!"

"Visualize the actual center of the earth, the very core. And then just push away from it."

She did as he instructed, but in the next second she shot upward, nearly out of sight. He caught up to her about two hundred feet off the ground and with no signs of slowing down.

"Wait! You have to control it! Pull yourself back in or you'll be on the moon!"

They came to a halt, hanging about a thousand feet in the air.

"This is w-wonderful! You're it!"

She tagged him on the shoulder and raced away, and they dipped and dove and soared after each other like young finches in springtime. Old

Missus Procter, who had lived next to one of Charley's grey boxes on the edge of town, saw them from her kitchen window, but she figured it was her bad eyes. She sipped from her coffee, laced as it was with Bundy rum.

"Damn flies. Ain't got a care in the world, buzzing around like that."

Carter and Kate were breathless and laughing as they returned to the ground. She reached up on tiptoe and kissed him lightly on the cheek. And they returned to Keyes-Smyth's musty room before a millisecond had passed.

The lawyer from New York looked around the room as if he was seeing it for the first time. He picked up his briefcase and glanced in the direction of the door. Big Bug and Hot Pants thought he looked ill, out of breath and gasping as if he might collapse before he could make his getaway.

"Hey, soldier, don't ya'all go running away now."

Carter sat back down in the nearest chair. Keyes-Smythe was going on about what to do with Kate. He pursed his lips and hissed through his stubby yellow teeth,

"Florida social services is ready to accept her with open arms, but I can get her into a good boarding school."

"You'd better," Carter Flinn said, taking a deep breath to calm himself.

"Well, what about my trust?" Kate asked,

"We'll take care of it, sweetie-pie," Keyes-Smythe said.

"No, I'll take care of it," the New York lawyer said. "You'd better burn that document you've been mousing. There has to be a law against falsification, even down here in the Confederacy. I'll send you a copy of the real one."

But his lawyerly pronouncement caused everybody to mill about in anxiety and concern, and Carter saw there was no chance, at least for the moment, that he was going to be able to get to his feet and walk out of that room.

CHAPTER ELEVEN

death shifted but not averted

Kate's happiness evaporated as she looked around the room and saw that there wasn't going to be a happy ending to the discussion. As was her long standing custom, she blanked reality out and let her mind drift. She was no longer in Keyes-Smythe's office, but this time her mind betrayed her and she found herself in one of those cheap black-and-white sci fi horror movies. Robbie the Robot was there, only he was Evil Robbie, cackling with a reverberating sound from his metallic innards. What was he laughing about? She looked to Carter for help, but he was stiff as a brick, frozen in time. She was on her own here. All the people in the crowded office were quick-frozen, caught like holographics, their mouths open, their eyes in mid-blink. But not everything was still. There it was, a bot-mosquito racing at her at the speed of light. Well, no, not the speed of light. Something more like a racing meteor. That would only be 67,000 plus miles per hour. No, wait, nothing like that, It was coming in at less than a speeding bullet, less than the speed of sound. This was going to be easy.

"You're too slow," Jesus said. "You're going to owe me for this one." To Kate it seemed as if life resumed its normal pace, rushing forward but now measured in ordinary seconds.

"This poor girl is not going to end up at that convent school," Bibbie Mae, the social worker spat out with sudden venom. It looked like this might provide a complication to the legal proceedings, but at that moment Jesus moved to intercept the speeding thing. He flicked one finger in the air, and an advanced model human with slo-mo vision would have easily seen the odd looking homemade dart as the Savior brushed it away from its primary target, only to bury itself in Bibbie Mae's neck.

Jesus plucked the dart from Bibbie's blackening skin and flicked it into the lawyer's waste can, and the unfortunate lady crumpled to the worn and dusty oak floor without a sound, her eyes staring wide at nothing and her mouth open without any air coming in or going out. It was clear she had left not only the discussion but the normal plane of mortality as well.

"How did you do that?" Carter asked.

The New York lawyer was staring at Kate, his mouth open. Kate gave him a warning look. She put her fingers to her lips and allowed him a brief sideways nod of the head. "Better be on your way, Lawyer-boy-wonder," she whispered. At that, without saying a word of goodbye to anybody, Carter took his chances and bolted out the door.

"Isn't what you did against one of the ten commandments?" Kate asked Jesus.

"I didn't do anything."

"Did, too. I saw you. Carter and I both saw you."

"Us, too," Jefferson righteously chimed in, speaking for the presidents and the dusty bust of the dead satirist.

"Maybe it was just Bibbie Mae's time to go." The Savior raised one eyebrow from under his baseball cap, trying to avoid a confrontation. He gazed down at the crumpled body lying on the floor, and his face showed a look of divine resignation. "Sometimes one look and you can just tell. Bad health management, poor posture, and that gum smacking was really getting to me."

"Somebody call 911," the Fire and Police Chiefs both said in the same voice.

"Convent school it is, then," Keyes-Smythe decided with a note of finality as he picked up the phone on his desk. Nobody was sure if he was dialing for the nuns or an ambulance.

Meanwhile, across the street, Fritz frantically rushed to load his final dart, but he was excited and out of breath and when he went to take his killing puff he inhaled and the dart ended up in his own mouth. He managed to spit it out without sticking his tongue or the inside of his mouth, but there was a rotten taste like cheap Korean kim chi. He went limp and rolled off the roof to fall ten feet into a dumpster bin located beneath him in the alley. By the time he woke, it was dark. Fritz dragged himself over the edge of the metal dumpster, made his way around the side of the Steady Eddy Burger & Taco Joint and limped along the deserted street toward his rental. His head was ringing and he felt saddened by the awareness that he still hadn't made his bones in the black op assassin business.

CHAPTER TWELVE
another airplane adventure

Carter Flinn came to believe he would never get out of the lawyer's office, much less the state of Florida. As he finally made his way out the door, he overheard Keyes-Smythe talking to the police chief. "Bug, can't we find something to jail that there carpetbagger?"

"I don't know...maybe lawyering without a local permit?"

"How about driving a foreign car? You know, like giving him a parking ticket?"

"That dang feller looked sneaky," Henry Phipps, the local coroner, joined in with his two cents worth, "You ought to hold him for something or other."

Henry also doubled as funeral director and ran the Fancy Dairy Princess soft ice cream shop and, as one of the few locals who hadn't scored with Bibbie Mae, was weighted with a suffering of unfulfilled desire for the lady, who by now had turned a light shade of purple that nobody was going to attribute to bad eye shadow or the Goth look.

"There's gonna be multiple clouds of questions to be answered and suspicion-of-guilt papers to be filled out."

Big Bug nodded uncertainly. The police chief had his own set of concerns in the criminal direction, and even the fire chief had a start up thought that he might want to know where Carter was in that long ago time when the Twillinger place and Gund's old motel lit up the night sky.

Big Bug got the siren going in his black-and-white Ford and blocked the road out of town before the New Yorker could sneak away, but Carter was cool and even friendly under his grilling and after a half hour or so the officer of the law ran out of questions. They ran outside to intercept him before he could get away.

Days passed until the youngish looking lawyer was finally given permission to leave town, but then his Bentley wouldn't start, so he had to make arrangements to have it trucked to Orlando and then ferried back to the Big Apple. Last minute seats on the trains north were unaccountably filled and Carter couldn't connect with any bus lines. So he had to get on a cursed airplane after all.

And that was how it came to be that, somewhere in the middle of the night and 26,000 feet up over Atlanta, Carter Flinn woke to find himself in a comic book adventure, or more exactly, in a three dimensional animated video of what life would be like in such an alternate universe.

Once he got over his surprise he nodded to his companion, "Unreal! We have to stop meeting like this, Vladi."

"How can you tell all of this is not real?" Vladimir Podofski asked from the seat next to him.

"It is totally bogus. Look, in the first place, I'm not scared shitless, so it must be a dream. And the little things. Notice, the lovely stewardess's skin is too smooth. No pores. And you look more like a plastic bust of Lenin than the real thing."

"Ah! It is always the details."

"What do you want, Mr. Podofski?"

"You did not perform your assignment. According to the Charley version of everything, that means we have to kill you."

"You never told me why I had to shoot the girl."

"One of you is bad enough. Two, never. You will take out the universe, and all sentient life with it."

"I thought there were a bunch of us."

"Nobody quite as stable."

"Oh, now I'm your version of stable. Me, the guy who is supposed to blow up the world."

"Universe. The known universe."

"Okay, let's play your silly game. Why was Charley – and now you – after me to fix your mess? "

"Don't be silly. One must tinker around if ever progress is to be made. That's what evolution is.

"I see. We're all just experiments."

"Yes, of course. But don't go into the feeling-sorry-for-yourself routine. Such a waste of time. From our view, you were born with the silver spoon. You had every opportunity, and yet you have failed every test we've ever given you."

"Maybe I can pass this one."

"Doubtful, but here's a clue. Everything not forbidden is compulsory."

"Oh boy. Some clue. Wasn't that something Max Planck said?

"No. Murray Gell-Mann. But he borrowed it from T.H. White."

"Wow, that's helpful. Tell me, why did Charley lie to me about everything?"

"Nobody knows why Charley does anything. Charley is a goofy-ball."

"You talk about him like he's not dead."

"Nobody is dead forever everywhere. Not anymore."

"More of your disintegrating universe theory?"

"I will do a metaphor. God is an old grandmother. She bumbles about fixing things, but it is difficult with all her grandkids knocking about. Pretty soon she cannot fix everything. A broken toy here, a cracked window, a lost stocking, a wheel off the tricycle. We were the bad children and we took over from grandma, smashed a few pots, broke a few windows. You have to help us fix what remains, before we are to be spanked, before we burn the house down."

With that, the odd Russian dissolved until all that remained of his animated presence were his glowing eyes. Unfortunately the rest of the airplane was wavering into nothingness along with him.

"Remember, young fool, the tick-tock can be speeded up as well."

In a few more seconds the glowing eyes seemed to hesitate, and then popped out like flashbulbs, and Carter was once again falling down through the icy night sky. But this time he was pretty sure there would be no saving wake up call.

He had about 200 feet to go before he would smack into solid ground when sheer fright brought blinding revelation. He could speed his presence through time – control it, actually…Podofski was referring to the fact that he could slow it down as well! Of course he could, if he could only control his panic! There was no difference between dipping around over Orange Glory with Kate and a plunge from the sky at 20,000 feet. A mental push in that direction and he found himself slowing. Another and another, and still one more and he found his fall screeching to a halt. He was hovering mere feet above the hard surface of a cobblestone pavement in front of what looked like an antique shop. He let go of his push and tumbled awkwardly the few remaining feet to the ground. He stood and brushed himself off. A nearby street sign said he was at the corner of Peachtree and Bennett Streets.

By an odd random connection Bennett was the name of the College he'd attended as an undergraduate. He visualized the old building where he'd lived in a dorm room, remembering the high tension wires that had run to a grey box located outside his window.

He shivered. It was bitterly cold with an icy sleet settling in his hair and running down his shoulders. Somewhere a dog barked and a small raccoon or a big rat scrambled in nearby bushes.

Carter resolved that, should he get out of this mess, he was going to live the quiet and uneventful life of an ordinary corporate lawyer. He would take no chances. He would make sure everything about the Katherine Twillinger file was in order and then he would put it on automatic pilot so that it would run without him, forever if necessary.

Carter walked the nearly deserted streets until he came to an all-night diner where he ordered a ham-and-eggs breakfast. He dropped quarters into the operated pay phone, and had a taxi pick him up and take him to the airport where he rented a big Ford sedan that he drove all the way back to New York City.

Over the next few weeks, Carter promptly attended to the small matter of Kate Twillinger's financial affairs, and that was a good thing, because a few days after he'd set up the eternal trust, one night when he was working late at the office some cleaning men in ordinary overhauls that said Goodwill Cleaning Service snuck up behind him and battered him unconscious with a baseball bat. They stuffed him in a soundproof duffle bag that looked like it was meant for transporting dirty laundry, and flew him to an island that was conveniently off the ordinary navigational maps.

The bag was totally wrapped in plastic and hot-band sealed so not even a breath of air could get in or out, and that was a good thing, because without that experience Carter might never have realized he could go for days or even years without breathing. He simply had to slip out of the time zone.

CHAPTER THIRTEEN

some decades later

To illustrate the average student's lack of understanding of eternity, nun and priest schoolteachers, inspired by hallucination or driven through frustration, sometimes describe the immensity of all of creation with the image of a white dove's wing that flicks a shiny steel ball every ten thousand years. When the ball is worn to nothing, that is but a blink in the eye of God. So, easy then to imagine several decades passing by and not even a minor scratch on the big ball of life. Young Kate, not at all so young as she looks, is now going by the name of Sister Mary Katherine. At her present rate of growth she may outlive Methuselah. This came as no surprise to Charley Birch, who, midway through the project roughly calculated the DNA alterations among the subjects who survived to become zoomins might allow them to live for several centuries. Just another reason to snuff them all.

Practicing invisibility, Kate only answers to Katherine and allows no one but Jesus to call her by the shorter version.

She settled in an undistinguished way within the ranks of young girls at a Catholic boarding school in Central Florida where she was considered harmless, something of a spaced-out geek who absorbed details so effortlessly no one ever thought for a moment she had actually learned them; as no human could learn that fast, and as her social skills were about as polished as a lump of coal, it was widely assumed that not much was sticking inside her rattle-brained head.

Sitting on a Saturday afternoon in the stuffy dead-air library, she dreamed of Carter Flinn and wondered what he was doing.

She cleared her mind and sent him a mental message.

What you up to, lover-boy?

We're not lovers, he answered, his voice clear in her head.

Just haven't gotten around to it yet. Something to look forward to.

You still married to Jesus?

Yep. But not for long. I feel a change is coming.

Send me some of that. I could use a little of that.

You still in the dark?

Yep. Going on 20 years now. I think they buried me.

I'm coming to get you, you know. I promise.

I'll be here.

Kate sent him a goodbye kiss and signed off. She had gathered all the novels of mystery writer Dick Francis on the desk before her and was rapidly turning pages Shifting time gears, she picked up Driving Force, read it through and set it back down before anyone realized she had moved. Then Longshot, The Edge, Hot Money, Bold and A Jockey's Life.

The librarian, Sister Ubergheen, stopped by. She was a nasty little nun with naturally pursed lips. "You can't hog all the Dick Francis, sister."

"I'm just getting the publication dates."

"You can do that from the card catalogue."

"Yes, sister."

Kate shifted into the next gear up. In the next second she read Reflex, Second Wind, To The Hilt, Come to Grief and Wild Horses. She saw what Francis was doing, and decided she'd read enough. Shifting back to standard time, she gave Ubergheen a snappy little salute.

"I'll put them all back."

"See that you do." The librarian retreated behind her desk, but Kate could see she was watching to make sure the books were returned to their proper shelf. She could have winked them back in a blink, but she got a book cart and rolled them back down the aisles. *It would give her something to do until the Messiah comes.* That old hippy expression came back to her. Her mother,Tillie, used to say that with a bemused expression on her face. Taking out the garbage or weeding the garden or anything small and simple and needing patience gave one *something to do until the Messiah comes.* She wondered if the Messiah had come to her mother often, and if her mother had found him as whimsical and unreliable a companion.

Sister Katherine was known as drifty-minded and even a little loopy, but young maidens were not lining up in droves for the celibate life, so her superiors sighed, nodded knowingly at each other and moved her along with the rest of their little flock of ewes.

When she began to blossom into young ladyhood, the religious order cunningly moved her across the country to their branch outfit in Southern California, carefully arranging so the support and tuition checks followed from New York to the Sunshine State and on to the Golden State. Of course, Kate never saw the actual money, having agreed to certain vows of poverty (as well as chastity), albeit with crossed fingers on both subjects, the final arrangements, in her own mind, to be determined later.

Kate had graduated high school and college, had taken the increasingly severe eternal and everlasting vows of her holy order with a raised degree of nervous apprehension and the same crossed fingers, and upon graduation with the equivalent of a college degree in something or other began teaching Natural Science with a passion girls usually reserve for shopping and stalking attractive young men.

Safe in the enfolding arms of the church, in January of each year she signed a document that empowered Mr. George Minson, the Florida lawyer who had taken over her affairs a few months after Mr. Keyes-Smythe coughed up a 32 ounce size mayonnaise jar of blood and passed on to his reward. Mr. Minson didn't bill Kate directly, though perhaps he should have, considering she received a monthly stipend that barely covered shoes and clothing. On the other hand, she had some resources, a bank account and a U-Storage room hidden away for her by Carter before his abduction.

Sister Katherine was considered by her peers to be a fool for devotion, but that may have been because by this time she had considerably sharpened her art of invisibility. The station of a nun was too low to allow for visions or miracles, so she kept all that *timer* business to herself and her life quietly drifted on, the months building into years. As her nun companions sadly drooped toward middle age, she remained, at least in appearance, to be in her early to mid-twenties. Nobody seemed to notice or care. Age isn't a thing of much interest when you are a lackey in the service of the Eternal Lord.

Once a month, when it was her turn to help with the grocery shopping, she would send off a postcard to a person the sister superior thought of as her harmless old uncle, one Carter Flinn, believed to live in Manhattan and said to practice law in New York City. Not knowing of the lawyer's disappearance, they figured he might some day of value, that is, if Sister Katherine should be persuaded to sign over more lasting and permanent financial attachments to the order. As Sister Bonavita, the assistant to the Mother Superior, would speed-read the postcards when Sister Katherine came to buy a stamp, the good nuns were confident there was never any communication of importance passed between the two of them. And, as Kate never touched the small but growing funds in any of the secret checking and investment accounts the clever Mr. Flinn had set up for her before he had done his own disappearing act, they were as invisible as if they, too were hidden out of the way on an uncharted island and not moving a muscle.

It had been a busy bunch of decades as well for Fritz Harper and grim faced Ollie Krell. The two of them had evolved into a two man zoomin-catcher squad. Oddly enough, Ollie the sniper looked like he had been born old, and Fritz maintained a sort of frozen, acne-pimpled adolescence, though he seemed to be getting heavier featured, and even a bit stooped over.

On one particular morning, Ollie's disdain for his partner came to at a particularly high boil. He was working on a jam in one of his antique AR-15's; parts were either missing or rattling between his feet on the floor, and nothing was right in his world.

"It's your fault we never kill any of them."

"Sure, blame me," Fritz grunted. Over the past few years, he'd been having trouble twisting his tongue around actual words, or maybe it had something to do with his vocal cords and all those unfiltered Camels he was smoking. The upshot was, he tried to keep his words brief and his sentences short. Ollie didn't seem to notice, or maybe he was grateful for the long silences.

"I feel like some sort of cheap bagman," Ollie complained.

"Bag man?" Fritz stared at him in open mouthed puzzlement.

"Yeah. We score by netting zoomins. We're supposed to snuff them, for crap's sake.

"Crazy Charley…warned us…"

"Right. And we're not paid to think. Look, you're just a low-brow fuckup, but I was born a shooter."

"A zoomin in the bag is good as one in the coffin."

"Yeah, you keep telling yourself that, Fritzie-boy."

The younger man's face flamed beet red. His forehead wrinkled until his hairline seemed to touch his heavy eyebrows. "Your fault. You been in charge."

It was Ollie's turn to show outrage. His thin lips were a gash across his skull-like face, "You're blaming me? Why you Neanderthal throwback!"

This was the worst insult Ollie Krell could heap on his partner, who had over the years indeed slumped into an appearance more than faintly pre-human. But Fritz's reality was, he was far from stupid; he had been waiting for an opportunity like this to throw his marksman buddy off his stride. He pretended to ignore Ollie, instead taking a solid gold krugerrand from his fatigues pocket and flipping it in the air, catching it and turning it over on his wrist, playing a little game of heads or tails with himself.

"What's that," Ollie asked, his eyes intent on the glittering coin.

"Krug'rand," Fritz said, forcing the difficult word out.

"Where'd you get it?"

"Bought it."

"Give it to me."

"Sure."

Fritz tossed it to him as if it was a fake foil wrapped chocolate coin. "I got more," he said.

"Give them to me."

"No."

"Why not?"

"I give, you give."

Ollie sighed. They'd played this game before. He always got the best of his partner, but it was so easy it was wearying. "Okay, what do you want."

"Next Zoom-down, I lead."

"Fuut! Impossible."

Fritz reached out and snatched back the coin, moving so fast Ollie couldn't stop him. He turned away as if the discussion was over.

"Wait! How many more coins like that do you have?"

"Seven more."

Fritz had been living for the day he would be in charge. He would show Ollie and their quietly invisible superiors who should be leading the squad. He would finally take a couple of the target enemy down and gain the respect he deserved. For years now all he could do was glower underneath his sloping forehead and thick eyebrows, plotting and planning and weaving complicated little webs, sure he would eventually snuff out one of the last remaining subjects of the Orange Glory project. And fate seemed to be giving him a bump in the right direction.

"Okay," Ollie said. "Eight gold coins. You're in charge." He held out his hand, "Hand them over."

"One now," Fritz said, flipping the heavy round marvel across to his partner. "Seven more after."

By this time Fritz had gotten to know his partner very well. Ollie the assassin could not be trusted, but he was a greedy hoarder who would do anything for money. This was great for Fritz, because money meant next to nothing to him. With his life savings he'd been able to buy eight South African krugerrands. That amounted to eight troy ounces of 99.9 percent pure gold. And his plan was working, at least at the start. Once he dangled those shiny coins in front of Ollie's face, old skull-head agreed they would handle the next operation any way Fritz wanted. As the operation leader, Fritz would show Orange Glory that it was he, and he alone, who was the real professional!

And, as if fate was agreeing, word came down the very next week that he and Ollie were to hitch a ride on a military cargo plane heading for Los Angeles.

Kate's collision with the calm makeup of her known universe began on an ordinary Thursday a week before Spring Break. It was early morning and her sophomore girl students in their fresh uniforms would not be trickling in for another hour. She was in the biology lab, putting the finishing touches on her prized Eco-Bio-System, an entire nearly-self-sustaining little desert ecology system in a clear plastic globe not much bigger than those beach balls the fans bounced around the stands between innings at Dodger Stadium in

Chavez Ravine. At least, she had heard they did that sort of thing. She had never been to an actual baseball game.

Kate was not in a pleasant frame of mind. She had unwittingly allowed some of her personal special relationship to the entity she knew as the son of God the Creator to creep into her teachings. It was not the first time, but as the West Coast progressives were exerting a sniping set of pressures on classic creativity theorizing, she had been several times warned to tiptoe her way around the church's interpretation of evolution. A war was going on, and Sister Kate was fighting steel with bronze, not that she cared one way or the other. To Kate's mind, trying to explain God's plan in human terms was silly.

"See how the lilies grow, they neither toil nor spin," she told her pal Jesus, fresh back from a vacation in South America, he said, where he had videotaped a dramatic documentary on the awesomeness of a pair of galaxies randomly colliding way out there in the great somewhere. She wondered how he had managed to do that in Uruguay, but she did not pursue the line of thought. Jesus could be stubbornly silent when faced with doubting Thomas questions.

"I said that first," he murmured. "That business about the spinning lilies."

"No, old testament, I think," Kate replied.

"Nonsense, purely my literary invention. Maybe I came up with it for my Sermon on the Mount."

"You should have slapped a copyright on it, then."

"That's the problem, you read everything. You're getting too damn smart."

"The son of God is not supposed to use cuss words."

He dissolved away to wherever he went, muttering in some ancient tongue. She thought she caught the phrase, "...at least she doesn't speak Babylonian."

The pickle in which the nuns found themselves was that the war of Divine Creativity VS. Scientific Evolution was politically incorrect on the one hand, and anathema to church teachings on the other. Kate probably should have paid a little less attention to Triassic, Jurassic and Cretaceous and a little more to threading the needle with the papal interpretation of the Divine Creator's intentions. When the summons came from Mother Superior, Jesus had already given her advance warning that trouble was on its bloody fine way. (He admired London street slang, but was sadly shy of any mastery in that direction.) There was no time to get her work done and at the same time listen to a lecture on the mind of God, so Kate decided to join battle in a direct confrontation. She picked up her Eco-Bio globe and marched down the hall. The quiet years since she had left Grandma Lu's place were now at an end.

She had nearly made her way to Mother Superior's office when she was neatly intercepted and blocked off by her arch-enemies, a trio of nuns her own age. Too bad for them, Kate wasn't in the mood for fooling around.

"Perpetua. Resolutia. Florencia. If you are purposefully blocking my path, your intentions are misguided."

Perpetua, who looked a little like Rosie O'Donnell after she let herself go to frump, took a wide legged crouching stance and held her hands out like she was revving a big Harley Davidson.

"Our intentions are fortified by the strength of the Lord! Sisters, start your engines! Vrummmm, Vrummm!"

The other two flanked Perpetua's hulking form, ready to engage the enemy, gave their own motorboat sounds.

Perpetua reached for Kate, thinking to pin her to the wall, but Kate proved as slippery as ice and left her grabbing thin air.

"Help me with these poor fools, Jesus," Kate whispered, "but try not to kill anybody." Without conscious thought, she ground one heel down on the big toe of Perpetua's left foot. The hefty nun yelped and Kate easily slipped out of range without too much damage to her Eco-globe, though clearly she was going to have to mini-rake the sand later when calmer weather prevailed.

"Disadvantage of sandals, Sister Pet," she taunted, "They leave your toes open."

"I'd have given thirty pieces of silver for a pair of Adidas in old Jerusalem," Jesus nodded at her side.

"You want a piece of this action?" Kate gave him a skeptical look. Jesus didn't say anything, but she knew he wasn't going to get in the game. Tough lesbo women were one of his big weaknesses; he may have been the son of God, but he was, after all, half man. Last thing in the world he wanted was to go one-on-one with big, bad Sister Mary Perpetua.

"Any more special messages, Sister Katherine?" Perpetua was trying to shake off the stinging pain in her big toe as if nothing had happened. She chanted "Du-du-du-du. Du-du-du-du!", in a pathetic off-key rendition of the theme music from Rod Serling's old Twilight Zone television series.

"Supernatural visions?" Resoluta added, seeing that game was still on, "Woo-woo-woo-woo-woo!"

"Prophesies from the beyond?" This again from Perpetua, who was running out of theme music and could only say, "Dum-da-dum-dum!"

"Winning lotto numbers?" This new shot from Florencia, who was hoping she had come up with the topper. "Bing! Bing! Bing! Bing!" That was her version of special sound effects like the payoffs at the big slots in Vegas before they went quietly electronic and more efficient, like silent assassins on your wallet.

Kate's hands were full with the eco-ball, but all it took was the twitch of her left shoulder and the nuns scattered like flies shooed off a big load of horse poop. They moved aside just enough so she could slip on through, but they yelled after her as she continued down the hall.

"Did sweet Jesu Christi come to your bed again last night?

"Were his hands strong, and yet understanding, and oh so gentle?"

"Jergens Hand Lotion is good for the Stigmata!"

"Calms the itching, soothes the burn! Well, some of it, anyway."

"Come and get it, you chicken-hearted bullies!" Kate knew they wouldn't follow her to the principal's office. And with that, she made her way down the hallway and was gone with the blink of an eye.

"You see that?" Sister Perpetua asked, "She's a devil-woman!"

"I didn't see nothing."

"Me, neither."

But in spite of their denial to each other, the three nuns were quaking with fear. Everybody had seen something. Kate had been *right here*, and then she was gone.

It was Fritz's idea to borrow the Golden Burrito Taco truck to use as their mobile base of operations. Ollie, of course, didn't like it.

"This is your dumbest idea ever! Suppose somebody wants to buy a taco?"

"We hire Mex chicks." Fritz grunted, "And you drive."

"I'm not driving no rolling diarrhea wagon!"

"We have deal," Fritz said. He flipped Ollie another krugerrand. The glittery gold coin tumbled through the air and the grim assassin snatched it before it hit the ground. "

"Okay, you get one shot. If you miss, we bag her, right?"

"Right," Fritz agreed, but it didn't count because he had his fingers crossed behind his back.

One of Ollie's rare smiles showed a mouthful of splintered and missing teeth. "This will be my first nun," he said. "I'm looking forward to it."

"My first," Fritz corrected him.

Kate paused to collect herself before a door on which was stenciled "Principal" in metallic lettering. She was breathing hard and felt the flush in her face, still overheated from her confrontation with the three monkey-bitch nuns from the dark side. .

"You did good not to say anything to the little strumpets," cowardly Jesus whispered in her ear. "Better that way."

"I wish I'd hucked my Eco-globe at them!"

"Wish, I wish upon a star; How I wonder what you are…"

"Some help you are. You call that advice?"

"You're going to have to shoulder more of the load from now on."

"What is that supposed to mean?"

"It's just that I've got places to go, planets to save, that sort of thing, and you're getting to where you've got to fend for yourself." He looked over her shoulder to where the dark trio was discussing the advisability of a second offensive. "Now is not really the time…"

"Right." Kate hitched the heavy ball a little higher and used her shoulder to push her way in through the frosted glass door to the council of higher authority. Mother Sister Mary Agathena turned from gazing out the window to face her. Sister Mary Bonavita looked up from where she was pretending to be sorting through a file on her desk, a smaller roll top snuggled up next to the principal's.

"So, we don't knock anymore," Sister Bonavita said.

Kate ignored her as she spoke to the Mother Superior.

"You sent for me?"

The Mother Superior hesitated. Not one for confrontation, she was set back by Kate's direct gaze.

"The complaints continue, I'm afraid," the older nun said. "The parents are unhappy."

Sister Bonavita nodded with a smug look. The secret cunning expression on her face angered Kate so much that she had to turn away, and in so doing, her gaze caught Jesus's eye, looking down on them in a kindly manner from a framed wall print while he held his own Sacred Heart out for their inspection. He saw her disgust, shrugged, and made the heart fade away.

Jesus shook his head and gave a disapproving glance over at the two older nuns. "It's a lie, Kate," he said. "A bald-faced manufacture. Ask them which parents."

"Which parents complained?" Kate asked. "Name me some names."

"Just drop your fascination with the monkey-people and the hand of God coming down to bless them and all that crap," Sister Bonavita snarled.

"Names, please. Oh, that's right, you don't have any, do you?"

Mother Superior, never a good fibber, shook her head and looked away. Sister Bonavita thinned her lips, hoping she could glare her way through the unpleasantness. Kate tossed another look to Jesus.

"What do you suggest?" she whispered.

"Turn the other cheek?" suggested the guy who, a moment before, had been holding out his own heart like a glowing lump of meat.

"How'd that *other cheek stuff* work for you, big fella?" Kate asked.

Jesus gave her a so-so wig-wag of one hand. Kate turned her attention to the Mother Superior, "A word with you? Alone?"

The old woman glanced in Sister Bonavita's direction and gave her a nod, indicating that she was to leave the room. The little assistant stood and huffed away, but she remained close by, frowning in their direction through a glass window in the next office.

"Anything I can say in my own defense?" Kate asked.

"Sister, sister, sister…" the Mother Superior dismissed her question with a small shake of her head. "You should never have…"

Kate knew the long, authoritarian lecture the Mother Superior was about to launch. She felt the little patience that remained to her begin to wilt.

"It's all just so much crap," she muttered.

The Mother Superior gave her a stunned look of disapproval. "Crap?! Sisters do not use that word! Why, whatever do you mean?"

"I mean God sends down his Son and we kill him. The Son, who's dead, sort of, figures out a way to talk to the few people who still love him and are willing to listen, but nobody believes it."

The Mother Superior shook her head and gave Kate a wary look. "Not this again…" She eyed Kate with a mixture of dread and anger, and the silence lengthened between them. When the Mother Superior spoke again, it was with the firm and lofty certainty of her lecturing voice, "God speaks to every one of us, child—through our consciences.

"Yes. It's all the same thing," Kate nodded.

Mother Superior bit her lip and gave a confused double nod, first agreeing, and then to the negative. Clearly this meeting was not about doctrine, but about who was in charge and who was simply an ordinary young and foolish nun with nothing at all special about her. "If that were true, Sister Katherine, we could all do your little…tricks."

Kate saw this wasn't going at all well, but Jesus certainly wasn't giving her any direction, dead ink in his frame on the wall, and so she felt she had to continue. "Well, maybe people are too preoccupied or stupid or something."

"I don't want to hear it," the Mother Superior said, putting her hands over her ears. "La, la, la, la, la, la la. La. I just don't want to hear it."

"Exactly," Kate said.

Sister Bonavita, who had been waiting her moment, rushed back in and pushed Kate toward the door. "You're making Mother Superior ill! You, you sinful devil-spawn!"

Sister Katherine looked at the Sacred Heart, who gave her a sympathetic shrug, "That is pretty harsh."

"Some help you are!"

Kate looked around the room, but there didn't seem to be any answers anywhere. She could feel her anger and frustration moving up to the boiling point.

Sister Bonavita, who didn't get to be second in command at St. Rita's, without reading body language, decided to push the young nun a little, to see if she'd pop her cork.

"Having trouble with our anger management problems again, are we, sister?"

Kate glared at the globe, and then slowly raised it over her head.

"That's hardly turning the other cheek, Kate," the Sacred Heart warned in mild reproach.

But Sister Katherine was over the edge, now quite beyond recall.

"I – don't – have – anger management problems!" she yelled.

And with that last explosive bit of denial Grandma Lulubird's granddaughter slammed her precious Eco-Bio globe down on the floor. Shattered plastic and bits of vegetation and damp sand rained and splattered everywhere. The big lizard hissed "Hey, what's up, babes?" and scampered under Mother Superior's desk, while a hairy Southwest tarantula Frisbee-ed across the room like a furry dinner plate to stick onto Sister Bonavita's black habit. Bonavita stubbornly whisked it to the floor with the back of one hand.

"Be gone, devil's creature!" she shouted. It made a dry pretzel sound as she crunched it with one of her hard leather shoe heels.

Kate wasn't sure whether the mean little bitch-nun was talking to the spider or to her, but it made no difference at all. *She was out of there for good.* And perhaps it was coincidental that the first quivers of a coming earthquake shook the building a little. It was just a 3.6 on the Richter Scale, but a lot of really big things start small like that.

The premonition that bad business was on its way had been floating down like dust from the ceiling of her life for a few years, and so when the argument up finally came, Kate was prepared. She could no longer stand the sight of herself in the mirror, trapped in the black-and-white outfit of her religious order, dressed like some sort of morality cop car.

She pushed aside the lurking trio of nuns on her way back to her classroom. They stumbled and fell over each other in a heap. Perpetua's hands clutched the crucifix on her oversized waist to floor rosary, and the metal edges of the cross neatly punctuated the palms of her hand, unfortunate wounds that seemed not to heal for the longest time, and when they actually did, they left thin scabby scars that bled every year during the forty days before Easter. Or maybe, the other nuns said behind her back, that was just because she picked at them.

As Kate pulled a gym bag from under her desk she saw that a small cluster of students already settled in their seats.

"Sister Katherine! Did you feel the earthquake?!"

"Oh, that's just the hand of God," she replied. "You have not seen anything yet."

In a way that was true; in five minutes she'd ditched her nun garb in the nearest toilet and walked out of the teacher's lounge wearing a tight fitting pair of jeans and a hot red tee shirt with the promissory slogan NUNS DO IT BY HABIT printed in big golden letters across the front.

CHAPTER FOURTEEN

Good times in Uruguay; better times at the Golden Burrito

Jimmy Jinx Warner was sitting in a Starbucks off Avenue Italia in downtown Montevideo. He was wearing a snappy black leather biker's jacket with a lot of chrome snaps, faux-worn jeans with an American flag sewn across the butt and a pair of ultra-soft mocs that would have set him back a pretty penny if he ever had to pay for anything. He'd just miracled himself up a vente mocca when the real Jesus walked in. Real Jesus was wearing nearly identical clothes, though he featured hip hugging black designer jeans, and a black Greek fisherman's hat, where Jimmy Jinx was sporting his blue and white La Celeste soccer cap 180 with the bill in back. Both men looked at each other through identical aviator's sunglasses. The newcomer spoke first, his voice the soft one of command and absolute mastery that would have instantly cowed Jimmy Jinx if he'd had a deferential molecule in his body.

"You know who I am."

Jimmy gave him an appraising look.

"Some sort of Jesus impersonator?"

"Wrong answer."

Real Jesus miracled Jimmy's mocca into a steaming cow pie.

"Oh, did you have to do that?"

"Yes. Because you piss me off."

"You must have a very low threshold for rage. Have you tried anger management? I hear you can send away for home courses."

Jimmy smoothly miracled the cow poop back into his mocca.

"And keep your bloody stupid magic off my drink."

"Miracles are not magic. And it's not your drink. You didn't pay for it."

And with that, Real Jesus changed the mocca into a large toad. The creature craned its plump neck and gave off a frightened noise that sounded like *Gronk!*, and then hopped off the table. A girl in a red halter top and a short skirt who was walking by stepped on the toad, spearing it dead with one of her high heels.

"You just killed that frog," Jimmy Jinx said.

"Did not."

And with that, Real Jesus snapped his fingers and the toad shrugged himself alive and hopped out onto Avenue Italia where it was run over by a motorcycle. Real Jesus shrugged and turned his full attention back to Jimmy Jinx. The air vibrated with his anger.

"I am here to command you to stop imitating me."

"Don't be so egotistical. Any resemblance between me and the shroud of Turin is purely coincidental."

"You're pretty slick," Real Jesus nodded, miracling himself up a vente latte.

He had it to his lips and was taking the first sip when Jimmy Jinx turned it into a lump of dog poop.

"Take that, you phony!"

Real Jesus dropped the big lump of poop. He grabbed Jimmy's tan Starbucks napkin and wiped his lips. His anger went up another notch and the room began to tremble, the beginnings of an earthquake the likes of which Uruguay hadn't seen since the big one at Rio de la Plata in 1888.

And that's when a lean Russian who looked a lot like Vladimir Ilyich Lenin took a seat at the table.

"I'll have tea. Black tea. Honey and milk on the side."

Jimmy Jinx, who seemed to have better reflexes than Real Jesus, miracled him up a samovar and poured him a steaming cup of tea and presented him with a plate of Russian tea cakes.

Real Jesus frowned, not liking being upstaged like that. He started to conjure up an even bigger samovar with rubies and gold inlay, but the Russian raised a hand to stop him.

"Gentlemen, just what is the argument here?"

Jimmy Jinx again got in the first word.

"This fellow who looks a lot like me is angry because I look a lot like him."

"No! He is a bad impression of me! He runs around the world miracling things up wherever he goes, but he has no moral judgment, he doesn't know good from evil!"

"I do, too!"

"Do not!"

The Russian sipped his tea calmly while the pair of Jesuses railed back and forth at each other. He finally raised one hand.

"You both have to stop."

"What?"

"Why? That's ridiculous, I'm the Son of God."

Jimmy Jinx, on hearing that claim, held up his own hand.

"When it comes down to it, we're all sons of God.

Real Jesus pointed a stiff hand at Jimmy Jinx, who had to duck out of the way as a lightning bolt shot past his left shoulder. A barrista behind the counter wasn't so lucky as the electricity lit her up. She crumpled to the floor without a sound.

"Blasphemy!" Real Jesus shouted.

"Not at all. "I'm a bit of a miracle, myself. I don't know how to stop miracling things, and I don't see why I should."

The Lenin look-alike spilled some of his tea as he hastily set down his cup. He was getting a bit hot under the collar, himself.

"We are all to blame, here. You, Real Jesus, made the first mess when you did all that water into wine and multiplying loaves and fishes."

"But the Father told me I could. And remember he stopped the sun."

"Well then, he's at fault too."

"My Father can do no wrong."

Podofski found he was grinding his teeth.

"Look, right or wrong, what happens when anybody miracles things, it screws up the way things are. The universe isn't ready for it. It is supposed to run on a multi-dimensional linearity. It wasn't built to take your sort of fustering and muckling around."

"I don't muckle," the Savior said, stiffing his spine and laying a haughty gesture on the Russian.

Jimmy Jinx eyed the imitation Lenin curiously.

"How do you know these things?"

"Because I am the second one to screw things up. My partner Charley Birch and I accidentally created a batch of humans who have abilities similar to those you possess. We call them 'zoomins'.

"So we're zoomins?"

"Well, you would be something like them if you were alive, but you're both sort of dead guys."

"Sort of?"

"Well, yes. You, Real Jesus, died on that cross. And you, Mr. Jimmy Jinx Warner, got nailed by electricity somewhere high over an airport in Florida."

Jimmy scratched behind one of his ears.

"Then what are we doing here?"

"That is a big question mark. Since the three of us started fouling up the universe, things aren't predictable anymore."

"Hey, it wasn't just us. What about Buddha? What about Mohammed? How about all the saints?"

"Yes. Them, too. I don't know where they are. I can't help any of them."

"Well, you're not helping us, either," Jimmy Jinx said.

Podofski stood and with his own quick flare of displeasure he started a small earthquake of his own. A crack appeared in one of the walls and bags of coffee and special coffee mugs tumbled off the shelves. His image began to crumble around the edges like a photograph that was draining pixels.

"Gentlemen, you have been warned."

And then he was gone.

Jesus waved one hand and the fancy samovar disappeared with a soppy little pop noise.

"Hey, I bet we could have pawned that."

"See, Jimmy that's what I mean. You have the morals of a Sinai swamp rat."

They went outside and stood together, waiting for a taxi. Real Jesus noticed the toad lying all flattened and bloody in the street.

"I don't care what that strange Cossack fellow says; I'm not giving up my miracle-izing."

He waved one hand and the toad stood up and looked around with a groggy stare. The creature took three hops and was flattened by another motorcycle.

"Me, neither," Jimmy Jinx said.

He waved his hand in an imitation of the Savior's gesture and the dead toad sighed, unflattened itself and hopped away.

Meanwhile in Southern California Fritz and Ollie parked across the street from the convent in their taco truck, and soon were pestered by an intermittent gaggle of teenage kids lining up for tacos and churros. Ollie had his hands full wrapping sugar coated pastries and counting change, but he was still the professional, and when he spotted a young woman in a tight red t-shirt and jeans who came boiling out the front door of the convent he yelled, "Shoot her, shoot her, shoot her!"

Fritz, who thought this was some sort of trial run, managed to get off one burst with an ancient Korean War issue burp gun, but his aim was bad and bullets ricocheted around inside the truck.

A container of boiling oil caught fire. Ollie, desperate not to have his cover blown, got in the driver's seat and the Golden Burrito lurched on down the street with flames and puffs of black smoke trailing behind.

Kate caught a bus in front of the convent and returned a half hour later behind the wheel of Mama Tillie's imported 1955 Datsun, a now ancient but fairly well preserved cream colored little sedan with 15,000 miles on it that had been in storage and transported cross country after Keyes-Smythe died.

The nuns, confused as to Kate's intentions, formed a thin skirmish line in front of the convent door, but they scattered like the Wicked Witch of the West's black monkey troop when she picked up an iron rod tool the gardeners used to turn on the lawn water sprinkler system.

Sister Bonavita called the police, but as she tried to dial there was a somewhat strong pre-quake and the phone lines went dead.

"My books. My stuff," Kate said, wheeling a collapsible but tough little handcart with two heavy boxes of text books and one containing her solar system maps and chart of the universe, her pictures of Darwin and Jesus Preaching On The Mount, her battered black leather-and-brass telescope still attached to its collapsed tripod, and the plastic skeletons of T-rex, Bronco, and the other dinosaurs she'd painstakingly constructed from Discovery kits.

Sister Perpetua thought to muscle her from behind, but Jesus yelled, "Kate, look out!"

Kate pulled a big crystal geode from the top box and reared back to fling it, and that pretty much was that, Perpetua, who already had blood smears on the palms of her hands, fell back with a frightened little yip, "Holy rat shit, you are crazy!"

So there Kate was, on the street outside the convent, loading up the dusty Datsun. As she packed the last of the heavy boxes into the trunk, a black crow sitting on a nearby tree branch yelled down to her.

"Waa-hoo—freedom, baby! Where'd you get that hot tee shirt?"

Kate gave him a disgusted little shake of her head, "I don't mean to complain, but they send a lousy blackbird to see me off?"

"How should I know," the big crow shrugged. "I don't make the rules."

Kate eyed the oversized bird for a moment, then went back to loading her things in the trunk.

Sister Bonavita and the Mother Superior watched from inside the convent.

"You saw her!" Sister Bonavita looked up from her futile efforts to call the authorities, "In your office, she talked to that picture of the Sacred Heart on the wall. Now there she is, in communion with a devil bird! That's most certainly Beelzebub, right there!"

She quickly signed herself with the cross and then sat down, gasping for air.

"Good riddance to bad garbage, I say."

But the Mother Superior was having second thoughts.

"We're going to miss those checks from Florida." She paced nervously around the room. "We're on hard times. We're going to miss that money that fell like gentle rain on our deflated bank account."

"Nothing is free," Bonavita said."

":It's more than the money. Did you consider that we might actually be turning away the personal friend of Jesus…you know, like she claims.

"Oh, right. That dumb little twit was hand-picked to send down messages of wisdom and salvation. My God, there's already too much foolishness in the world. On the other hand, I do see your point about the money. All that money. Such a lot of money.

"Sometimes…I just don't know…"

Sister Bonavita's lip curled.

"Too late now, Mother Superior! Too late!"

A smile broke out on her stern features as she saw Kate was having trouble closing the trunk on her grimy beige car. The trunk was too full and there was no way it would close. "Huh. Look at that. God's little interpreter, can't even close a car trunk. She'll never make it out there in the real world."

"You don't think so?" Mother Superior asked, more and more convinced she had made a wrong decision. "Maybe you should go get her?"

"Not me! She's certifiably over the edge."

"Maybe her Jesus will protect her out there…"

"Right. Like he did in here."

Sister Bonavita's smile broadened, the seldom-used grin muscles working against the ordinary stern lines etched in her face until it looked as if she might crack like hardened plaster.

"They are going to eat her alive."

Outside, Kate slammed the trunk and pushed on it with all her strength, but her weight and energy were not enough to close the few inches she needed. The black bird fluttered down from his tree branch and sat on the roof of the Datsun.

Inside, looking out the window, the two nuns gasped and looked at each other.

"Let me help you wit' dat, sweet-cakes," the crow said.

Kate tried to brush him away, but he just hopped out of reach and peered at her, cocking his head like a wise old bird.

"Hey, you're crying, babes. I can see it."

"I'm sorry, I'm just upset. I tried so hard, and I wanted it to work out."

"Well, sweet-meat, sometimes it don't. Now let's give it another try."

Kate sat on the trunk and began to bump it up and down.

"Close, but no cigar," the crow commented. "Here, let's do it together."

With that, he fluttered from the roof to the trunk lid, and perhaps it was just that little extra weight, but there was a click and the latch caught.

"Thanks," Kate said.

"No magic," the crow said with a quick nod of his head. "It's just physics…see ya."

He spread his wings and did a little hop toward the end of the trunk.

"Where you going?" Kate asked, even though she already knew the answer.

"Gotta be about my father's business," he said. And with that, he fluttered off in the direction of whatever it was that crows did next.

Kate watched him flap away over the nearest rooftop, and then she got in her car. She was momentarily flustered when she couldn't find her keys. She patted her clothes in a semi-panic and was about to run around the back of the car, hoping she hadn't locked them inside.

"Try the overhead visor," a voice suggested. It came from the Bakelite plastic Jesus stuck on the dashboard.

Kate grabbed the right key and turned it in the ignition, but in her semi-panic and inexperience she forgot to push in on the clutch and the car jerked forward and stopped. She blew out a big breath of air to steady herself, and tried again.

Inside, behind the safety of the convent window, Sister Bonavita thought dark thoughts she hoped would rain down evil on the little car, but it finally pulled away from the curb, stopped at the corner, and then disappeared into the traffic of the world that lay beyond.

And that was when one of those unexplainable mini-quakes hit the convent, causing structural damage that would cost a fortune and bankrupt the nun's order to where they had no alternative other than allowing themselves to be restructured under the dire financial auspices of the diocese accountants. No more ruby rosaries or pilgrimages to Lourdes and Fatima.

CHAPTER FIFTEEN

North to the land of oil, citrus and nuts.

Entranced with her new freedom and a feeling of adventure, Kate was wide-eyed as she gad-flied the dented white Datsun through the brisk traffic, looping in and out of lanes as she headed north on Topanga Canyon Boulevard through the city of Chatsworth toward the 118 Freeway. Plastic Jesus was tightly hugging the dash with the suction cup under his sandals, and a plain black rosary hung from the rear view mirror with its silver plated cross swinging idly back and forth in a movement seemingly random but actually precisely determined by the laws of physics, which are God's laws as well, as any proper modern theologian can tell you.

Kate was not thinking about any of that. She was singing in that peculiar off-key way of hers.

"I don't care if it rains or freezes/ Long as I have my plastic Jesus. I don't care if it rains or freezes/ Long as I have my plastic Jesus."

Her voice was something short of professional, and after a few minutes, things started to get tedious, but Jesu Christi just grimaced and decided to ride along with it. When they got to the 405, Kate carefully drove through the curved onramp to the 405 North. She grinned and said, "Hang on to your testacles, Jesu Christi! Here we go!" They were moving so slowly that a big Home Depot 18 wheeler honked them from behind, but in no time at all, Kate had her mother's old Datsun in one of the moderate-speed middle lanes, heading north up the incline toward the Grapevine.

It was oddly amusing that the radio was playing, because she hadn't turned it on. Or maybe the music was in her head. It didn't matter, because it fit her mood and she liked it.

It was ambling, chunking-along, happy calypso music, with somebody like Bob Marley singing in a plaintive tenor, a little something plastic Jesus had whipped up to distract her. The Bob Marley voice sang:

It don't matter no how no mo
Close out de light/ an' open de do'
One thing begin/ the other end
Only 'portant/ we be friend
Cause it don't matter no how no mo
No, it don't matter no more.

Too soon old/ an' too late smart
Dat be the shape/ of 'd' human heart
Too soon old/ an too late smart
Dat's d' way/ of d' human heart.

She couldn't be actually singing along, but she believed she might be, or if she wasn't actually singing, what she heard in her mind's ear was the same as if it actually was pouring at her out of the radio. The Bob Marley sound-alike sang:

Mother Theresa/ Where d' way
To d' golden/ light of day?
Firefly winkin'/ in d' night

Should I run/ or should I fight?
Mother, give me/ One more day
Run d' sun/ an' dance an' play
I don't do wrong/ I wanna do right
So should I run/ Or should I fight?
Should I run/ Or should I fight?

Kate drove steadily uphill until she got to Valencia, not minding the steady stream of honks as the cars and trucks moved around and passed her. The island voice was in her head and life was good:

Too soon old/ an too late smart
Dat's d' way/ of d' human heart.
'fucious, Plato/ Play your part
Teach me t'know/ d human heart
Teach me t'know/ d' human heart

At the so-called top-o-the-vine, the Datsun hummed steadily through Gorman pass and then started the steep sled ride down into California's Central Valley. Miss Katherine Twillinger, the former Sister Katherine, now thinking of herself as just plain Kate, concentrated on the road and talked to herself as she drove along, "You're going to like Taft Union High School. You're going to like Taft Union High School."

Finally, Jesus could not stand it any longer. "Why are we going to like Taft Union High School, Kate?" he asked

His plastic lips moved as he spoke, but she was not surprised. Talking with Jesus was as natural to her as breathing or making love to the universe.

"About time you asked," she said. "It's Taft, Taft, Taft, because I'm clearly not daft, daft, daft."

"Debatable," Jesus muttered, "but go on."

"I need a job," she said.

"You've got Granny's money from the orange ranch. And your monthly allowance. And you're due a really big bundle from the family trust when you turn 35."

"I'm way past 35, mister. And it's a little late for you to start in about that Joys of Poverty stuff. You can sell that to Sister Bonavita and her Ruby Rosary Bunch."

"The Ruby Rosarys. Good name for a rock group," Jesus said.

"It is at that," she said, taking her eyes off the road ahead to admire his trim little form.

"But how about you, Kate?" When he looked at her, she saw a few worry wrinkles appear in his smooth pink forehead.

"What about me, Dashboard Savior?"

"This car, your clothes, your little stash of cash? Remember you actually did take a vow of poverty. You were supposed to give everything to the order."

"Every girl needs a parachute, Big Jesu, in case things don't work out. Didn't your mother tell you anything?"

"I never listened to my mother," Jesus said, thinking it over.

"Well, that's it, right there.".

She sounded glib and confident when she said it, but a gloomy silence settled between them, and Jesus could see she was seriously thinking over the decisions she had made of late. That was one of the things he liked best about his Kate. She did not treat him like a holy card or a string of beads. She actually listened and thought about his ideas. And he knew in his Sacred Heart of hearts that he actually had some good ones. After all, had not God the Father told him so? Or was that God the Mother? Sex didn't seem to matter all that much on the cosmic scale. In a way, everything was creation.

And then there was this other thing. She believed he was the real Jesus, and until he'd met the real thing down in Montevideo he'd at least part-way thought he was, too. Now he wasn't sure who he was. On the other hand, if the universe was really coming apart as the strange Russian had claimed, did it really matter? Maybe he wasn't a moral guy, as Real Jesus had claimed. But still, he had been trying to do the right thing by Kate. That had to count for something.

After chugging a few miles across the broad valley that lay before them, Kate took an off ramp and parked in the gravel space by the side of the road. She walked up on the overpass and put her elbows on the rounded guard-rail, watching the intermittent stream of cars flowing by under them.

T. Vernon Biggs was having a devil of a time. A few days ago he was a CPA who ran an income tax company that had been caught chiseling the

United States government out of over a half million dollars a year. That may not seem like much, but he'd been at it for over two decades. One night when everything had seemed hopeless he'd tried a little snort of coke that was left in the bottom drawer of his office desk and woke up to find himself drifting over his body that was lying on the floor beneath him. He struggled to get out of the room, but the ceiling wouldn't let him. He found an open window and dove head first out of it, only to find that his body had joined him again, but now they were thirty stories up and plummeting down onto Figueroa Street in downtown Los Angeles. It wasn't too bad all the way down, but after that things got totally whacko-bird, an expression he didn't know where he'd come up with, but that fitted his circumstances to the letter 'T'. He was in a warm place with a roaring fire and a big guy dressed in a devil outfit gave him his choice, roast around down here for a while or go back to the other place as a recruiter. T. Vernon looked around at all the burnt flesh and the howling and decided to go back.

He was wearing tight black pants that clearly showed his junk, and a nipple-hugging shirt colored a flashy fire engine red with black racing stripes and little glow strips for night peddling. He was on his first assignment, biking it up over the freeway. There she was, a gal in the tight jeans and red t-shirt. A sudden feeling came over him as he took in the neat, rounded curves of her butt as she leaned against the railing, watching the cars approach only to streak under the overpass. *Woow,*

woow, woow, pretty mamma! Vernon applied the brakes and skidded to a stop next to her.

He eyed her in what he hoped was friendly innocence as he took a long pull from a water bottle cleverly inserted in a wire holder on the frame of his bike.

"You're not thinking of jumping, sweetie-pie?"

The scene reminded Kate of that time when Satan tempted Jesus by offering him everything far as the eye can see if he would only bow down and adore him, and it seemed she may may have been right about that one.

"Trying to tempt me, devil-biker?"

She smiled politely to show she was not really serious about calling him a devil.

But T/ Vernon decided it had to be some sort of come on. Yes, he was a tricky little devil, and what woman could resist him! Her car was deserted and there was nobody else nearby. It excited him to see dozens of cars racing by under the pass, and the two of them, man and woman were on display; *Why they could do it right up here if they wanted! And why the hell wouldn't they?*

He hopped off his bike and moved behind her, "Hey, sweet baby, what are you watching down there?"

"Oh, I don't know. Just the rest of the world rushing by."

"Hey, let 'em be on their way. We've got our own little island of pleasure here."

While he spoke, he moved behind her and pressed his swelling loins against her and *Glory be it is as if they were made for each other!* He reached around her and cupped her breasts, but his moment of joy was interrupted when she yelped at him with a thunderous, stentorian howl.

"What are you doing?!"

He jumped back, staring at her.

"Come on now, sweet cheeks, you know you were coming on to me."

She stared at him, a look he sadly mistook for the beginnings of passion. T.Vernon moved in to gather her in his arms, at the same time grinding his pelvis against her body. This was a grave mistake. He felt an instant burning sensation in his penis. In a flash all thoughts of passion dissipated with the Central Valley breeze. He staggered back to his bicycle and managed to peddle away.

He yelled back over his shoulder, "I'll kill you, you bitch!"

Of course, it was just an idle threat. To his mind, that should have been the end of the story, the crazy bitch who came on to me and then knifed me in the dick (or whatever she did), but unfortunately it was not.

The fiery pain in his groin continued and Vernon Biggs limped around like an old man for several weeks until he woke one night to find his penis lying next to him under the covers. There was no bleeding, just a new scab where his prized organ had been attached. Once he recovered from the shock he gingerly rolled the severed organ in Saran Wrap, stumbled to his red Ford Mustang and raced over the grapevine for help. The urologists at the UCLA medical hospital had never seen anything like it, but over the next few months more and more cases of the same nature came in until they decided it had to be a new, highly specialized form of disease never before observed. They called it IPD, short for Involuntary Penis Detatchment and told him he should be happy to know he would live and what was more important, enjoy an otherwise long and healthy existence.

Kate drove on, north through the south end of the Central Valley. Dashboard Jesus finally broke the silence.

"That's bad karma, Kate."

"You mean that biker-pervert?"

"No, of course not."

"What then, Jesu, Holy Lord?"

"I'm referring to you keeping all your stuff."

"Oh great. You believe in karma?!"

"Well, I certainly do—"

"That's probably why they hung you up on the cross. Always sermonizing, all your holier-than-thou crap."

"I've got my problems, too, you know."

He wondered if now was the time to tell her about Jimmy Jinx Warner and meeting Real Jesus and all the rest, but then the moment had passed and she was blathering about something else.

"You're the first of your kind, you know."

"What do you mean?"

"How many human children did God Almighty have, anyway?"

"There could be something to that," Jesus Jinx admitted. Maybe it wasn't a good time to get into that sloppy truthfulness about who and what he was, particularly as he himself had more questions than answers. He quickly changed the subject.

"Hey, where we going?"

By now, the 405 had merged with the 5 freeway, still headed north through nut and cow country. But Kate had pulled off the 5 at Lamont Avenue. She clicked her left turn blinker and waited at the stop light.

After a moment, when she didn't answer his question, he added, "By the way, did you know you can be pretty abrasive?"

"The truth will set you free, Little Big Man."

He found he easily fell back into the role. Maybe he should have been an actor. Jesus Christ Superstar, the role of a lifetime, right up there in the lights on Broadway.

"That crown of thorns really hurt."

"Not my fault, Big Jesu."

"I died for your sins."

"Don't try to lay that one on me. I wasn't even born yet."

Having crossed to the west side of the freeway, Kate turned the old Datsun into a roadside cluster of gas stations and fast food outlets. She spun the wheel and parked in a handicapped zone.

"You're not handicapped," he chided her.

"Mentally, I well may be," she retorted. "Think about it."

She flipped down the sun visor on the driver's side, revealing a blue placard that still had a year left on it.

"Where did you get that?"

"Lifted it from Sister Bonavita back at the convent."

"She wasn't handicapped, either."

"Emotionally. She was an emotional cripple."

Jesus threw up his tiny plastic arms in an exasperated gesture, or maybe he was giving her his blessing. He did look a bit like that big stone statue on Sugarloaf Mountain in Rio, the Lord giving his stiff and never-ending blessing over the mass fornications of carnival and the naked tits and string bikinis of Ipa Nima.

Kate entered the Starbucks and looked around. She was feeling uneasy at this unfamiliar contact with the outside world. The place was crowded with long distance travelers, mostly tourists and truckers and salesmen. No one in here was a local; everyone passing through from L.A. to San Francisco or heading back the other way, or maybe taking the long route to Tahoe and the High Sierras. The 5 was notorious as the most boring freeway in the world, and it certainly was that for anyone who had never driven through Kansas heading from Chicago to Denver or back again.

Of course, the Starbucks Mermaid spotted her right away. The fish-gal winked from her sign up over the counter and greeted Kate with a voice that boomed like Yogi Bear, "Hey, hey, HEY! It's Sister Kate! Long time no see, sweetie-pie!"

"Just Kate," Kate replied through gritted teeth, not wanting to be singled out in the crowd.

The mermaid winked at her, nodding in the direction of her Datsun in the parking lot, "About time you gave up on plastic Popsicle Pete."

Kate shook her head silently, trying her best to ignore the gabby coffee lady.

Al, a tractor and mower salesman standing in line in front of Kate, turned to her and thought he might strike up a conversation, and who knew where that might lead?

"Headed north or south?"

Kate jumped at the sound of his voice and ran her hand through her short curly reddish blond hair. She tried to compose herself, but it had been a long time since she'd talked to someone she thought of as a *wild male*, that is, anyone who wasn't a father or possibly the grandfather of one of her students.

She gave out a nervous, self-conscious laugh. "Goodness, you startled me!"

He was over forty, overweight by about thirty pounds, and, she was certain, full of testosterone-driven over-confidence. The silence lengthened between them until she realized the man was still waiting for an answer. "Uh, west, actually. Taft. I'm going to the town of Taft."

"Then this is your last outpost." He grinned and put on a mock-stern face, acting like Jerry Seinfeld's Soup Nazi.

"No more Starbucks for you!"

She stared at him, puzzled and not getting the reference. After the televised nightly news, her life had been evening vespers and then grading papers and to bed before ten.

Al tried to dig his way out of the mess he was making of their conversation.

"You've never heard of the Soup Nazi? You know, Jerry Seinfeld…the comedy show? Been in reruns for about a thousand years?"

Kate eyed him seriously, not wanting to appear retarded or stupid.

"No. Then there is a Starbucks in the city of Taft?"

"Town. Taft's not really a city. And no, there isn't. That's the point, you see. Jerry wants some soup, but he offends the Soup Nazi and then—"

"Grande Latte for Mike and Al," a voice sang out, rescuing Al from his sad dilemma. Al shrugged as if he had no choice and hustled forward to pay for his drink. On the way out, both men glanced back at Kate.

Mike jostled Al with one elbow and scoffed, "Nicely played out of the rough, old man."

"Aaah, shut up. How did I know she was a hermit?"

"Only men can be hermit's, idiot. Women are her-mites."

"You mean hermaphrodites."

"No, Aphrodite's…Hell, I don't know what I mean." And so saying, the two chummy fellows exited Starbucks, laughing at their own sad puns.

"Afro-dikes?"

"No. That would be a black lesbian. Aphrodite, you asshole. The Greek goddess of screwing."

And so they retreated on down the freeway of their lives.

Jimmy Jinx was loitering in his favorite Starbucks when a middle aged white man with a spear shaped piece of Lucite through his heart came in, looked around to orient himself, and then sat at his table.

"Care for a drink?"

Without bothering for a response he miracled up a steaming carmel macchiato.

"Please don't do that."

"Why not?"

"I'm Charley Birch, and I'll tell you why not. Every time you do one of your little tricks, you weaken the fabric of the universe."

"I don't care. Maybe it needs to be weakened."

"It won't take too much more and it will pop like a balloon."

"You know, just last week a crazy Bolshevik was in here, spouting the same nonsense."

Charley gritted his teeth. The drink in front of him looked tasty and so he figured what the hell and took a sip. He was rewarded with a little earth tremor. Dust fell from the ceiling, but nobody else seemed to notice.

Jimmy Jinx smiled and nodded.

"They're getting used to it."

"I'd like to put the fear of the Almighty into you."

"Too late. I'm already scared to death. I just don't know what to do about it."

"Did the Russian guy explain how your miracle-izing is destroying everything?"

"Something like that. I didn't understand a word of it."

"Okay, tell me what's the largest city in the United States?"

"I give up. New York?"

"No, Upper Norcoville."

"I never heard of it."

"Exactly. Not in your universe, right? Well, you see, it used to be, but now it isn't. One little tear in the fabric and twenty million people are gone from history, gone as if they never were."

"And that's because I whipped you up a little caffeine?"

"People like you, all of you, it's a cumulative effect, pressure on the fabric of our space-time dimension…"

"Oh, man, now you're losing me. Could you just cut the Einstein crap?"

Charley stood and screamed at the man who looked more than a little like Jesus Christ.

"You have to listen! Everything not forbidden is mandatory!"

"Who said that? Quai Chang Caine, I bet. Okay, I'll bite; who gets to decide what is forbidden?"

"God does! That's my point! You can't just have a whimsy to pop this – this *creation* – out of nothing. It's not allowed!"

"Okay, you've got my attention. Now what?"

"You have to convince the very dangerous Katherine Twillinger to give up her powers!"

That set Jimmy Jinx back on his heels.

"Wooh, that came out of nowhere. How do you know about her?"

Charley sighed and sat back down at the table. "It's a long story."

"Go ahead, the soccer match doesn't start for a few hours and I'm a good listener."

Kate sat behind the wheel in her white Datsun. A policeman pulled into the parking spot next to her. He eyed her blue placard, hitched his equipment belt a bit higher around his ample waist and headed for the mermaid's place to snag a cup of free java. Kate watched the sunlight glance off the windows and the metal shine of the cars and the trucks as they made their way into the roadside stop. After a while, she sighed and took a sip from her cooling café mocca.

"What a joyful morning it is!" she exclaimed. "Just look at those mountains in the distance."

"Hills, actually," Jimmy Jinx corrected her. "It's the start of the Sierra range."

"Thank you for all this," she said.

"Don't mention it," he said. "I mean, you're welcome."

He hoped he'd put enough sincerity into his delivery. For the first time he was starting to have misgivings about his own go-along-to-get-along attitude. He hadn't asked to be lightning bolted. He hadn't asked to become the non-living sort of spiritual being that he was. He just played along with it. And what if this Charley guy was right? What if people like him and Kate could pop the universe like a starry blue-black birthday balloon?

And even if that was true, if it was an absolute fact that everything was one or two steps from absolute *kablooie!* how was he going to convince Kate to give up her – what had Charley called them? – her 'zoomin' powers?

Kate had her own concerns. She took a thoughtful sip of her coffee. She could see the policeman, now standing in line inside Starbucks. She thought he might have turned around, maybe to take a closer look at her.

"I'm actually crazy, aren't I?" she asked her plastic companion.

"What do you mean?" Jimmy asked in return, gently trying for a little time to think by skirting the original question with one of his own."

"Well, I usually get on as if I'm perfectly normal," she said. "But here I am, chatting away with you."

"You've always chatted with me. And you used to talk with your dollies when you were a kid."

"Well sure…" Kate was remembering back to those times, Pappa trying to run away with his whore-secretary and Mamma forced to get seasick on his horrible fishing boat so she could accidentally push him overboard. She didn't know how she knew these things. Maybe she had been there, on the boat, and had suppressed the memory all these years. "But I was all alone on the orange ranch."

"You had Grandma Lu."

"You any idea how many times she punched me in the head?"

"Hey, I had the stations of the cross, remember? After the first dozen whacks or so, you lose count."

"Sorry, I retract my gripe."

"Damn right," Jimmy said. He paused, thinking what he knew about Real Jesus's past joys and hardships. What he knew would have to do. He easily fell back into the role, "I wish more people would talk to me, I mean, really talk to me. Why is it so hard? Billions of sentient beings around here—that is, counting the dolphins, the whales, the elephants and the krill—and yet they only ask me for stuff they think they can't do without. Tastier mackerels. Another Notre Dame win. More bananas. Sometimes I get so lonely."

Kate found herself interested, in spite of her morose mood. "What do the krill ask for?"

"Some tiny thing-ies that they eat."

"I still think I'm crazy," she said.

"Hey, sweetheart, learn to live with it," Jimmy said in an imitation Groucho Marx voice.

"You might not be the best role model for sanity, you know," she replied.

Dashboard Jimmy-Jinx-Jesus stared straight ahead and didn't say anything more; apparently his Silver Screen Persona could not come up with anything appropriately snappy to respond to that dose of cold historical reality.

CHAPTER SIXTEEN

on the way to Taft

Kate pulled out of the Starbucks parking lot and accelerated on the 5, once again heading north. The radio, if it was a radio, came back on. Gnarls Barkley was singing “Crazy” from his St. Elsewhere album.

I remember when, I remember, I remember when I lost my mind

There was something so pleasant about that place

Even your emotions have an echo in so much space

The problem was, looking back, there was nothing pleasant about Granny Lu slapping her around. It was beyond evil, almost as if there was a mad scheme behind the old lady’s attacks. She didn’t need a rational reason to start using her granddaughter’s head as a punching bag, and her many sneak attacks, coming up from behind with a hard whallop, proved there had to be forethought in her malice.

Kate took the 166 off ramp and soon had her little Datsun sedan rolling west on a two lane blacktop. She listened to the lonely whine of tires on the asphalt and snuck peeks to the left and right at the solid walls of nut trees and the rows of cotton that stretched toward distant hills. The land was like a semi-arid version of the rural Florida farms and orchards of her younger days. No swamps or natural ponds, of course. Deep ditches ran on either side of the road, and there were red irrigation pipes, thick around as a man's waist, running here and there along the dusty ground, and water storage tanks 20 or 30 feet high, and grey oil pumps slowly laboring against a steely backdrop of blue-grey sky.

"My new job's one hundred and fifty miles north of Los Angeles," Kate said out loud, speaking to herself.

"North! To Alaska!" Jimmy-Jinx-Jesus shouted, causing her to jump after the protracted silence that had developed in her car.

"Jesus! Will you stop that?! Come on, God-man, hold it down. It's just Kern County."

"Sorry," he said with a sheepish grin spreading over his plastic features. "I just couldn't help myself. I always love a bit of an adventuresome frolic. You know, I once flew a DC-3 in and out of South America."

He thought he might get into his real persona, the messiah bit could be tiresome, but Kate shut that one down with a cheerful snort.

"Not likely, miracle-man. Not at all likely."

Route 166 ran straight as an arrow, heading west through the orchards, the cotton fields and the oil rigs. Kate muttered, "Cotton, citrus, oil, nuts. My brave new world, particularly the nuts."

"And the grapes," Jimmy reminded her. "Don't forget the fine California wines. I did some of my best work in vineyards."

"You're a commie rat bastard, did you know that, pal Jesu?"

“Watch your potty-mouth,” he replied. “Why do you say that?”

“I read my New Testament. Nobody in their right mind pays everybody the same. You preached they should pay the same wage for a day’s work, no matter when the lazy bastards showed up. Pinko red commies preach that.”

“Well, I thought of it first.”

Kate felt he had actually made her point, so she decided she didn’t have to say anything more on the subject. Just like a man to want to take credit for something, even if it was something stupid and against actual common sense.

“What do you know about common sense, anyway?” Jimmy asked in that sometimes peevish way Jesus had that passed for righteousness.

“I know a lots,” she answered. “And stop reading my mind.”

And in a flash of inspiration, Jimmy saw his opening.

“Cranky, aren’t we. You know, I actually think you have it too easy.”

“How can you say that?”

Jimmy was nodding his little plastic Jesus-head.

“Yep, too sweet a life, cruising through with your time shifting and flying around like a June Bug.”

“I could survive without...well, I haven’t flown in years.”

“But you could. But here’s the thing. You couldn’t survive without your *advanced powers.* I bet you couldn’t.

"Of course I could."

"I think I'll take them away for a while."

"You couldn't!"

"Of course I could. I can do anything I say so."

"You wouldn't?"

"Just the time slipping and the flying. How about that?"

"No. I'd rather you didn't."

"You don't always get what you want."

"Beetles?"

"Rolling Stones, actually."

She couldn't do any flying because she was driving, but she tried a little time slip and it didn't work at all. The failed attempt left her feeling naked and a little afraid.

"I think you should give them back."

"Who's that up there?" he said, changing the subject by pointing like a semaphore with one of his tiny plastic arms.

She looked and saw that, about a hundred yards ahead of them, a man in shabby work clothes was waving excitedly to slow them down.

"I don't know…dirty clothes I think he's an illegal alien?"

"You shouldn't judge a man by his garments," Jesus said, his voice sullen. "Give unto the poor, you know."

"I wasn't judging him. Don't be so pissy," she said. "Sometimes you can really be a pain in the ass."

He didn't say anything out loud, but she looked over and caught his little lips silently voicing the words, "You too."

She slowed the Datsun as the man motioned with broad and excited gestures that he needed a ride. She pulled to the side of the road, careful to park on the dusty edge, half off the asphalt, but away from the ditch. She leaned over and opened the door, then started to throw some books and blankets from the front passenger seat into the already crowded back seat to make room for him. She was just in time as the man, all grime and underarm odor, piled in with a rush. He was about fifty, a sunburnt Latino with a shock of unruly black hair.

Recoiling a little from his nearly overpowering scent, she managed a weak smile.

"Hi, I'm Kate. I'm heading for Taft."

"Andale! Andale!"

There was great urgency in the excited pitch of his voice.

"What? Oh, you mean 'go fast.'

"Jesus, Maria, Jose! *Andale!"* The man glanced frantically back down the road, the way Kate had come.

"You mean, Let's go," Kate instructed.

"Si! Rapido! Mucho fast!"

"Okay, okay, keep your shirt on." She began a slow acceleration back onto the asphalt, driving in her usual cautious way, while the laborer waved her on with both hands. Then he gave up, cupping both hands and burying his face in them.

"Noooooo…nonononononon…."

Even as she crept past thirty miles an hour, she managed a glance in her rear view mirror, and what she saw was not comforting. A large, shiny maroon colored Dodge Ram pickup truck was approaching at high speed, and it was going so fast that a collision seemed inevitable. The pickup zoomed uncomfortably close behind her small white Datsun, flashing its lights and blaring an annoying loud horn.

Kate hunched her shoulders, both hands on the wheel, determined and grimly intent on the road ahead.

"This stupid odd-jobber thinks he owns the road! Well, you can just go around, me Bucko-boy!"

The laborer beside her looked like he was trying to duck down and hide himself, but her car was small, and his was a move of desperation and quite impossible. In another moment, the maroon Dodge Ram had pulled alongside her, and a burly, sunburnt middle aged white man yelled at her and shook his fist while he drove with one hand. There was a Mexican in the passenger seat of the Ram, and he too was very agitated, yelling at her in Spanish and pointing at the man she'd picked up along the road. She caught the word *pendeho*, which she rightly assumed was a very bad thing to call some stranger you didn't even know.

The driver shouted in English, as if that might clear up her confusion, "Hey! Pull over, you stupid, dumb broad!"

Kate rolled up her window and shook her head No. She set her jaw and stubbornly continued. "I don't have to pull over! Who does that numb-nuts think he is?"

But in the next few seconds, the maroon pickup roared ahead of her car and then swerved directly in front, forcing the Datsun off the road. She slammed on the brakes and skidded along with the wheels on one side of her car just inches from the steep roadside ditch. The Datsun came to a wide-eyed, skidding halt.

She exhaled a breath of air in the sudden quiet.

The two men hustled out of the pickup truck. The white man banged on her window, and then on the roof of her car.

"Open up, lady! Nobody's going to hurt you. My name is Rod Harris. I'm a rancher around here. And that spic gentleman you got inside there is a dirty, rotten thief!"

Kate numbly shook her head.

When he saw she wasn't going to open the door, the man who said he was Rod Harris slammed his hand on the roof of her car and shouted to his companion, "Don't let him get away!"

The second man, a clean-cut Hispanic who looked like Rod's assistant, hurried around the Datsun and reached for the handle on the passenger door.

Kate got her hand down on the lock mechanism at the last second. "Go away, you—you savage pricks!"

The man who said his was Rod Harris slammed his fists on her roof in rage, "Lady, you got my thieving worker in there!"

She was frightened, but still determined.

"He's a human being!" she yelled. "He's not a piece of meat!"

"He's a stinkin' spic and a no-good thief, is what he is!" Harris took a few steps to the bed of his truck, rustled around in a toolbox, and returned with a heavy metal crowbar.

"You wouldn't dare..."

Harris didn't bother to answer. He threw the crowbar to his foreman, who caught it mid-air and in the same motion smashed in her passenger side window. The window exploded in a hail of glittery fragments. The foreman reached in, unlocked the door, yanked it open and reached for the man cowering inside.

Harris rolled his eyes, giving a look toward the imaginary heavens. "Why is it always so frickin' hard?" Unseen to anyone but Kate, Dashboard Jesus gave a little plastic shrug.

Kate was outraged. Obviously her Savior wasn't going to go out of his way to save anybody. She would have to do the heavy lifting by herself

"You can't just take this man!" she shouted. She grabbed one of the laborer's arms with her own and gripped the steering wheel with the other. The foreman forcefully grabbed the laborer's arm, and an unfair tug-of-war took place. The foreman was bigger and stronger, and even though Kate had the advantage of holding on to the steering wheel, she had to give way. She soon lost her hold, and the laborer fell from her car and tumbled into the roadside ditch.

The foreman went down into the ditch after him, pounding him a few times with his fists, and then getting him in a headlock. He dragged the laborer back up to the roadside and over to Harris, who punched the the sagging man on the top of his head. This was not the smartest move, because the man who called himself Rod Harris hurt his own hand.

He turned away, swearing and trying to shake the sting out.

"God damn, son of a bitch!" He kissed his hand, glaring at Kate through the windshield, and then looked over at the laborer, who was still snared in the foreman's headlock. The foreman steered his bucking captive over, and Harris dug his good hand in one of the man's pocket. The hand came out with a bunch of rusty screws and nails. Harris threw them on the hood of Kate's car. The metal clattered on the hood and the individual nails and screws bounced and rolled in all directions.

Harris gave another savage glare into the Datsun. "Nobody steals from me!" he shouted. "Nobody!!" He turned his attention to the man in the headlock. "Hold him up a little," he instructed his henchman. The foreman turned him into a more favorable position, and Rod hooked him in the stomach with a vicious upper cut. "Feels good," he commented, and then hammered the man with a second, and then a third savage blow. The laborer, who had been out with the first punch, collapsed to the ground without a word.

"Throw him in back," Harris said. He climbed in the driver's side of the Dodge Ram pickup as the foreman dumped their victim in the bed of the truck like a sack of potatoes.

Kate wound down her window a few inches.

"Nails?! Are you crazy? You're killing that man because he took a handful of your nails?

The foreman, who was returning to his side of the truck, swung the crowbar at her window almost as an afterthought. It exploded with a satisfactory shower of sharp, glittery particles, and he threw the crowbar in the bed of the truck, where it bounced off the laborer's head before coming to rest in a corner of the flatbed.

"We're not killing him, Lady—just teaching him an honesty lesson."

"What about my broken windows?" she yelled.

Rod Harris's sunburnt face flamed even redder; he was clearly beside himself with anger.

"Yeah, you harbor a criminal! That's your honesty lesson!"

"No, you're the real criminals!" she shot back.

Rod stuck one hand out of a window and gave her a savage finger as he swung his maroon Ram in a skidding U-turn and headed back in the direction he'd come.

"Tell it to the judge," he yelled. "See what good it gets you. He's my cousin, you know!" And his raw and ugly laughter dopplered away with him as he sped off into the distance.

As the roar of the big V-8 Hemi engine lessened Kate looked over at plastic Jesus in disgust.

"A lot of good you did…"

"You blame me for everything," Dashboard Jesus said.

"Useless in bed, useless on the battlefield. We were supposed to be married!"

"Come on, Kate—that's just a metaphor. How else do you think they get hot young girls to sign on for a lifetime of frumpy dresses and no sex?"

"Now you tell me."

"You know full well, you divorced me!"

"Well, I want my powers back, and I want them right now."

"No chance, baby. Let's see you learn to survive in the real world."

"Well, I'm frightened. I don't know how to do this."

The little plastic image's anger faded. He puffed out a tiny breath and sighed, seeing she was starting to cry.

"Okay, okay, okay…look, I'll send you a sign. But no superpowers. From now on, you've got to be more on your own."

"Right. A sign. You do that."

About twenty seconds went by and a scruffy looking blue, red, green and yellow feathered parrot fluttered close and then perched on the rim of the open window where the glass had recently been.

The parrot tilted his head and peered in at her, and then began singing in a screechy, lusty voice,

"I'm Perry, the Pirate Parrot/ I'm totally without merit!"

She tried to wave him away, but then she was struck by the fact that parrots, rather than being indigenous to California's Central Valley, were actually quite rare.

Perry took advantage of her moment of indecision to repeat himself, "I'm Perry the Pirate Parrot/ I'm totally without merit!"

Kate studied his colorful plumage with a mixture of admiration and disgust. "Just like every man I've ever met, Perry. That includes you, Big Jesu."

She cast a glance at Dashboard Jesus, but he was still as a statue, undoubtedly looking down the road to the adventures that lay ahead for them all.

"I'll steal your things," Perry squawked. "I'll take your stuff!"

"How about my heart, Perry?" Kate asked. "Will you steal my heart, too?"

"Awk!" Perry screeched. "Trouble! Trouble!"

Kate gave Dashboard Jesus another mean stare.

"Boy, some sign."

Dashboard Jesus remained frozen, and so Kate put her battered white Datsun in gear and pulled back on the highway. Perry fluttered in at the last minute and perched on the back of the passenger seat. "I'll steal your stuff!" he squawk-sang. "You give me trouble/ I'll give you guff."

With that, he hopped down in front of the seat and began pecking around as if there might be a few seeds or old cookie crumbs there. As the car, the bird and its driver stumbled and hiccoughed on toward the town of Taft, California, the plaintive voice began wailing again in Kate's head

> Too soon old/ an too late smart
> Dat's d' way/ of d' human heart.

CHAPTER SEVENTEEN

arrival at the new school

The torrid heat of early afternoon was burning down on Taft Union High. School was just letting out and the first yellow busses were parked in a long line in front of the campus. The students with wealthy parents, or those with middle class parents and part-time jobs, were ambling toward their own cars, SUVs and pickup trucks in the student section of the parking lot. Others were crowding around the bus loading areas or waving to friends lucky enough to have their own rides.

Kate drove in and parked in the teacher's section of the same lot. She jerked the hand brake and the white Datsun skidded a few inches with an embarrassing little tire squeal. Perry hopped on one window sill and twisted his head around in quick jerks as if he was looking for something to nibble or somebody to annoy. Kate's battered white Datsun was a sight, with the newly broken windows and the heavy books and stacks of her clothes in the back seat weighing the car down to where it looked as if it had bad springs.

Randy Harris, Rod Harris's favorite son and the only one he publicly endorsed as his own child, was one of the first to spot her. He and his best bud Joe, and their girlfriends Lucille and Judy, were walking hand-in-hand nearby. The boys were escorting their sweet-meats to their respective cars for an afternoon smooch and maybe a feel or two if they got lucky, after which the fellows would be hustling over to the baseball diamond for practice.

Sports at Taft Union High was more than recreation; it was a religion, and Randy was the current reigning high priest. As captain and quarterback of the football team, he could do no wrong from September through Christmas. And now that it was Spring, his fastball had attracted scouts from colleges as far away as Texas. Joe was less a talent, but as Randy had vowed not to sign without him, his college career at least was secured.

Randy wrinkled his brow at the sight of a hot broad talking to what looked like some bird that had been dipped in rainbow flavored sherbet. But before he could comment on the spectacular set of jugs displayed under the newcomer's tight tee shirt, Chester tried to sidle up to Randy's very own Lucille. Chester, it was widely known, was Rod Harris's bastard son, the one he'd tried unsuccessfully to run out of town for years. Chester, as Rod was eager to inform anyone who would listen, was a sneaky bastard. Nobody really knew where he lived or where he got his limited stash of cash to support his dusty old grey Chevy pickup, though it was believed he grew marijuana plants in various damp spots on the ocean-facing side of the hills west of town.

Lucille, who knew which side her butt was buttered on, rolled her eyes in mock dismay as Chester moved to intercept their tight little foursome.

"Hi, Lucille," Chester said with a furtive come on look in his sneaky glance that undressed her tip-to-toe all in one look.

"Oh, God help me," Lucille groaned.

Judy came to her rescue with a cheesy smile and a too-cheery voice, "Hiiiiiii, Chester."

"I wasn't talking to you, Judy," Chester said, not bothering to hide his annoyance. In addition to his limited funds, it was widely thought that Chester possessed limited intelligence, a rumor also quietly but persistently promoted by his father.

"Buzz off, Chester," Randy said, moving in a step or two and raising one muscled arm like he was going to backhand him across the face. "Don't you ever, ever get it? Lucille is with me. She's with me, Chester-Wester-Fester-Pester."

Chester ducked back two steps, just out of reach. "Why'n'cha let her speak for herself, Mister My-Daddy-Owns-The-Whole-Frickin' County?"

Randy did a quick forward move and gave Chester a vicious shove that sent him sprawling.

"Get a life, piss-for-brains," he said as he walked past without bothering to look back.

Lucille tossed her golden-streaked hair.

"Hopeless as ever."

It was at this moment that Kate made a lunge for Perry, but the parrot, who was proving to at least have the merit of quickness, easily avoided her outstretched arms and flapped away to watch the scene from a nearby carob tree. The tree was loaded with dry carob seeds, and this proved of interest to Perry, who set to work exploring the possibilities while Kate yelled that he'd better get back there right now or else.

"Sure, yell it," Chester muttered from his position on his back in the gravel parking lot. "That'll fix things."

From her safe spot surrounded by friends and her lover, Lucille was amused.

"You can fly, pretty bird..." She looked at Judy and they finished the thought together with a happy laugh, "...but you cannot hide."

It is doubtful that Kate even saw them. Still working through her anger at being dominated and (she believed) humiliated by Rod Harris's bullying ways and her old pal Jesus's chicken-hearted cave-in, she yelled up into the tree, "Come back here, you stupid parrot!" For his part, Perry snagged another dry pod and stripped half of it away, revealing a line of plump brown seeds. He was thinking they tasted a little like chocolate, and maybe he was going to live out the rest of his life right here in this parking lot where he could eat chocolate and poop on all the fresh young humans coming and going.

The four friends slowed to watch Kate, just to pass the time of day and maybe see what the new lady and her pet bird might do next, and even Chester sat up on his haunches. It may not have been a circus, but there wasn't much else going on in Taft, and so Kate's arrival was passing for entertainment.

"Bet she's the new sub for jack-off Fisby," Joe guessed.

"You're probably right, dip-shit," Randy said.

Kate leaned in the window of her car, looking to them like she might be talking with somebody, but that couldn't be, because the car was empty. She was saying something, but it was too far away to make out.

Head inside the car, Kate gave Dashboard Jesus her meanest nasty look.

"What is this damn bird all about?" she asked. "A sign is supposed to mean something!"

But once again Jesus was dumb as a plastic statue. Even so, she saw he was cheating, his tiny little eyes following her.

From the view of the friendly foursome just passing by, Kate looked more than a little sexy, particularly from their advantageous angle that highlighted a profile already brought into focus by her tight red tee shirt and even tighter stretch jeans. Randy thought he might get a little rise out of Lucille.

"Hey, nice knockers—for an old broad."

Lucille punched him in the arm and gave him a warning look.

"Hey, Mister," she said.

Judy also thought the new person, whom they pretty much had decided was Fisby's replacement, was actually talking to somebody…or maybe into a cell phone hooked to her ear…or maybe she was crazy lady talking to her very own self, ever a possibility.

"What's she doing?"

Joey grinned at her in his good-humored way. "Looked like she was talking to her bird." As he looked into her eyes, his ready grin widened, "I'd like to talk to your bird."

Judy grabbed his arm and snuggled next to him, "My bird wants to flap around with your bird."

Lucille caught on right away, and put her arm around Randy's waist and brushed the front of his jeans with her other hand—and then pulling back with a little gasp as if the gesture just might have been an accident.

"Oh, yeah," she said. "Come on, let's take your bird out for a little walk, Randy. Could I please, please, huh, huh?"

They all laughed about that, but by then Kate had retrieved her slim carrying case from the back seat of the car and was steaming in the direction of the administration building. Randy watched her retreating form, pleasantly set in her tight jeans. He wanted to make some comment about the nice ass, but a quick look over at Lucille told him she was already ahead of him, and that would not be a good idea.

And that left Chester, still sitting in the dusty gravel parking lot.

"Stinking rich fart-heads," he muttered. "Though that Lucille, now…I want me a piece of that…oh yeah, man, I wish to drinketh of that cup…Yea verily, just once, right before I shoot her dead between the eyes…"

There was something arresting about Chester. He was calm and about as quiet as a country mouse. But the flickering fluid venom of his dark stare offered a hundred-proof guarantee that he wasn't kidding.

CHAPTER EIGHTEEN
seeking justice

Kate paced like a caged lioness, three steps one way and then three in the other direction, walking in front of Principal Horace Huckelby's old wooden desk which was decorated with carved oak leaves, shields and quill pens, all ornaments of erudition in that rural neck of the woods.

"And these—these roadside gangsters just swooped out of their pickup truck like vigilantes and dragged that poor man away!"

At one end of her pacing, she looked up and her gaze made contact with a picture of Abraham Lincoln that was hanging on the wall. Abe raised his eyebrows and spoke in a huffy voice, "Gangsters?! Bald-faced ruffians?! What in the name of the Great Army of the Republic is this world coming to?"

She whirled away from Abe without giving him the courtesy of a reply. Principal Huckelby, however, was a matter cut from the actual cloth of reality, and had to be addressed.

"Most frightening for you, I am certain, Miss Twillinger. "And you didn't know the thieves? Never seen them before? Had occasion perhaps to meet them in a restaurant?"

His line of questioning was so fruitless that she ground her teeth to keep from saying some bit of common sense that might get her fired.

"Of course not! I'm new from LA, just got here! I never saw them until that very moment they forced my car off the road!"

"Yes, yes, how very unfortunate." The Principal made a gesture with his hand, resting it on his telephone as if he was preparing to call in to report the crime that had taken place on the way to their city.

"Ahh, um…two men, one white and one Hispanic. And what color did you say the pickup truck was?

"I didn't say, but it was maroon. It was one of those big, shiny trucks with a big chrome grill up front. I would know it anywhere."

"Ahh," the principal said, taking his hand from the telephone and resting it with the other on his lap. He cleared his throat, "Perhaps we should let matters lie, Miss Twillinger. Now, about your biology class…"

"But they broke the law!"

"Miss Twillinger—Katherine, if I may—from your description, the owner of that maroon pickup truck is Mr. Rod Harris, who also helped build that beautiful new gymnasium you saw on your way in here."

"Yes. I remember, that is exactly who he said he was!"

"If Mr. Harris says that fleeing stranger you picked up on the road is a thief, his word is good enough for anyone in this town."

The principal wrinkled his brows and looked at the copy of the portrait of Lincoln on his wall, as if they might be sharing some moment of quiet agreement. Then something else occurred to him.

"Do you have good insurance on your car?"

"No. Actually, I don't have any."

"Well, that is unfortunate. You shouldn't be on the road, actually. That is a very clear law, and our teachers have to set an example for our students. I think we can probably let it pass this time, but…"

"But that's—that's—that's—" she began to sputter.

"That's Taft, Miss Twillinger," the principal cut in to finish her thought. "Mr. Harris is a builder and a grower. We all aspire to be builders and growers around here."

Kate was finding his line of non-logic bewildering.

"Builders…?"

"Yes, builders and growers."

He clasped his hands over his plaid vest, which itself plumped out as if the man might be growing a watermelon or a giant pumpkin in there.

"What about you, Katherine Twillinger? You are our new teacher. We have selected you from a veritable hoard of applicants, our special selection. It should be your natural inclination to build things up, and to nurture them, so to speak, rather than tearing them down and crushing them underfoot."

At that moment there was a crack like thunder and the room shook a bit. It was as if God spoke in agreement with Principal Horace Huckelby. Kate glanced around in stunned amazement, but the rotund little man, apparently used to being on the proper side of divine reasoning, merely nodded a bit.

"The gravel pit north of town. Occasionally they use a bit too much dynamite."

He distastefully brushed bits of dust from his desktop with one shirtsleeve, but the interruption only served to illustrate his lecture. “People working together to build a better society,” he said, fixing her with a beady-eyed stare.

“Yes, sir,” Kate said. She backed out of the room, biting her lip to make sure none of her fire-and-brimstone thoughts leaked out through her mouth.

Math teacher Benjamin Rice was walking down the hall with his best and only pal, English teacher Vince Carrey. Of Benjamin, it could be said that one plus one actually did add up to three. Poor Benjamin had bloomed only once, and late at that, though with an early Spring flower; and then, having knocked up the poor young object of his inclination, had the common sense if not the decency to marry her. His Nancy had only been 15 at the time, but since he had a steady job and the girl, though pretty in the Kern County sort of way, had no other prospects… Once the pregnancy started to show, the good citizens of Taft looked in the other direction when Ben and Nancy applied for their marriage license, quietly whiting out the five and replacing it with a seven.

Benjamin and Vince were walking down the hall, reluctantly shuffling toward their last classes of the day when the well-stacked young woman in the red tee shirt came boiling out of old roly-poly’s den, her face glowing red and angry as a new-born baby’s. The young woman, who they took to be in her mid-to-late twenties, brushed past them like a tornado through a haystack, leaving the two men looking after her with heightened curiosity.

"Woow!" Ben said.

"New biology teacher. Replacement for poor, diddly old Homer, I do believe."

Ben thought about it for a beat or two. "Nice ass," he reflected.

"You're married, Ben," his friend reminded him.

"I'm just saying, Vince. You go after it, then."

Vince shrugged, looking after Kate who was relentlessly churning toward the far end of the hall.

"Maybe I will," he said.

CHAPTER NINETEEN
settling in to a new life.

But Vincent didn't get around to screwing up his courage to talk to the new teacher until he dusted the blackboard and swept up his classroom after his Trig class. And that only after another ten minutes to brush his shoes, comb his hair and rinse out his mouth with mint flavored Scope. By that time, Kate had contacted an ad in the paper that proclaimed Room To Let, had called to close on a three month lease, and was driving her dusty, overloaded Datsun with the busted out windows to see the room, which proved to be on the upper floor of an old Victorian with a big yard that included three ancient, gnarled apple trees, the last remnants of an orchard that had been split into parcels when the town had a growth spurt about seventy years before.

Kate frowned and paid a month's rent and a month's security in cash. Her new landlady, Mrs. Rainey, plopped herself in a rocker on the front porch and counted her money while examining Kate's things as she watched her haul them in from the car.

Mrs. Rainey frowned as she approached. "I'm a widow, child. Did I mention that?"

"No, I don't think so," Kate said, staggering up the steps under the weight of a carton loaded with heavy books. "Sorry. Can't talk now. Heavy books."

Mrs. Rainey's frown deepened when she realized her new boarder wasn't going to pause, not even to be civil, mind you. She listened as Kate clunked her way up to her designated room on the second floor. Listening carefully, she gauged her next comment carefully so that Kate wasn't past before she got out the sense of it.

"Did I tell you, 'No dogs or no cats nor any of them stinkin' lab rats or dissect-ory frogs?'"

"Yes, you did," her new boarder said, and she hurried on past practically before Mrs. Rainey could put two words together to come out with the next sentence. "That there means no pets whomsoever," Mrs. Rainey called after her.

"Whatsoever," Kate corrected her automatically, but under her breath.

On her return, the elderly lady got in another shot.

"And did I say, 'No gentleman visitors?' I don't care if they're white, red, black, brown or green. No gentlemen callers, whichsoever."

Kate hissed, again under her breath, "Whomsoever." Her comment was a bit clearer as this time she was facing the wrinkled old lady seated in her chrome yellow wicker rocking chair. Fortunately it wasn't that clear, as the pile of clothing in Kate's arms served to muffle her delivery

"What was that, dearie?" Mrs. Rainey said.

Kate dropped the load from her arms onto the steps in front of her.

"What happened to your last renter? The old biology teacher?"

"Homer Fisby? That wicked, wicked old pervert!"

"Yes, Homer. What happened to him?"

"He was convicted of flashing his thing, right in the park down the other end of Main Street!"

Kate tried to catch her breath. One or two more loads, and she'd be all packed in. She bent down to pick up the clothes scattered on the steps in front of her.

"So he died in jail?" she asked.

"Don't be silly, child. Homer-the-Roamer got off with a slap on the dick, him being Mr. Harris's uncle on his father's side and all. That show-and-tell business was ages ago. Homer hisself died of AIDs only a couple months ago."

"Too many gentlemen callers?" Kate asked, gathering the last of her frilly things and marching on across the porch and through the front door.

"Close that door! You're letting in flies!" Mrs. Rainey shouted after her.

"Hope they're not fruit flies," Kate said, smartly but unwisely getting in the last word.

That evening's dinner, the board part of Kate's deal, proved to be microwaved Kraft's Macaroni and Cheese in individual containers, and Snapple Peach Flavored tea, in the bottle. As there were no other boarders, the two women ate at a small kitchen nook.

Half way through the meal, Mrs. Rainey smacked her lips and said, "You didn't say grace."

"Did, too," Kate responded. "I snuck it in while you were microwaving that extra 30 seconds." Mrs. Rainey reminded her of Grandma Lulubird more than she'd care to admit. She kept waiting for the blow to the side of the head that, so far, hadn't come.

The old woman went to a cabinet behind the refrigerator and returned with her half empty bottle of iced tea full to the brim.

"What are you putting in your tea?" Kate asked.

"What you mean?"

"Well, either it's a miracle or you're adding some pop to your Snapple."

"My, ain't we the observant one. Here, gimme your bottle." Mrs. Rainey scurried behind the refrigerator and returned with the bottle filled to the top."

Kate took a swig and her eyes widened. "What is this stuff?"

"Raison wine," Mrs. Rainey said. "Make it myself"

"Wooh, that is strong!"

"Yeah, I distill it some. A few years ago one of my boarders got caught with a meth lab. I made a few adjustments and it seems to work just fine for turnin' out liquor."

"Really strong stuff," Kate said. "Look, about the bird…it's really not my pet. It flew in my car and now it has been following me around.

"Horace says you talk to Jesus," the old woman said, her eyes bright as bird's eyes, eager for a little inside dope on Kate's personal life.

"Horace Huckelby, the principal of Taft High School, told you I talk to Jesus?!"

"Not that Horace. Horace Harris-the-Mailman. But I do rightly think the first one did tell the second. They are cousins, you know."

Kate didn't know whether to be outraged at the invasion of her privacy or amazed at the speed that information traveled in Kern.

"I don't think it's anybody's business," she said.

"Interesting theory," Mrs. Rainey said. "But you see that ship has sailed. So what are you going to do? Here, let me get you a fill-up."

Kate watched her pour them each a refill from a gallon wine jug with a tattered Gallo Hearty Burgundy label. The strong raison brandy was relaxing her.

"Got plenty more where this came from," Mrs. Rainey said.

"Is everybody in this town related?"

"Well, sure," Mrs. Rainey said, as if that was the natural order of things.. Back after they chased off the no-good Indians, there was jest the Huckelby's and their chicken farm and a few head of cattle. And then Little Huck struck oil. Rumor was he killed Big Huck, but nobody knows for sure nothing about that. Oil was everything—and like I said, the few cows, 'til some som'bitch figured out how to steal the water from up north. With the water came a bunch of outsiders sneaking in from Bakersfield, and even up from Los Angeles."

"Outsiders like me," Kate said.

"I didn't mean it like that. I guess we got off on the wrong foot. You don't seem like a bad sort.

I mean, I ain't buying that story about your miracle parrot pal, but we all got our quirks."

"Like talking to Jesus."

"Yeah. Like that."

Later that evening, distant dry lightning flashed to the southeast, low on the horizon in the direction of Death Valley. Lightning had never frightened Kate, though she'd had several near misses while out in the family orange fields. She wondered what Mrs. Rainey's reaction would have been if she'd told her she'd not only held intimate conversations, but had made love to Christ the Savior, not once but dozens of times. It was her job as his wife.

Kate felt buzzed from the homemade brandy, but it was too early to go to bed so she busied herself by unpacking her books. Her room, though small, had one wall of built-in bookshelves that could hold the books she'd brought, which could be divided into three topics: evolution, spiritualism, and romance fiction. Her room also featured a large window with a view of the closest of the shrunken and withered old apple trees. She had a narrow single bed, and a glass-faced oak cabinet into which she placed her framed photos of a sweetly smiling Jesus with his Sacred Heart, one of wild-haired Einstein, another of haughty Darwin, and gruff Sigmund Freud with cigar posed in hand, giving the world his knowing look, and finally a fuzzy photo reproduction of the young Edgar Casey wearing a bowler hat, his prim wife beside him.

Kate had found a special spot on the night table for her worn prayer book and was propping up a favorite prayer card picture of Jesus, who was standing in a small fishing boat while several men pulled in enough fish to threaten a sinking and with the clouds in the background thickening toward dark and ugly. The picture card of the Savior kept falling over, and she was stabilizing it with her worn black wooden rosary beads when she heard a familiar voice.

"Meatball!" the voice called from outside the window. "Hey, Meatball!"

"Perry!" She hurried to the window. It stuck a little, but she managed to get it open. She felt a refreshing evening breeze. Perry fluttered like a helicopter in front of the window and then settled on a nearby branch of the apple tree.

"I'm Perry the Pirate Parrot!" he squawked, his voice a screechy imitation of her own.

"Where have you been?" Kate scolded him. In spite of the fact that he had deserted her, she was delighted to see him. After all, he was her sign, given her by her divine sidekick, Plastic Jesus, and it was some indication that her mission and her fate would not desert her, even in rural Kern County where she had no powers.

The moment was interrupted by Mrs. Rainey's whiny voice, complaining from the room below, "Shut up, bird!"

Kate heard a thumping knock on the floor directly below her. She was thumping on the ceiling , probably with her cane or the butt of a 12 gauge shotgun.

"Twillinger, I told you absolutely no pets!"

"Hey, Meatball!" Perry replied from his branch on the apple tree.

"I'll shoot you, you goddamn squawk-box!" Mrs. Rainey shouted.

"Life is tough, and then you die!" Perry said. "Awk! Awk! Awk!"

From her window, Kate saw the colorful bird fly away. She sat down on the plain, straight-backed wooden chair that had come with the room, feeling frustrated and alone. Maybe taking the job in Kern hadn't been such a smart idea. At least in the convent there had been the busywork routine, classes and vespers and food and to bed with Jesus, and then up the next morning to do it all over again. Here there was nothing but a frightening new job with godless teens and rurals who, like as not, believed the earth actually had been created in seven days, and that 5,000 years ago by the active hand of God. Kate believed God was guilty of the act. He had done it, alright, but the job had taken quite a bit longer, millions of years, truth be told.

Her bout of dark mulling was interrupted by another series of thumps from the ceiling directly below her.

"Come down here with that damn bird!" Mrs. Rainey's muffled voice clawed at her ears.

Kate said nothing in reply. The expression that crossed her face was just a twitch, but had Mrs. Rainey been in the room to see it, that look might have made her uneasy…indeed, might have sent her scurrying for the door in retreat. Jesus, who had personally taught her that look, called it

Moses-On-The-Mountain and she thought she'd once overheard him bragging to St. Paul that properly applied, such a look might bring down lightning and melt solid rock. .

The next morning, as Kate clattered down the steps from her room with her hands full of books and was hurrying out the front door, Mrs. Rainey was standing behind a drawn shade in the living room, watching as Homer the mailman approached. Some will say it was one of those mothers of all bad coincidence, while others, knowing a bit about Mrs. Rainey, will decide in favor of bad feelings and how they come to be.

Regardless, Mrs. Rainey was standing behind the shade and the heavy lace curtains next to the open front window as Kate hurried out the door, running into Horace the mailman and knocking him flat on his butt on the browned grass of the front yard.

"You!" Kate shouted, kicking him as, with the books in her hands, she didn't have a free hand to punch him. "Spreading gossip about me!"

Horace scrambled to his feet, dusting his mail pouch off and backing away. "Wait! No! Lady, back off! Everybody gossips in Taft! There's nothing else to do."

"That's just insane!"

"No, it's true! It's our native sport! Benny Rice the math teacher knocked up a Sophomore Cheerleader and had to marry her or go to jail. Horace Huckelby was seen through his window wearing his wife's panties and bra!"

“Who saw that?” Kate asked, shaking her head in disbelief.

“Well…I did,” Horace the mailman confessed. “And Chester who’s in your class at Taft Union, and Jimmy Frulandi and Jeeks Danner are all Rod Harris’s illegitimate sons, and Aggie Daniels, Julie Harris and Bunny Danner—“

“Okay, okay, okay. Kern County is Rod Harris’ personal breeding pen.”

“True enough,” the mailman said, ‘but that’s not my point. Bigs Martin, manager at the Taco Bell, has a whole second family in San Diego. Jugs Bridgestreet beat her husband to death with a mallet, but they couldn’t prove it so she moved to Hawaii. It’s just our own local soapie, stuff everybody knows. You talkin’ to Jesus barely ticks the meter. Hell, even your own landlady had a failed sex change.”

“Mrs. Rainey?” It was probably the information overload, but Kate couldn’t figure that one out. “From what to what?” she asked.

“Don’t matter, it failed, Horace said.

And with that, the chatty mailman wrinkled the broad forehead in front of his disappearing hairline and forced a See Ya Later smile, and then walked on down the street. And Kate threw her books in the back seat of her car and drove off in the direction of the high school. That left Mrs. Rainey standing alone behind the yellowed lace curtains, grinding her teeth and muttering “I’ll kill that bitch. I’ll kill her and send her straight to hell. We’ll see if her pal Jesus can save her from that.”

But when, an hour later, Mrs. Rainey looked in the mirror at the ruin of her self-image, or at least at the notion of whom she might have thought she was, she couldn't remember why she had been so angry or even the slightest hint of what it had been about.

It had been something…something…something really important, but now it was gone. When you're a kid, they tell you to eat your vegetables so you can grow up to be an old person. But what they don't tell you is that getting old really sucks.

CHAPTER TWENTY
trouble in a small town

After class, Kate sat alone at her desk in her schoolroom, with the tools of her trade around her. The lizard glared at her from his home in her new plastic Eco-globe. A dew of moisture at the top of the sealed globe indicated something wasn't right in there. Too much water for a desert habitat. She was going to have to do something to save that particular little world.

And, thinking about that, she began reciting the geologic epochs, which were spaced on cards over the blackboard, cards which had the relevant families of animals living during that period of time.

"Pre-Cambrian, Cambrian, Ordovician, Permian, Silurian, Devonian…"

Her quiet musing was interrupted by a knock on the door. '

"Come in," she said, losing her train of thought. Was it Triassic that came next?

Vince Carrey, the English teacher that she'd noticed had been sniffing around for the past few days, came bounding in. He flashed his toothy 100 watt smile and said, "Hi there. I'm Vince Carrey, English."

"I know. We've already met. I'm Katherine Twillinger, Natural Sciences, in case you've forgotten or haven't picked up on the stuff around the room."

“Yes, yes, yes. My pleasure,” he said, still acting like they had never run in to each other before.

“Good to meet you. “ She gave him an odd stare like he might be some form of obdurate monkey or primitive species of Homo Neanderthal. “…err, to meet you again.”

She nodded, admitting his mistake, but didn’t say anything. She looked up at him with a vague smile that seemed to indicate boredom or a lack of expectancy.

“How’s it going, Kate?” he said, blathering the first nothing-thing that came to mind, as if he was back in 6th grade.

Her smile was replaced with an irritated frown.

“Katherine,” she said.

“Katherine,” he repeated after her.

This exchange took some of the energy out of his approach. Vince relied on the belief that he was still quite a catch in the rural burg of Taft. While his sandy hair might be thinning a bit in the middle of the top, and while there might have been an embarrassing convex appearance to his abdominal six pack, he pretty much had his way with the feminine crowd, darting from flower to flower like an industrious bee, all the while avoiding any permanent embrace from their fragrant pedals.

Vincent looked around uncertainly while the silence grew between them. After a moment, he sat at a desk in one of the front row seats, and his patience was rewarded.

Kate looked up from a seating schematic that she'd obviously been studying when he entered.

"I seem to have the entire Taft Union football team and their girlfriends in my Natural History class."

"Why sure," Vince smiled agreeably, happy to be the senior teacher dispensing advice to the rookie. "They hold it off as long as they can, but they have to get through biology to graduate. It's a state law."

"I know what the laws are, Vincent…but these kids are dumber than amoebas. And worse, they don't care."

Vince gave her the shrug of a veteran teacher and survivor.

"Give them all "C's" and get on with your life."

"I can't do that."

"You have to," Vince said, leaning forward to look into her eyes with his best Mister Sincere look.. "C's or better for student athletes. It's the rule."

Kate felt a tightening in her stomach and her voice went up a notch, "I didn't see that in my contract."

"Take my word for it," Vince said with a wise older-teacher nod.

"I don't take anybody's word for anything," she said.

Vincent gulped down whatever pleasantry he was about to say. Kate's response didn't leave him any room for more of his patented pleasant banter. He said something vague about hoping everything would work out, and took his leave. Kate, head down and frowning at the seating chart in front of her, didn't bother with any sort of a warm send off.

A few minutes later a disgruntled Vince joined Benjamin Rice in the well-worn and musty teacher's lounge. Ben was eating a Sara Lee blueberry bagel and working the New Yorker crossword puzzle when Vince slammed himself down on a nearby sofa with its ripped leather arms and busted springs.

"How'd it go?" he asked his one-and-only friend in Kern County.

"You got butter on your mustache," Vince said with a sour look.

"That good, huh?" Ben said, rubbing his cheek with a napkin. "Better than egg on my face."

"The bald-assed truth is, it did not go exactly as I had visualized it beforehand," Vince said, carefully spacing his words so as not to reveal the extent of his deep seated irritation, a move that only served to further highlight his foul mood.

"What's a four letter word for 'struck out'?"

"Fail, " Vince said automatically, and then did a double take, realizing that wasn't in Ben's puzzle.

"She's a dyke?" Ben asked, trying to cut to the heart of the matter.

"No…I don't think so. Not dyke-ey…kind of spiky. Maybe a loner. I think she's got some serious problems lurking behind that wide-eyed and innocent strawberry blond business of hers.

"That's your problem, right there."

"What?" Vince said with the little snarl in his voice that revealed he was annoyed.

"You scare off too easy." Ben grinned to show he wasn't serious; it was just a bit of good-natured ribbing.

"Oh, yeah," Vince said, the heat now rising in his flushed face, "Like you would know, mister I-Married-The-First-Girl-I-Ever-Dated."

"Hey, that was different, and you know it."

"Everything is always different," Vince said. And with that, he jerked to his feet and slammed out the door, exiting the teacher's lounge like a crabby teenager.

With the clock slowly ticking toward midnight and lightening flickering low on the distant horizon, Kate sat grading essay papers at a small desk in her room at Mrs. Rainey's. She worked with a red Sharpie pen and a sense of ruthless abandon, and the corrected papers were covered with red ink and exclamation points.

She came to one brief report that stunned her teaching sensibilities. "The monkey with the biggest, reddest butt," she read, "be the prime-time bad-assed ruler of the wildernest king-dome."

Kate set the paper down and rested her chin on one hand while she stared out the window at the far away lightening. After a moment, she went back to reading the rest of the essay, "He be the ruler of all with his big, red butt. That is the law of the jungle." And that was it. She marked a giant "F" on the paper and tossed it on the pile with the other "D's" and "F's".

And that was when she heard a call from the window.

"Awk!" a shrill voice shouted, "I'll steal your stuff!"

And with that, Perry landed on her window sill.

"Perry!" she whispered. "Get in here, you're supposed to be my sign!"

The colorful parrot eyed her from his perch on the sill, but made no effort to hop inside.

"No merit!" he squawked. "No merit!"

Kate broke off a bit from a Trader Joe's Cranberry Oatmeal cookie and held it in an outstretched arm. He twisted his head from side to side, eyeing the morsel of food, and it looked for a moment like he might go for the bait, but then there was a loud thump from under the floor as Mrs. Rainey pounded on the ceiling with her cane.

"No pets! I said no pets!" her muffled voice came up from below.

Kate held out the bit of cookie, "Shush, Perry…be quiet and eat a yummy cookie!"

"Awk! Meatballs!" Perry squawked. It looked like he might hop over and take a peck at it, but in the next second there was a loud bang on Kate's door. She'd had the good sense to lock it, but that only gained her a few seconds. There was a key rattle in the door, and Mrs. Rainey jerked it open, glaring around the room with a baseball bat in her hands.

"Damn you, Child—I said no pets!" Mrs. Rainey shouted at the top of her lungs.

Perry, who had flown the coop at the first sign of trouble, was now eyeing them from the safety of a branch in the apple tree.

"There's no pet in here," Kate said, spreading her arms wide.

"I heard that damn squawk, squawk, squawk! If I catch you just one time, Missy, you will be so out of here!"

"I think maybe you're imagining things, Mrs. Rainey. The irony of the situation started to amuse Kate, and she let out a half-snort, half –giggle. "Maybe I talk to Jesus and you talk to birds."

That set Mrs. Rainey off the other way, and she steamed downstairs, intent on getting out her shotgun, the one she and old Fisby used to use to go a ways out of town and blast rabbits and such-like before Homer got all twisted and crazy. She actually did pull out the shotgun, but somewhere between that and when she started loading in shells, her mind came apart like a nest of wet noodles and she couldn't remember who she was going to shoot or why she was so blamed angry. So she set the shooting aside and headed to the kitchen for a jar of raison's finest.

CHAPTER TWENTY-ONE
bird brains

The next day Kate read to her class while they sagged in their seats, displaying various degrees of boredom. She only had ten students in the class, five footballers and five girls, and they were far more interested in each other than in anything they could get out of a book.

But this was her job, and so Kate read in a calm and steady voice, "And where is the place of understanding? It is hid from the eyes of all living; and concealed from the birds of the air."

She set the book down and eyed the individual members of her class, one by one. This was evolutionary stuff, very close to the heart of why she liked being a teacher,

"That's from the Book of Job in the Bible. It is also the quote that Jonathon Weiner uses to open his epic book, The Beak of the Finch, our modern-day bible that proves evolution is as real as…as this dinosaur." She pointed to a plastic scale model of T-rex on her desk.

The lesson passed on to the unworthy, she dropped her gaze to her attendance notebook and began to check off the names of those who had actually showed up. She suspected that Horace-the-Principal fudged the list when she reported the kids who didn't show, but that was his business, not hers. It was a complicated game where local schools siphoned federal tax dollars depending on how many kids they taught, but Kate saw it as taking from Caesar that which he was giving, that is, politics and not something judged by the ordinary standards of morality.

Randy, seeing Miss Twillinger was distracted, took the moment to show Lucille his essay with the giant red "F" on the front.

Lucille shrugged and gave him a sexy smile, "I got a "D".

"What you got don't matter sweetie honey-pot. I got a game Friday. And coach don't let me play with an effing "F".

Lucille gave him another of her come-get-me shrugs, "Oh, baby, just go up there and talk to her. She's new. She doesn't know the score.

"Yeah," Joe grinned from the desk behind Randy, "Talk to her."

The bell rang and the students gathered their books and moved in a slow, milling cluster for the door. Randy gave Lucille a shrug of his own, their own simple short-hand communication, Nothing to lose.

"You go on ahead," he said. "I'm gonna try it.

Lucille moved close so her breasts touched his chest and she reached up to kiss his cheek, "Just talk now, you sexy man-beast, you."

"Right," Randy grinned. "I suck up to lonely old broads."

"Be nice Randy-dandy. You need this, remember…"

Lucille gave him a playful whack on the back of the head and drifted away with Joe and Judy.

Alone with Miss Twillinger, Randy wasn't as confident as he had been bare seconds before. Kate was making marks in her notebook, and he had to shuffle on his feet before she noticed he was standing in front of his desk.

"Randy. Randy, Randy, Randy. What am I going to do about you?"

"I-I need to talk to you about this." He held out his failed essay paper, and from all appearances he had lost every ounce of the shallow arrogance he'd showed in parting with Lucille.

Kate sighed and gave him a shrug of her own. It hadn't taken her but a few days to pick up some few of the cultural nuances that were so integral to Kern County life. Horace Huckelby-the-Principal had shrugged, and Horace Huckelby the Mailman had shrugged, and Mrs. Rainey and everybody else she'd met in Taft shrugged at the slightest provocation. Even Jesus had picked up the habit, shrugging away her concerns and fears about her job and her new life in the few running conversations they'd had on the way to and from work.

"I understand I have to pass you at the end," Kate said. "But I don't have to lie about every rotten paper you do."

"No," Randy said, shaking his head in dismay, disheartened by the depth of her ignorance of the local customs. "It's week to week. I can't play if I have an "F". It's the rules."

Kate snatched the paper from his hand and briefly scanned it. "I've never seen a paper quite like this one."

That seemed to agitate Randy, who abruptly started to leave the room, then stopped and turned to face her.

"Sure, it's so easy for you, and for the rest of the kids, too. Me, I know the ideas when you say them. I actually understand them. I just can't write them down."

Kate said nothing, but Randy saw he had her attention, and so he plunged ahead, "Look, I know this stuff: The strong dominate the weak. The smart like me crush stupid guys like Chester. The big and the clever and those who can do their life-changes will outlast the dumb ones who can't a-a-adapt."

She nodded, "Well, yes…those are the main driving forces behind the theory of evolution, even stated in your own unique terms."

She handed back his paper, gesturing to see she more or less accepted his monkey butt analogy.

"But you were supposed to do a three page essay. You wrote three sentences."

"But I can't write it. I can't! I had tests that say I'm…I'm…I'm a moron."

"There's no test that says that."

Randy hung his head like a little boy who had wet his pants.

"The tests say I'm dyslexic."

"That's not a sin."

Randy was looking like he was about to burst into tears. If he was faking it, it was pretty convincing.

"My dad says I'm a moron."

"Your dad, the know-everything Mr. Rod Harris, said that?"

"Yes, he does. All the time."

"Here. Give me that paper." She took it and scratched out the "F" with her broad Magic Marker pen. "Will they let you play with a "D"?

"A "C" is better," Randy said, swinging for the fences.

Kate wrote a bold "C-", initialed it and handed it back to him. In taking the paper, Randy saw a book on her desk open to a photo of a parrot.

"I like parrots," he said.

"That's my parrot," Kate told him. "Perry the Pirate Parrot. At least, that's his species." The expression on her face clouded, "But Perry's flown the coup."

"Right. In the parking lot, when you first showed up at Taft Union. I think I saw that."

"He talks," Kate said. "He talks a lot."

"Animals know more than we think they do."

"Yes, they do," Kate said, reflecting on Perry's odd behavior and how Jesus had said the colorful bird was her sign. "He knows where I live."

"Maybe that's not the best test. Everybody in Taft knows where you live."

"Right," she grinned. "Horace the gabby mailman…anyway, Perry came back yesterday and sat in the tree just outside my window, just flaunting his freedom."

"I bet I could help you catch him."

Kate looked at him, admiring his youthful enthusiasm, his raw energy just bursting to get out and do great things.

"I wish I'd been more like you when I was your age."

She was thinking she might have done better with her life than retreat into the convent with Jesus."

"It wasn't a retreat, Kate," a familiar voice said next to her. "I find that really insulting."

She shook it off, and Randy mistook her expression for rejection.

"No, Miss Twillinger. I'm really good with animals"

"Give the boy a chance," Jesus, standing at her shoulder, said.

"Maybe you should be a vet," she said to Randy .

"Yeah, like I ever could…" Randy scoffed.

"I know a few tricks to get past dyslexia."

"I…I don't think so," Randy said, the stubborn look that came over his features reminding Kate of his angry bull of a father.

They stared at each other, both different and yet both similarly set in their ways. He looked frustrated and confused. Before she could say another word, he turned on his heels and stormed out of the classroom.

"Give him a shot, Kate," Jesus repeated. "What harm can it do?"

"A thank you for the C minus would have been nice," Kate said, looking after Randy's abrupt departure.

Darwin, from his picture on the desk, shrugged like a true Taft native. The dinosaur's grin widened with the understanding of a hungry raptor, and Darwin shrank back in fear.

"Stay away, you ugly creature!" the august man of science's voice piped from the photo in his tinny little voice.

CHAPTER TWENTY-TWO
sex and consequences

It was a hot and sultry evening. Grey moths the size of faux desert pear blossom petals fluttered around the blue-white drive-in fluorescents and heat lightning flickered and rumbled in the distance. Joe and Judy sat at one of the cement outdoor tables drinking diet cokes from big MacSlurpie cups and pretending to study. Lucille drove up in her daddy's dented Caddy, skidded into a near slot and sat down next to her pals.

"Hey, where's Dandy Randy?" Judy asked.

"I don't know. Something about helping his dad."

"Well, don't look now," Joe said, "But guess who followed you."

"Oh, crap," Lucille said, the whiny complaint full in her voice as she spotted Chester, sitting in his old pickup truck in a slot at the end of the MacDonald's parking lot.

"Technically, he was here first, so, much as we'd like to, we can't accuse him of stalking," Joe said.

"How about lewd staring?" Judy asked, frowning in Chester's direction.

Sensing the general mood in the heavy night air, Chester started up his truck and spun a little gravel as he made his way out of there.

Meanwhile, Randy was nowhere near his dad. He was in Kate's room, setting bits of apple on the sill of her open window and laying a small trail that led to the bed where they were sitting.

"Meatballs," Perry said from the tree.

"Here he comes!" Kate said.

"I thought we had to be quiet."

"It's Mrs. Rainey's bingo night."

"They still play bingo?"

"It's your town…quiet, here he comes!"

Perry fluttered to the sill, pecked at an apple, and then feathered down to the floor, pecking at the trail of apples. Randy lunged at the window and pulled down the shade. This startled Perry, who flew into the shade and fell to the ground. He lay there stunned and motionless.

"Randy! You've killed him!"

"Naw—look!"

Perry had indeed recovered enough to get on his feet and stagger around in a dizzy little circle. Randy carefully lifted the feathered creature and placed him in the glass-fronted cabinet with the pictures of Aristotle, Freud, Jesus and Darwin.

"Holy Crappers, he doesn't weigh much."

He threw in a last handful of apple bits, and Perry hopped around inside as if it was the right thing to do.

"I'm Perry, the Pirate Parrot!" he sang in his squawky way.

"Oh, that's wonderful!" Kate said. "I'm so grateful. He is like my only friend in my new town."

Randy smiled at her. "That's one fine talking bird. Singing, actually."

"Nobody's sure if they actually know what they're saying in people talk, but they've got lots of intelligence."

“I can see that,” Randy said. They were standing close to each other, and feeling flush with the victory of catching her pet parrot, and, looking at each other, neither could nor wanted to ignore the rising heat in the room. There were solid reasons why they should have moved away from that moment, but instead they drifted closer together, looking at the promise in each person’s eyes.

“I...we shouldn’t...” Kate said, feeling her lips so close they were nearly brushing his.

“Hey,” Randy said. I been set back five times. I could be a college grad right now.”

Still closer, now in his arms, she tried to protest, “Can’t...must not...”

But then they were kissing, at first gently and then overcome with the moment, they tore at each other’s clothing and fell together on the bed in a passionate embrace.

It was hours later when Kate woke with a start. She’d heard something. She sat up quickly, looking around in alarm, but there was no need for panic. Randy was gone. The noise she’d heard was probably him banging his way out the front door.

The window was open, and the glass cabinet door was also open a crack. She leapt to her feet, still naked, and wrapped the blanket around her. She hurried to the cabinet, but her worst fear had come true – Perry was gone.

She sat on the edge of the bed, and then got down on her knees on the hard wooden floor. She felt more devastated and alone than ever. The way Kate saw it, she had seduced one of her students, and that was so against her idea of who she was and what she stood for that she found the idea maddening.

"Oh, Lord Jesus, I had sex with one of my students," she said.

"Randy is almost as old as you are," Prayer Card Jesus said, speaking from his spot propped up next to her worn book of vespers and her rosary on her night stand.

"And I betrayed you," she said.

"What?:" Jesus shrugged, getting into the Kern County customs, "Didn't I have Mary Magdalena? And a dozen, dozen others you never heard of? Women come easy in the messiah racket. Come on now, Kate."

"Well, that's true enough he's older than your ordinary high schooler…"

"Older than most college graduates."

"Still, he's a student, and that's a line that must never be crossed." .

She stood naked in the window, staring at the distant horizon, moody and unconvinced by Jesus and his words of comfort. She didn't blame Jesus; she knew that was just the way he was, always trying to calm her jitters. .

Unseen under the trees across the street, Rod Harris sat in his maroon pickup truck.. As luck would have it, he'd arrived about fifteen minutes after Randy had tiptoed down the steps, snuck out the front door and left the scene. Looking up at her, Rod was thinking of a quick move across the street and up those same steps to have his way with their whacko new schoolteacher. She might not be able to teach him to talk to Jesus, but with a body like that he was betting she could get him to sing hallelujah. He started to get out of his truck, but the untimely return of Mrs. Rainey from her night of bingo fun put an end to that plan. Rod took a last look at Kate, standing still as a statue with her arms folded under her full breasts, illuminated in the faint light from a corner streetlamp. Damn, how could one woman be so crazy and attractive all at the same time?!"!

The night was a long and sleepless one for Kate. And the next day, as she walked alone to her classroom, she couldn't lose a sense of restless uneasiness. And worse, her mind was playing tricks on her. She'd always known she could read other people's minds. Now, as she headed for room 317, she was sure the kids she passed were whispering about her. Taft being the small, chatty town it was, there was good reason to feel this way even on an ordinary day, and so she walked faster, and then faster still until she was nearly ready to break out into a jog.

And, rounding a corner, she bumped into Vince.

"Hey, there!" Vince said. "You almost knocked me over."

Usually, she would have argued it was his fault, Vince cutting the blind corner the way he had. But she just pushed on past.

"Oops. Hi. Hey. Sorry. Wasn't looking where I was going!" This last sentence she delivered over her shoulder with a gay little laugh.

Vince, misreading her mood, tried one of his moves, "Hey, Kate, how about dinner tonight?"

She stopped long enough to give him a stony stare.

"Katherine," she said.

"Right, right. Katherine," he breezed, as if she should forgive him for being an idiot.

At that moment she was willing to say anything to get away "Right, okay. Sure. Why not?" She wave over her shoulder, "I'm late. Gotta be going."

Vince looked at his watch, puzzled to see there was still nearly ten minutes until first bell. But she'd said yes, so he chose to close the deal rather than worry about the time, "Eight o'clock, then?" he pressed.

"Right. Right. Date at eight. I have to go." And with that, she churned down the hall away from him. He rubbed his jaw, admiring the swing of her curvaceous behind.

As she continued down the hall, Vince was already forgotten; Kate was imagining more and more of the students were talking about her, even laughing behind her back. She lost her composure entirely when she could not get her key into the locked classroom door. Finally she did manage to slide the big brass key into the slot and gain entrance to her room. Once in, she turned the bolt from the other side, relieved to have a few moments alone before her class began.

She was flushed and unsettled as she tossed down her books and sat behind her desk. The big plastic T-rex on her desk opened his beady eyes and gave her a toothy yawn.

"Come on, Missy—get it together before these kids eat you alive.

Darwin huffed at the dinosaur, "Mastication is all you know, isn't it…?

This dialogue intruded on Kate enough to shake her out of her agitated state.

"I-I guess you're right," she said.

"Of course I'm right. We were a smart bunch, you know."

"What?! You were nothing more than a bunch of nasty beasts!" Darwin said.

"If it hadn't been for that big meteorite, I'd be sitting where she is, right now! And you—you'd be meat on the table!"

They bickered a little more about this and that, and Freud even woke up long enough to insult T-rex's mother, but Kate tuned them both out and looked at her faint image in one of the windows, taking the moment to straighten her hair and do a little magic on her lipstick.

At about that same time, Mrs. Rainey was shopping at the Save-A-Lot supermarket when she spotted Lucille and Judy giggling together as they tried on lipsticks in the cosmetics section. The old lady had no use for young people, and so she started to turn her cart around, but the wheels caught in a fuzzy toy cardboard display sticking out in the aisle. A green alligator and a brown monkey with a silly grin fell to the ground. Mrs. Rainey tried to pretend they'd been there before, but her wheel was still stuck and the alligator and the monkey were followed by a small shower of furry critters. Of course, by then it was too late to make her escape.

"Hiiiiiii, Mrs. Rainey," Judy said in her official the-game-is-on tone of voice. "Oh, these poor furry little things. Here, let me help you."

"I don't. I didn't I don't want…"

But before she could even come out with a proper sentence of protest, the two teenage girls had piled all the fur toys from the floor into her cart.

"There you are, Mrs. Rainey," Lucille said.

"Having trouble with your new boarder yet, Mrs. Rainey?" Judy asked, batting her eyes in an innocent way she had practiced since she was barely toilet trained.

"That would be none of your business," Mrs. Rainey sputtered. But then she stopped, thinking about it, and that's when she fell into the impromptu trap the girls had set up for her. "Why? Why do you ask that? Should I be worried about something?"

"Well-l-l-l…" Lucille said, following up on Judy's opening thrust, "…the rumor is, Miss Katherine Twillinger had a big, bad drug habit …you know, from when she was back there in the big bad city of Los Angeles where she came from…"

"You do seem to pick the real losers, Mrs. Rainey," Judy added, giving the old woman a sympathetic pat on the shoulder.

"Damn it, child! I don't pick them! On my limited income I have to take whoever comes my way!"

"Well, be careful she doesn't burn your house down, what with cooking her dope and things."

"Done it before, I heard, burnt clear to the ground" Judy said with a solemn nod of her light brown curls.

"Well, we gotta run," Lucille said. You had to know when a hook was well placed, and then move on. The two girls scooted off, leaving Mrs. Rainey staring in suspicious places around the store as if she was about to be attacked by wolves.

CHAPTER TWENTY-THREE

big date, little consequence

Vincent had to wait at the kitchen table for a half hour with Mrs. Rainey, while Kate went upstairs to change into something presentable. The older woman, who was known as somewhat the village crank, was drinking some vile yellow liquid out of a jelly jar.

"What is that stuff?"

"Spiked tea," Mrs. Rainey said in her normal curt manner, fixing him with a stare that dared him to call the police chief if he disagreed. "You think she's really on dope?" Mrs. Rainey gave a nod and shrugged one shoulder toward the room upstairs.

"Dope? Miss Twillinger? I hardly think so. Where'd you hear that?"

"School kids was talking about it, down at Save-A-Lot. They warned me, Be careful, Mrs. Rainey. I was touched by that. Most young kids these days aren't raised to be so thoughtful, thinking to warn old people about drug trouble and nakedness perversions like there is everywhere you look."

"Yes, that's right," Vince replied. "Did they say what kind of dope?"

"Hard stuff, I think. Something they cook on a burner. You any idea what that might be?"

Vince had a very good idea, having tried it for some months of his life that nearly cost him his college scholarship.

"No, Mrs. Rainey, I don't," he said. "What about the naked perversions?"

"Well, I ain't so sure about the specifics of that. You heard she talks to Jesus?"

"Well, I had heard that…"

Mrs. Rainey's battered old face assumed a crestfallen look. "That Homer the mailman…he gets to everybody before me."

But before Vince could think of anything to say in Homer's defense, Kate bounded into the room. Her collar was disappointingly high, but she was wearing a fuzzy light blue sweater that showed her ample breasts to spectacular effect, so all in all he wasn't that put off. Kate reached across the table, gathered up Mrs. Rainey's jelly jar and took a big gulp of the vile, brownish tea with the little whatevers floating at the top of it.

"Hey, take it all, why don't you?" Mrs. Rainey grumped, but her snarly ways didn't seem to put Kate off at all.

"There's plenty more where that came from," Kate said by way of a reply.

And to Vince's amazement, Mrs. Rainey gave her a conspiratorial smile in return.

"Yep, there is," the crafty, two-faced old bitch said.

As the English teacher escorted his date out the front door, he looked back to see Mrs. Rainey giving him a broad, two-handed gesture of warning, her face twisted up all witch-like, her hands raised with the boney fingers hooked like claws.

Vince was hoping for a quiet interlude at the La Salsa Tex Mex, but it was somebody's birthday and so his evening with Kate started out unsettled from the get-go.

Kate dawdled over the menu, until Vince was pretty sure that she wasn't used to hot-and-spicy food. He couldn't figure out why everything he did with her seemed wrong. Maybe he should have asked where she'd like to go, but she didn't know any place in town, and that wasn't the way men did things in Taft, anyway.

Once again, he tried to pick up the lagging conversation, "Sooo, Katherine, how do we stack up to life in the big city?

"I don't know," she said. "I was in the convent, you know. Until they threw me out."

There was an awkward silence while Vincent's brain scrambled madly for solid ground.

"Ahh, I actually didn't know that," he said. "You were a nun for real?"

"That is who lives in convents."

"Ahh, yes…well…what was that like?

"Not as quiet a life as you might imagine, Vince, except for the sex. That was very quiet.

The conversation ground to a halt. Kate was wondering if Jesus would have anything to say to the fellow, and just like that he popped up. It was a small square dining table for four, and the Christ chose the seat to her left.

"I'd ask him what he thought of the King James version of the Bible," Jesus said.

Kate nearly blew his cover of invisibility by answering out loud, but she only shook her head, instead.

"What?" Vince asked.

In a moment of semi-confusion, her gaze swept around the room and lit on a large poster taped to the window behind the cashier's booth. The poster proclaimed the benefits of the Red Rock Canyon Haciendas, the clean air, the beauty of the natural surroundings and the proposed community swimming pool and a nine hole golf course that would offer recreational opportunities. The poster claimed the project was now in the development phase, and advised readers to get their money down to take their pick of the condos.

"What is that?" Kate asked, nodding toward the poster. "Red Rock Canyon Haciendas?"

"Oh," Vince glanced over his shoulder at the poster. "That's Rod Harris's new deal."

"Rod Harris again," Jesus said, raising his eyebrows.

"He has his fingers in everything around here," Kate said.

"He's the man," Vince said.

"No he isn't," Kate said, looking at Jesus, who humbly dipped his head and blushed a little at her compliment. Kate turned her attention back to Vince. "Tell me about this Red Rock thing."

"It's an area east of here, maybe 150 miles or so. Near the rim of the Mojave Desert, actually. Rod laid claim on the canyon through a deed his grandpa supposedly filed. You ever been to Mojave?"

"No, I haven't. What is it like there?" Kate asked.

"Well, like this used to be before we got the water from up North. Really pristine, desert canyons, a few springs, some dramatic cliff faces. Good place for dirt bikes."

"And he's going to build there?"

"Yeah. It's a big project. Retirement home condos. The idea is, people from Los Angeles make piles of money and then need a place to get away from the smog and the city taxes. They'll be able to come out to Red Rock Canyon and garbage things up."

"And you're for it?"

"No, against, actually." Vince's expression turned sour. "As much as I can do…I mean, it's tough around here. Rod Harris gets what Rod Harris wants.

"Does he have a trophy wife? What's his wife like?" .

"He doesn't have a wife. He did, about fifteen or twenty years ago."

"And?"

"She ran off with an oil rig mechanic, had a kid."

"And?"

Vince toyed with his menu, thinking about the past. "Rigger had a bad accident, got his head crushed in by a load of concrete pipes. His ex-wife came crawling back for a little bit, then went missing."

"She came back and then left again?" That seemed strange to Kate, and even Jesus shook his head doubtfully.

"She was dumb to come back in the first place."

"And the kid?

"Lives with his grandma. He's in high school. Chester, the Molester."

"Chester is Randy's half-brother?

"Yeah…it's like dumb and dumber met rich and poorer."

"I'm not really hungry," Kate said.

Jesus had already gotten up from the table, eager to be on his way.

"Yeah," Let's get out of here," Vince said unhappily.

As busy as the La Salsa Tex Mex was, the streets of Taft were already fairly deserted, considering it was only eight in the evening. Vince drove along in silence, wondering if he should transfer to a high school in Bakersfield where he'd have a better pool of available women on whom he could flash his effective smile. He'd just about given up on Katherine Twillinger, but he hated silence, "Sooo…what's your story, Katherine?"

"I don't know that I have a story," she said, and that promoted another long silence.

"Everybody has a story," he said after the silence extended so long he thought he'd scream. He realized he'd rather be having his teeth drilled without anesthetic than be going through this agony. If it weren't for the tempting ripe fruit of her plump breasts, he was ready to dump her out the door at the nearest street corner.

"You mean, why did I leave the convent?"

"Yeah, okay…that" he replied, grasping at any straw he could find.

"I had a falling out with Jesus's handmaidens."

"Who?"

"The other nuns."

"Oh…and are things better now?"

"No," she said. "Worse, actually."

Again, Vince didn't have any answers, and the silence lengthened between them. At long last they pulled up in front of the old Victorian house in his faded blue Mustang convertible.

"Well, here we are," he said, leaning over hopefully for a kiss and maybe a bit of romance time. But the sweet moment was avoided when Kate noticed something was not right in her room.

"Hey!" she shouted, turning her head away from him to look out the window. "There's a light on in my room!"

"What?" he asked, startled out of his dream of a little smooch and a few grouping feels under her sweater.

""Somebody's up there! That bitch!"

Vince looked for himself, and it did seem there was a moving shadow, somebody had the light on and was moving around up there in Kate's room. He was about to say something, but Kate was already on the move. She grabbed her purse and was rushing away before she realized she hadn't said goodbye. She paused, then turned and rushed back to the passenger window, which was half down because his air conditioning was on the fritz.

"Vince. I'm glad you're against those condos. Next time, I pay. I had a good time. Bye."

And with that she was gone.

"Yeah, me too…I guess…" Vince said to the empty passenger seat where she'd been. He thought he might have heard a soft and pleasant voice from the back seat say, "Me too," but Vince immediately blanked the notion from his mind, deciding that was just some craziness brought on by his own frustration. God, that Kate had terrific bazoomies!

"Totally terrific," the voice from the back seat agreed."

And with that, Vince slammed on the radio. A retro C&W golden oldies station had Waylon Jennings wailing *She's a good-hearted woman/ In love with a good-timin' man.* His key turned in the ignition, he hit the gas, and his Mustang peeled him on out of there.

CHAPTER TWENTY-FOUR

lust in the country

Randy and his bud Joe and Lucille and her gal-pal Judy were seated at an outside table at the McDonalds. They were drinking cokes to wash down a shared super-sized order of French fries and using the fat plastic straws to shoot spitballs at the grey moths fluttering around. Judy, who was the president of the Photo Bugs Club, had her camera bag on the metal table, and was busy dusting off the new video camera the club had purchased.

"They got it all grimy," she said.

"Who did?"

"Some silly sophomore chumps who wanted to film sunset on the desert."

"Excuse to catch some sandy-butt nooky out at Red Rock," Joe grinned.

"Shoot the bush, shoot the sky. Rah, rah, go! Taft Union High!"

Her camera bag had "Taft Union High Photography Club stenciled on the side, and the logo "Shoot 'em up!"

"Yeah, shoot the bush," Joe grinned.

"Why don't you put that stuff away for a while and come on over here so I can inspect your gear."

Judy gave him a wicked grin. She blew breath on a big lens and polished it with a worn cotton baby diaper. "You seen my latest brushfire on YouTube yet?"

"The whole world has seen you," Randy said. "You've got the most famous scrub in history.

“They should call it PubeTube.”

“That was nothing. I’ve got plans.”

Joe yawned as if he’d heard it all before. He knew she was working up to inviting him to do a sex scene. He had two problems with that one. First, he was afraid he might wilt under the big lights, and second, she might be able to hold it for a bargaining chip to get him tied up in Holy Matrimony. Time to change the subject.

“Hey, Randy. What did you have to do to get that “C”?

Randy, caught off guard, gave him a guilty look. “C minus,” he said.

“Right, C minus. Come on, give with the details, Oh Romeo. What exactly did you do to get it? You boff the Twill? Lay the love-lump on her?”

This was so unexpectedly funny to Lucille that she snorted, the Coke running out of her nose.

Randy’s face reddened. “Oh, man, come on, get real…”

“Well,” Joe asked, “what did you do?

“Actually, I played the poor old *dyslexic me* number on her.”

“No! Christ—The Twiller from Maniller bought in on that?”

Randy’s sly grin broke into a laugh and they high-fived.

“C minus!” Randy said.

Meanwhile, across town Kate burst into her room to catch Mrs. Rainey sniffing a pair of her orange silk panties. “What in the world are you doing, you ancient, twisted, vile sex pervert?!”

"I'm the pervert?!" Mrs. Rainey shouted back even as she dropped the panties and some rubber object she was about to inspect more closely. "You should talk! Look at this madness!"

She reached for the pink rubber object, but Kate slapped it out of her hand.

"Don't touch my stuff!"

"I got a right to inspect what you bring in here! There's druggies and hopped out nuts like you up from L.A. all the time. I can't be too careful. I got a reputation, you know."

Kate's voice slowly began to rise as she spoke, "What reputation? I never heard such crazy crap in my life! Get out of my room! Get out of here, you droopy, snoopy, sagging old witch, before I put a curse on you that will wither and rot your flesh right off your bones and send your soul to burn in the eternal fires of hell forever and ever and ever!"

Mrs. Rainey's mouth opened, but no words came out. She had been carrying her baseball bat…but it bounced to the floor as she began a retreat, inching toward the door.

Kate was thundering now, her voice loud enough to be heard out on the street as she repeated at the top of her lungs, "Rot – the – flesh – right – off – your – bones! And send you on a one way ticket, your personal elevator ride straight down to hell!"

Mrs. Rainey managed to scamper out the door as Kate slammed it shut behind her.

She caught a glimpse of herself in the mirror, her hands raised like demon claws. That started her giggling. She was one of the witches from

Shakespeare's Macbeth. She mugged a little, going over the top with a half-mad laugh

'So much for you, my dearie!" she cackled.

Jesus frowned from the prayer card, shaking his head in disapproval, but he had the good sense not to say anything.

CHAPTER TWENTY-FIVE

not much goes on in a small town

Later that night, the room was dark except for the soft ivory glow from Kate's night light, which featured an etched carving of an angel watching as a little girl escorted her younger brother across a rickety wooden bridge over dangerous rapids.

She started awake. She was sure she heard something. She fished around for Mrs. Rainey's Louisville Slugger baseball bat, which she'd placed next to her bed, and got ready to let out a scream to wake the dead or bring Jesus back from the brothels of Jerusalem, whichever came first.

Before she could do anything, she heard Randy's voice, "Shush…Miss Twillinger…put down the bat. It's me, Randy..."

He took the bat from her hand and began to smother her mouth with soft kisses.

"I had to come back to see you."

Kate glanced over at Jesus, who had one hand up to his face in alarm and was vigorously shaking his head.

"No," Kate said, "No. What we did—that was just that one time."

But with a smooth athletic move Randy knelt above her on the bed and pushed her down. He poured a shower of kisses on her, now working his way down from her ear to the softness of her neck.

"No, Randy…we'll get caught!" She tried to protest, though she seemed to be running out of energy in that direction.

"No, we won't," Randy reassured her. "I used a ladder to climb in your window. And I made sure Mrs. Rainey is asleep."

"Randy, no, we shouldn't..."

But he again smothered her objections by unbuttoning the front of her flannel nightgown and burying his head in the soft fullness of her bare breasts.

"But we can't..." These were simply worthless words, because by that time she was helping him unbutton the last few buttons to fully open her nightgown to him.

Noooo," she said. "Nooo...ohhhhh...ohhhh...oh, oh, oh, oh, oh, oh..."

And by then she was hopelessly caught up in the ancient ritual that had kept all of humankind going through its darkest hours.

Randy was young and strong, but he didn't like to linger. He had his reputation to consider; nailing a teacher with a bod like the Twill's was a feather in his, err, butt, but too much of that and he'd get a rep as a tweedy needy weedy, some kind of a perv like Chester, even. So he had his fun, was done, said he had to run.

And on just the other side of twenty heated minutes he was pulling up his surfing shorts and tiptoeing back down the ladder. It gave him a little heart bump when it scraped the wall while he was taking it down and putting it back behind Mrs. Rainey's tool shed where he'd found it, but no lights went on in the house, no sirens started from the street. He took a deep breath, gave a last look up at Kate's darkened window, and trotted on down the street toward the parking lot where he'd left his car.

`So it was just after ten and Randy was gone, leaving Kate feeling dirty and used—and hot and bothered at the same time. She thought a shower might cool her off, but when that didn't help, she threw on a pair of shorts and a halter top, laced up her running shoes, and headed downtown.

The night air was warm, with no coastal onshore breeze this far on the eastern side of the low Pacific Range. She alternately jogged and walked, heading toward a deserted patch of dusty ground that served as the town square. Her hair, which she hadn't bothered to comb out, was soon dry. However, it was curly and disheveled and, without any makeup, she took on something of the haunted look of a crazy lady. Recognizing this as she stared at her silent form in a darkened shop window, she was oddly pleased.

"Form follows function," she whispered to herself.

"They say that about buildings," Jesus chided gently, throwing a comforting arm around her shoulders.

She shrugged his arm off and walked away. "Oh, go away," she said.

"All right, I will," he said. And when she turned around, he was gone.

"Good riddance to bad rubbish," she muttered.

"That's very close to a sin," his voice whispered from his close invisibility.

“I said away, not just out of sight,” she yelled out loud.

“Okay, okay, Miss Touchy-pants,” he said.

After five more minutes of brisk walking, she realized she was passing a Catholic church.

“There are no coincidences,” she muttered.

“Except for actual coincidental events, I believe that would be true,” the gentle voice at her side murmured.

“Jesus H. Christ, will you stay out of my head?!” she shouted.

And then she was still, realizing there was a third person who had heard her. It was a dim figure standing in the dark in front of the main door of the church.

“Who are you?” she stammered.

“I am Father Ricotto.”

“You could just be saying that.”

“I assure you, I am,” he replied in a calmly reassuring way that sounded like Jesus himself might have given the fellow voice-coaching lessons.

“You’re just a dark figure in a dark doorway. You could be a pervert or a rapist.”

`“Child, I assure you I am who I say I am. Look, I’m wearing a robe.”

“I’m not your child.”

“Of course you’re not. It’s a figure of speech. Now how may I help you?”

“I actually wish you could help, but you can’t. You haven’t got a clue.”

The figure took a step backwards, as if physically struck by Kate’s bitter tone. Since he didn't seem to have anything else to say, Kate turned away and walked on down the street. As she passed a park bench, a solitary figure in shabby clothes, a tattered raincoat and a dusty beret saluted her and took a pull from a bottle in his hand.

"Who are you?" she asked him.

"The town drunk," he said with a note of pride in his voice. Every town this size has one. Or at least they should." He held out his bottle, "Here, you want a taste of the devil?"

"I don't think Jesus would approve," she said, turning on her heel and walking back toward her room in the boarding house.

"What? Wrong brand?" the town drunk asked. "I didn't think the almighty Creator was that finicky."

Well, he is!" Kate shouted over her shoulder as she picked up her pace and broke into a dog trot. Sometimes, she was thinking, small town life could really get a person down.

CHAPTER TWENTY-SIX

suspicious minds

One of the problems when people get involved is that they lose their sense of separation in public places. So, although their connection was becoming a talking point among a variety of third party observers, Kate and Randy were oblivious as they stood together in the hallway in front of her classroom. True, she was pointing to a page in a book containing illustrations of brightly colored birds, but they were standing very close as Judy and Lucille rounded a distant corner and spotted them. The two girls pulled up short with that sixth sense young predatory females have, not wanting to be spotted but rather wishing to blend in with the vegetation and gather more information.

"My, my, my, they do seem to be getting on," Judy said, licking her lipstick.

"Well—that doesn't mean anything," Lucille protested. "She's helping him with his dylex-dylex…his reading problems."

"I dunno," Judy said. "Seems like Dandy Randy's going the extra mile for his "C" minus."

"Oh, that's just dumb, Judy." Lucille turned and headed the other way, toward her locker. "Forgot my notebook," she said.

Judy didn't bother to point out she was carrying it in her arms. "Meet you in class," she said. She'd decided she would hang out to see what she could see.

Churning toward her wall locker, Lucille nearly ran over Chester, who was slumped back against his own locker, playing a hand-held version of Kill Bill.

"Uh, Hi Beautiful," Chester said. He gave Bill one last Boom!, and put his game away. He fell into stride next to Lucille.

"Oh, hi Chester."

"What I got to do so you take me serious?"

"Oh, Chester, maybe in another life—but in this one, I'm in love with Randy."

"No, uh-uh. No, you ain't. You just don't know yourself yet."

"That's crazy talk, Chester."

"What if I was a rich boy, like Randy…or famous, like…like Bonnie and Clyde?

"Chester, get it in your head: I'm with Randy, and that's a forever thing."

She turned away from him, heading back the way she'd come. Then she paused for a moment, having thought of something.

"And, by the way, dummy, you'd have to be Bonnie or Clyde."

And with that, she walked on past, their discussion already out of her mind as she tried to imagine Randy serious about an ancient-aged school teacher, and to figure out what her next moves might be, just assuming the ridiculous for a moment, that maybe her boyfriend was, well, not in actual love, but was suffering some schoolboy infatuation.

Chester remained behind, facing his wall locker with a space of two inches between his eyes and the chipped grey painted metal. He was talking half to himself, as he often did.

“Well, Clyde, then. I could be Clyde. Clyde. Clyde. Clyde. Clyde. He began to bang his head against the locker to the beat of his own words. He didn’t remember what series of events led him in the next ten minutes to be standing in the bathroom, staring at his image in a cracked and bloody mirror. “Clyde,” he said, “I could be Clyde.”

CHAPTER TWENTY-SEVEN

let the lusty times roll on

The days and nights passed like a heady blur in the thriving rural community of Taft, as Randy visited Kate's rented room in Mrs. Rainey's house almost every night. It was as if he was hooked on crack, and she in turn couldn't say no. Meanwhile, Jesus had retreated to his lonely vigil on the prayer card from where he could empathize with the suffering and the needs of all of strong spirited but weak willed humankind.

And worse for Kate, she began to agree to meet Randy around town, at little frequented bars and failing burger joints where nobody from the school ever went. No matter where they met, Randy would leave usually leave her before eleven. Kate would go to her room at Mrs. Rainey's, or if already there, she would lie back on her bed and look up at the ceiling, tormented by her feelings of guilt...and, truth be told, her fear that their relationship would be discovered. She was seducing one of her students, and she had nowhere else to go from Taft. When she'd left the convent, she'd sent no forwarding address back to New York, and her supporter, Carter Flinn was out of the picture. This was the end of the world for her. There was no hope or peace in her foreseeable future, and for the present, the nights were full of sleepless wandering. After Randy scurried away, she would take a shower, throw on some running shorts, and walk the town streets.

She asked herself what could she possibly be trying to prove? She had seen the stripping of her zoomin powers as something of a trial by fire; at least, that was the way Jesus had presented it, some sort of test. She'd almost immediately regretted her decision, but her abilities were gone by then, disappeared as if they'd never been. Why had she allowed herself to be talked into this impossible situation?

One night while walking alone on a street bordering the dusty square that passed for the Taft village commons, she reached the town drunk, who was sitting on his regular bench across from the church.

He hailed her as he had many times before, "Hey, sweetie-pie, how are you."

She started past him without replying, but then she paused and eyed him suspiciously. She squinted down at him.

"You seem harmless enough, in a dirty, disgusting sort of way."

"You too, actually," he said. He was so drunk it came out 'act-chew-al-ly'.

"*Act-chew-aly*, You don't look so well, yourself," she said.

"Well, it ain't an easy job, being the town drunk. There's standards to uphold." He cackled at his own joke and held out his flat glass bottle. "Here, catch yourself a snort."

Kate eyes the bottle thrust in her direction. "What is it?"

"Fish turds and rotgut."

"Swell. You're a comic, too."

Kate eyed the bottle, thinking penance.

Encouraged to see she hadn't said no, he pushed it further in her direction.

"I heard that line in a movie one time. Always wanted to try it out. Here. Go on, sweetie. Have a swig."

"Right, my penance. Five Our Fathers, five Hail Marys and a swig of rotgut."

She sat on the bench, as far as she could scoot to the edge away from the man. She took the bottle and carefully wiped the lip on a corner of her tee shirt. At that moment, the dark form of the priest became apparent, watching them from the shadows of the church.

"Keeper of the town secrets," the town drunk sneered, nodding his head at the shadowy figure across the street.

Kate raised the bottle in a little salute in the priest's direction.

"How come you don't like him? Everybody is supposed to like a man of God."

The drunken man sneered again, but before he could answer, there was a rough engine roar from down the street and Chester's pick-up truck went flying past. Kate saw Chester's arm fling something she thought might be a cigarette butt, and a few seconds after he passed there was a powerful explosive Boom! at the church door where the priest had been lurking.

The drunk chuckled, "Chester got his own war against religion. Every Spring, when kids is knocking down mailboxes with baseball bats,

Chester M-80's the church. You can count on it, like the swallows coming back to Capu-chino."

"Well," Kate said, "I guess the show is over. Thanks for the drink."

She stood up, handed him back the bottle of cheap booze, and walked on.

"That's what I'm here for."

Though it was nearly midnight, there were bright lights and loud speechmaking emanating from the town hall meeting place, a building that also passed for the Congregational Church on Sundays. Kate was curious as to what could be going on in Kern County at that hour of the night. Standing in back of the hall, she saw that about fifty people were sitting together on folding metal chairs in the front one third of the meeting place. Up on a low stage, a foursome of plump, middle aged men in suits faced the gathering. These men were wearing suits, and looked like the lawyers, bankers and prosperous businessmen that they were.

What was more, a man stood in a single spotlight up on stage, illuminated as if by a ray of light from God The Father Almighty, Himself.

"Vince…" Kate whispered to herself.

"Right," Jesus said, always at her side for a little commentary. "Why are you so surprised? I said I would send you a sign."

It was Jesus, life-size and in the flowing robes, standing nonchalantly sipping from a plastic McDonald's cup.

“They really should get a Starbucks. I miss my café mocca.”

“Why don’t you just conjure yourself up one?” Kate asked, falling into their old conversational ways without thinking about it.

“Against the rules,” he said. “

“Vince is my sign? I thought you said Perry was my sign.”

“I never said that.” Jesus eyed her calmly over the plastic lip of his Mac-Coffee.

“Perry is a false prophet?”

“Perry is just an annoying parrot.”

“Now you tell me.”

Kate gave him an angry glare and started to storm away, but Jesus took her by the arm and held her back.

“No, I’m serious. Maybe this guy. Take a look, Kate.”

“It’s just Vince Carrey, the English teacher from Taft High with the fake smile on his badly enamel plated teeth.”

Jesus smiled patiently. “How do you know I don’t want to enlist him to save the world?”

“Oh, great. Why didn’t you enlist me?”

He gave her his gently reproachful smile, “Kate, he can’t see me or even talk to me, like you can. And, believe me, right now, he’s scared silly. Frankly, I don’t think he’s going to be able to pull it off.”

As always, Jesus’s gentle and kind way had her feeling guilty.

“Oh, Jesu Christi, I don’t mean to be so…so self-centered,” she mumbled her apology.

She turned to look at the Christ and explain how badly she felt for her behavior, but he was gone. She shrugged, continuing the conversation even though she was talking to empty air, absolutely certain he could hear her anyway.

"But still…come on, mousy little Vince Carrey?"

She looked again at the stage, and through perhaps some trick of stage lighting, it did look like a bolt of divine light was illuminating Vince in a radiant, glowing halo. And that started her thinking that she should give the sad fellow a chance to prove himself. Kate found herself compelled to move forward, walking almost as if she were in a trance, until she found an empty seat right behind the end row of the crowd that had gathered.

It was interesting to hear Vince speaking with passion about something he cared for. The fake plaster-cast smile was gone as he went on about a place that sounded like a small slice of paradise pie. "It's where our people go on picnics," he said. "It's where they take their families for reunions, and teach their kids to climb rocks, ride dirt bikes and shoot .22 rifles.

The four men seated on the low stage wiggled on their plump butts and stuck a finger in their tie-bound necks. It didn't seem to Kate like they were sympathetic to Vince's petition, or plea, or whatever it was. In fact, they looked downright bored.

"Rod Harris doesn't need this," Vince went on. "He has all the money he'll ever need."

That perked Kate's interest. The subject of the meeting came to her in a flash. This was one of those public meetings about land development, and they were talking about Red Rock Canyon!

From the crowd in front of her, a heckler shouted, "Yeah, Vince? What are any of us going to do about it?" Kate saw a shadow of hesitation cross Vince's face. *Oh, Vincent, Vincent—if only you weren't such a weak vessel of the Lord!*

"Well…sure, we have to be careful," Vince answered the heckler.

But that only raised a stronger voice against him, "Careful, hell! We can't do nothing, and you know it! And when Rod gets wind you're here shooting off your mouth against his precious Red Rock Project, you're gonna lose your fancy job at the high school, mister teacher-boy-wonder!"

One of the plump men in suits harrumphed at this, and felt compelled to rise from his chair. "This is a Land Use Committee meeting. I'll ask for a little of the proper decorum here."

But that only raised another voice from the crowd. "We're just wondering what the hell interest Vince here has in being here?"

"I'm just a concerned citizen, like you!"

"Hey, I ain't concerned. Rod gets what he wants and he leaves me alone. That's a fair deal, I'd say."

"Yeah," somebody else shouted, "Rod already got the outcome sewed up in his pocket. He don't have to be here!"

"It isn't a sure thing," Vince shot back. "Just find one rare and endangered species out there, and we could stop this thing!"

"That right, Mister Commissioner?" Another jeering voice raised itself.

"Yes," one of the plump officials replied, "That is correct."

From her seat in back of the crowd, Kate stared at Vince as he tried to fluster his way through the jeers from the dubious audience.

"Some sign," she muttered to herself. "Some goddamn sign. You'd think the son of God would be better at picking winners by now."

As she rose to leave the room, Vince was encouraging the crowd to get out there to Red Rock Canyon and find that special plant or desert life animal.

"Rare and endangered," Kate shook her head. "See, there's always some hang-up. Where the hell is divine intervention when you really need it?"

CHAPTER TWENTY-EIGHT
maybe he should have seen it coming

Father Ricotto stood in front of his church, angrily pointing out to the fat Taft City police chief exactly where the big firecracker had gone off. Rod Harris pulled up alongside the police car in his maroon pickup truck.

"It's willful desecration of religious property," the priest insisted.

"Crackered the church again, huh?" Rod yelled from his open window.

"Oh, hi Rod," the Chief looked over at the newcomer with a smile, and his voice was friendly and conversational.

"It's a hate crime!" The priest said, his voice going up another notch. Father Ricotto clearly didn't like that the Chief seemed to be deferring to Rod, who was ignoring him the way he always did.

"I heard it on the radio," Rod told the Chief by way of explanation. "I was tuned to the police band. Look, I'll handle this."

"I'm going to press charges!" the priest burst out. "Hate crimes are a federal offense! The FBI will be here in no time!"

"Oh, you don't want to do that, now Father, do you?" Rod's voice was smooth and calm, but there was an underlying something, a hint of unpleasantness. "This isn't really like somebody spray painted Nazi signs on your walls or burned a cross on your lawn."

"Well," the priest puffed out his cheeks, "We can't have people exploding dangerous bombs around here.

"For God's sake, get a grip—it was a fire cracker, Ricotto!" Rod snapped at him.

"A big, dangerous fire cracker bomb! We can't let ruffians run wild like they own the town.

"Oh, hell—"

By now Rod had slid out of his seat and joined the two of them. He dug in his front pocket and came up with a fat roll of twenties, and began peeling off the bills, letting them fall in a little pile at his feet. The priest said nothing as the number of bills grew and grew.

"Chester's one stupid and confused young fellow," Rod said, "and he's got some lumps coming," Rod said. "But this is a family matter, and I'd appreciate it if you'd allow me to deal with it."

Rod winked at the police chief and got back behind the wheel of his truck. He drove slowly away, his eyes automatically flicking left to right, scanning the area for any sign of Chester's battered pickup truck.

Back in front of the church, the police chief gave Father Ricotto a look that could have been anything from mild annoyance to contempt.

"Better pick up your money before the night breeze blows it away," he said.

As he drove away, he saw by way of his black-and-white SUV's large rear view mirror that the priest had dropped to his knees and was scratching around to gather in the money.

A few blocks away, Kate entered Artz Liquor & Deli. She wandered down the aisles, pausing in front of the cheaper bottles of whiskey. She picked up a bottle of rum and a bottle of vodka. "The Pirate's Choice or Russian Roulette?" she muttered. And in the moment when she was about to choose the rum she overheard someone talking in a low, urgent voice in the next aisle over.

"Your money or your life!" the voice said. "Shit, that's stupid. How would Clyde do it? Gimme all the money. No, wait. Gimme the money in that cash register…Jesus, no…Gimme all the money in that there cash register –right now!"

Kate rounded the corner of the aisle and caught Chester play-acting with a snub-nosed police .38 pistol as he looked into the image of himself reflected in the sliding glass doors of the soft drinks cooler.

"Oh, shit…" Chester said.

"Chester, what on earth do you think you're doing?!" she said in whispery outrage.

"No-nothing, Miss Twillinger," Chester said, crossing his arms in a vain attempt to hide the pistol.

"Yes, I'll say nothing," she said. "You were practicing to rob this store!"

"I most definitely was not," Chester said, trying for dignity. "People don't practice to do a thing like that."

"Yes, you were," Kate insisted. "And you know something? You'll screw up your life forever and ever and ever."

"W-what are you talking about?"

"You'll get a life sentence for armed robbery! A life behind bars for you—with perverts behind every bush who have nothing better to do than tie you upside down with your head in a toilet bowl while they corn-hole you in the butt! Corn-hole," she repeated for emphasis. I have read the penmanship and seen the graphic illustrations in the bathrooms"

Chester panicked at the thought. He looked around wildly.

"Agg! Crap!"

He realized he had the pistol in his hand. "Here!" He shoved the .38 in her purse and scrambled down the aisle like an Olympic walker, making his way for the door.

The East Indian night manager looked up from a magazine he was reading as Chester rushed past.

"Via con Dios," the manager said.

"Yeah, Dude," Chester managed to reply on his way out the door, "Con Dios. And may Allah bestow you 40 virgins."

The night manager cocked his head sideways, thinking about the possibilities. "Thank you," he said, his attention sliding back to the magazine he was reading. He looked up again as Kate placed a bottle of rum on the counter.

"So, that nervous young man-boy was going to rob my store?" he asked.

"Yeah," Kate said. "I saved your life."

The night manager shrugged with a sad smile and pulled out a huge, heavy Dirty Harry type Magnum .44 pistol from under the counter. He dropped it on the counter with a heavy metallic clunk.

"No," he said, "Most probably his."

Chester walked down the street away from the liquor store to where he'd parked his pickup truck behind the old city hall building. He was feeling frustrated and angry, wondering why his plans always seemed to backfire on him. It more than the loss of the quick money he'd hoped to pick up…this was a bad start to his career as the new Clyde, Robin Hood Robber of the West.

He was tiptoeing through the dark alley toward his car when a powerful arm reached out and captured his head in a choking arm lock. In another minute he was slammed against a blue dumpster and a clawed hand grabbed his throat, cutting off his windpipe while his assailant's other hand, balled into a fist, hammered his abdomen and groin.

As he began to black out, the claw relented so he could breathe a little, and the voice he recognized as his father's snarled, "Disturbing the minister again with your stupid 4th of July shit, I hear."

"He's a priest, not a minister," Chester managed to choke out.

"I don't give a diddly crap, little boy bastard of mine."

Rod gave him a violent push and Chester's body slammed into the rusty blue dumpster behind him. His back felt like it was cracked, but he'd been beaten and hammered his entire life by his father.

"Go ahead, kill me," he said.

"You only kill somebody as a last resort, boy."

"Yeah? You got it all figured, do you?" Chester taunted.

"Yes, I do, Chester the Fester. You want to crush somebody, you stamp out their dreams."

"That what you did to mama?" Chester asked.

The punch to his face came with such violent force that Chester's head snapped back and slammed against the dumpster.

"With that smart ass remark, you just used up your good will in this town, boy!" Rod said, rearing back to deliver a killing blow. But Chester, even dizzy and bleeding from one ear and his nose as he was, still managed to duck the punch, and to slip away, running down the alley in the direction he'd come from.

Rod knew he didn't have any chance to catch his son on foot. Chester was a track and cross country runner, and he may not have been the super star that Randy was, he could still run a ton as the Taft Union track coaches liked to say. And, in a way, that was Rod's mistake, because Chester stood panting behind a nearby dark corner as Rod's maroon pickup truck roared by. Chester's back throbbed too much for him to go more than a few paces, but his face was dark and hating.

"You crush their dreams...Oh, yeah, Daddy...Thanks for the advice. I think that's just what I'll do."

CHAPTER TWENTY-NINE

you can't keep a secret in Taft

Something was up and every kid at Taft Union High from the most savvy Senior to the dumbest out of it Freshman could sense the vibes, even those few who didn't already know what was going down. The halls had been buzzing, and probably the only person who knew nothing of it was Lucille, who had called in a sick day to go with her father to watch the Modesto Nuts semi-pro baseball team get their nuts cracked. She could barely stand even one inning of watching baseball, which she found about as exciting as watching paint dry or listening to Miss Twillinger rattle on about wooly mammoths and dodo birds. But Daddy, who was Rod Harris's lawyer, had promised her own credit card with a $2,000 limit, and she figured she could endure any short term pain for a big time shopping gain.

Mercifully, the game had finally ended after nine outcomes, or whatever they called them, and her dad had tooled them back down the freeway to Taft and dropped her off at the McDonalds to meet Judy, who had texted she had some very important, vital and even critical news.

Lucille's dad had barely driven off in his Lexus and she hadn't even sat down, much less ordered a Coke-and-fries when Judy shoved a grainy 8 x 10 black-and-white photo in her hands.

Lucille's eyes bugged. There was the Twill, that frumpy bitch with her back against that beat up old car of hers like any easy bar babe or cheap pole dancer—while Dandy Randy, her boyfriend, leaned over to kiss Twill full on her Botox middle-aged lips!

"What? What? What!!" With three words, Lucille ran the emotional gamut from uncertainty through dismay to vengeful fury.

"Five hundred millimeter lens and high speed black-and-white, and you'd be surprised what you find after dark in the school parking lot.

"But—he…that sloppy-assed bitch!"

"I'm not the pres of the Shutter Bugs for nothing," Judy said. "Here, take a gander at this one." She passed over another shot, this one with Randy's hand clearly inside the Twill's silk blouse. And another one, this one at extremely long range. A casual observer would have made out that it was a man lying on top of a woman…both were naked, and the woman's legs were draped around the man, who obviously had his thing deep inside her. But Lucille, who knew the fellow in the photograph, gritted her teeth so hard they made an unpleasant grinding noise.

"That no-good, dirty dick-licker! I can't wait to kick her ass!"

"How about his ass?" Judy grinned.

"Her first. Then Randy Dweeble-dick."

"What did you have in mind?" Judy asked.

Lucille bolted to her feet and did a roundhouse karate kick, her foot whistling through the air. She followed this with a one-two knuckle punch.

"First, the roundhouse. Then I punch her in the throat."

I got a better idea," Judy said. She opened her laptop on the round cement table, punched a few keys and turned the screen in Lucille's direction. "Don't you just love YouTube?"

Lucille started laughing after the first two or three shots. There was an entire montage of Randy having his way with the Twill, all set to the beat of an old Harry Belafonte love song.

Love, oh love, oh careless love
Love, oh love, oh careless love
You've broken the heart of many a poor guy
But you'll never break this heart of mine...

For Kate, the day had started with a languid shower and a bracing strategy meeting with Jesus where they plotted how to inspire some experts to take a trip out to Red Rock Canyon to find those rare, endangered plants and lizards that could doom Rod Harris's condo project.

"But you're already an expert," Jesus reminded her.

"Just swamp stuff. Not on the local desert plants and wild life."

"Why don't you Google it?" Jesus asked.

So Kate sat down at the small table in her rented room and opened her laptop. And, before getting into the research, she clicked through her junk e-mail, deleting as she went. Her hands flew over the keys, going so fast she almost missed the brief note from slammabamma directing her to a site on YouTube.

One click on the site indicated and her mood and her life changed forever. Someone had been stalking her!

Common sense told her she should pack her books and clothes and head out of town. The problem was, it was two days until payday. She didn't know what she was thinking, somehow hoping against hope that news didn't fly like lightning on the internet.

Of course, she was wrong about that one, and by the time she made her way down the hall to her classroom, she knew it was a bad mistake.

"Here she comes!" a boy she'd never noticed before whispered. Three members of the football team moved to block her way, much as the nuns had the day she was fired from being a nun.

"Hey, Miss T," one of them asked with a smirk and a bad attempt at civility, "How come you play favorites."

"I'm every bit as studly as Dandy Randy," the second one said.

"Oh, baby, try me," the third panted.

Kate angrily swung one fist at the nearest of her taunters, but they simply stood aside to let her pass.

"Hey, Twilly-baby," they hooted after her as she retreated down the hall. "How many hits did you get today?"

"You goin' viral, Baby!"

"New queen of the dot com scene!"

They were still in a group fifteen minutes later when she came storming out of her classroom, wheeling her collapsible handcart with her books and pictures and the plastic T-rex. They laughed nervously as she headed directly toward them, but nobody tried to stop her.

Vincent and Ben were about to go into the teacher's lounge, and so they saw her on her way out.

"Disappointing," Vince said, loud enough so she heard him.

She paused and glared at him, "It wasn't like that."

"We don't want to know what it was like," Vince answered.

She struggled to say something, but as she couldn't think of anything that made sense, she tilted her loaded handcart and headed on down the hall. As she went past, Vince saw how agitated she looked. "Maybe we're being a little harsh…"

"What?' Ben looked at him in disbelief."

"Randy Harris is a shit, just like his old man."

"Yeah, but if you're a teacher, you set boundaries."

"You didn't, with your cheerleader."

"I married her!" Ben sputtered.

"Yeah, I know, Ben. But still…we don't know what exactly happened."

Ben held up a wad of Xerox copies he'd ripped off the walls from where they'd been taped in the cafeteria. "Yeah, I think we do," he said.

Randy and Joey were sitting on the steps of the gym when Kate came boiling out of the big front entrance and threw her things in her car. They watched as the Twill's white Datsun bounced and hopped a curb. Several students had to jump back as her tires spit up gravel, and she nearly lost control as her car skidded out before heading down the road.

"She ought to drive better than that," Randy said, shaking his head. "Little foreign cars aren't built to take that."

"There goes one nutty broad," Joey said.

"Nice tits, though."

Joey gave his buddy an approving grin and a high five.

"You would know, bro!"

After settling down, Joey had a moment of what passed for a shallow sort of serious reflection,

"Where the hell does old HH come up with them, anyway?"

"Ahh, nobody wants to live out here in the sticks," Randy said. "She only came because nobody else would take her."

"Talking about people having to duck out, here comes your own bundle of trouble." Joey nodded to where Lucille was approaching at high speed across the dry and dusty campus lawn.

"Come on," Randy said. "She can't follow us in the men's locker room."

CHAPTER THIRTY

getting out of town is hard to do

Kate drove up to Mrs. Rainey's house to find her belongings packed in grocery bags and boxes of various sizes with Amazon.com, HSN and QVC printed on their sides. As she got out of her Datsun, Mrs. Rainey called from the porch, "I took the liberty of packing your garbage. And I took back my baseball bat you stole from me." Mrs. Rainey short-gripped the Louisville Slugger and slapped her other hand with it, as if she might like to take a swing at Kate's head.

"You're throwing me out, so you owe me three weeks rent."

Mrs. Rainey tapped the bat on the wooden porch floor like a serious threat and held up her cell phone. "I got the Slugger right here, and the cops on my Fav Five. I guess you could say your old pal Jesus is on my side for this one."

She'd no sooner spoken when a Taft police patrol car pulled up in the middle of the street.

"Any trouble, Mrs. Rainey?"

"None whomsoever, Officer," Mrs. Rainey cackled. "If some comes, you'll be the first to know."

Kate felt like she might explode, but she threw her belongings in the trunk and the back seat of the Datsun.

"None whatsoever," she said in a low voice.

Packing her things took less than five minutes, and then she gave Mrs. Rainey the finger and drove off.

It was probably just another rash and stupid move on her part, but she went down to the police station to register a complaint against her landlady for the disputed $500 dollars. The police made her wait and wait, until from their hushed whispers she began to get the notion something unpleasant was in play. She tried to re-read a textbook on prehistoric man, Lucy by Donald Johansson & Maitland Edey, to keep the panic down as the minutes slowly marched by. Finally a clerk came out from a back room to tell her that she would have to return in the morning. By that time it was nearly six, and so she shouted she would indeed be back first thing tomorrow, and left as quickly and quietly as possible.

She had a strange longing for a burger and a beer, a combination she ordinarily never would order, and she couldn't figure out where in Taft she might go to get something like that. She filled up her gas tank at a Serve-Yourself gas station, and found herself parked behind Artz Liquor & Deli. After a while, the East Indian manager peered out the window and then gestured for her to come in.

"You should be leaving town," he said, his voice heavy with concern.

"I know, I know," she said. "I just feel too tired to run."

"How about can I get you something to eat?"

"I'll pay you for it," Kate said, starting to get out of the car. "Maybe a burger and a beer."

"Okay if I use microwave?"

"Yeah, sure, anything."

"You stay here," the man said. "I get it for you."

Fifteen minutes later, he returned with a plastic bag containing two hot hamburgers, and a six pack of Coors Lite. As she rummaged in her purse, the glass bottle of booze and the snub-nosed .38 special fell on her lap.

"It's okay," the manager said. "You pay me some other time." And he hurried in the back door. She sighed as she heard the bolt lock click behind him. But the burgers were a comfort, in their own way, and the beer was cool and refreshing. And after a while listening to the simplistic wail of country western singers, she fell asleep.

Kate woke some time after the sun had disappeared over the low western hills and the afterglow had faded to purple and then a blackish blue. A bright pair of headlights had flashed through her consciousness, followed by a beefy roar of tailpipes, but it turned out to be just a couple of kids who'd picked up a case of beer and were heading out to look for a party.

"I've been told I should get out of town," she said.

"Told me the same," Jesus said from his position leaning back in the passenger seat. "Don't these seats go backwards, Kate? This is really uncomfortable."

"Well, should I stay or should I go now, Lord?" she asked.

"You might stop ripping off rock songs for ordinary conversation."

"Nothing ordinary about you, Jesu."

"Sometimes I do wish I'd left sooner, maybe gone to Turkey or off in the desert with the monks." Jesus was silent for a moment, and then he spoke again. "I have the unholy feeling you won't make it out of town if you leave now. Maybe you better wait until after midnight, 'til that fat sheriff and his merry men go to sleep."

"Not a bad idea." Kate screwed off the cap on her rum flask and took a healthy pull. "Agg! Hair of the dog," she said, rubbing the back of her hand across her mouth. "I'm going stir crazy in here."

"Why don't you take a walk?" Jesus suggested.

"I think I will." He watched her go, but if he thought he was going to enjoy the rest of her rum, he was going to be disappointed, because she stuffed it in her purse and took it with her.

It was exciting, in a way, walking casually along the nearly deserted streets of Taft, peeking around corners to see if anybody was coming or if anything suspicious was happening. It was also time-consuming, and it took her nearly an hour to get from the Datsun to the town drunk's bench near the town square.

The smelly old boy gave her a morose look. He didn't say anything. But he did hold a hand out, and Kate dug in her purse and handed him the bottle of rum.

"Good," he said after taking a healthy swig and returning the bottle to her.

They sat in silence for nearly a half hour.

"Here, how about another?" Kate asked, holding the half empty flask of rum out to him.

When he didn't react, she thought maybe he hadn't heard her, so she pushed him a little with the bottle to get his attention.

"Here," she said. "It isn't going to kill you."

But instead of taking the bottle from her outstretched hand, he fell off the end of the seat, gone from dead drunk to simply dead, just one more small step for mankind.

"Men keep leaving me," she said, gazing down at the silent form.

A large shaggy haired mutt that had been walking along the sidewalk stopped to sniff at the body lying on the dusty grass at the end of the bench.

"Hey, this guy's dead," the dog said, raising an inquiring eyebrow in Kate's direction. With his kindly eyes and unkempt hair, he looked like Einstein-the-Dog.

"You're some genius," Kate responded.

"Actually, I was," the dog said. "But that was in another life."

"Well then, if you're so smart, help me out of my mess."

"What mess?"

"My life is hopeless."

"At Hiroshima, the simple translation of less than an ounce of matter into energy vaporized a million or so Japanese citizens."

"Yes, I know. E = MC squared."

"I worked on that bomb. I actually killed a million people. After that, my life was hopeless…and yet, here I am."

"So?" Kate elevated her own skeptical eyebrow.

"Soooo, darlink. Repent if you must, and then get on with the rest of it."

"Repent?" Kate hadn't expected that suggestion.

"Your church is right over there," the dog said, sitting on his haunches and raising one paw. Kate figured he was either pointing out the church across the road or looking for a paw-shake, so she held out her own hand.

"Thanks," she said.

"Pretty flip, aren't you?"

The dog gave her a one paw salute and ambled off.

The conversation with the shaggy canine started her thinking, and after a few minutes she got off the park bench, crossed the silent street and entered the church. Inside, it was candle-lit, and softly pretty in a religious sort of way, all shadowy and romantic in the direction she'd imagined her life was going to be after she'd married Jesus. A flickering green neon light glowed over the confessional, so after a few moments of inner debate, she entered and knelt to bare her soul in the traditional Catholic method of casting out guilt and renewing, if not innocence, at least a fresher outlook on life.

Soon she found herself spilling the beans about the messy business she'd shared with Randy,

"They're saying I had my way with him, but it wasn't like that, Father…I mean, he did as much to me as I did to him…"

The more Kate talked about it, the more she started to think maybe Randy had instigated the whole mess."

"Just how did this young student provoke the situation, my child?"

Well, I never had much experience with actual physical sex…I mean, with another actual living person.

"Perhaps if you described exactly what he did to you…?"

"Well, first he held me down and started kissing me."

"If I can visualize this, he probably held you down by your wrists, with the impossible weight of his big, strong, heavy body on top of you. You struggled, but obviously he was able to overpower you."

"That was about it," Kate agreed.

"Well," Father Ricotto urged, "That couldn't have been everything. What happened next?"

"Oh, right. Well, then he ripped off my blouse and took off my bra. I had to help him with that. I didn't want him to hurt me."

"Very understandable, my child. And how did that make you feel…I mean, your breasts out in the open air like that?"

"At first I was frightened, and then I began to experience those other feelings."

"What kind of feelings, my child?"

"Wicked feelings. Wicked, bad feelings.

"Would you describe them as feelings of arousal?

"Well, yes..." Kate hesitated.

"And did you feel a tingling excitement in your vaginal area? Perhaps a hot moistness...?

Kate looked around in the dark little closet. She had the sudden feeling the walls were closing in around her. She tried to push the door open, but it wouldn't budge.

"Answer me, child," Father Ricotto persisted. "How about your nipples? Had they become unexpectedly firm, hard as diamonds, actually, at the exquisite touch of his hands.

A hard and angry feeling overcame Kate. She looked up at the crucifix hanging over the heavy grill window, "Jesus, don't do this to me," she said.

The priest's voice went up a notch, "Continue, child. I have to hear more to know what penance to give you."

"What will I do, Lord?"

From his fixed place on the cross, Jesus murmured, "I will give you the strength of ten lions."

Kate stood and rammed her shoulder against the door. The lock was not a strong one, and when she put all her weight into it, the wood splintered and the door flew open. In two steps she was in front of the priest's side of the confessional, which was enclosed with a deep red velveteen curtain. She had no time to react as Father Ricotto's arm reached out from inside the curtains. The priest grabbed her wrist and pulled her toward him.

"Yes!" he let out a triumphant hiss. "A little bit like fishing for trout! Am I not a good fisherman?!" He grabbed her other wrist and began pulling her into his side of the confessional, at the same time trying to force her down to her knees.

"What?! NO! Disgusting! "Let me go!"

He was stronger than he looked, and she started to give up hope, but then Jesus's vow came to her, the strength of ten lions. Kate had once seen part of a Bruce Lee picture. The sisters had each pitched in twenty five cents to rent a DVD from Blockbuster. That night she'd been consumed with strange dreams of an Oriental Savior, lean and tawny with no hair on his bare chest, a holy man who kick-boxed and punched the evil and the misguided to their salvation. Now a war cry rose in her throat, and she managed to pull one wrist free. Blindly reaching in the purse that was still strapped to her shoulder, her fingers wrapped around the handle of the snub-nosed .38 revolver Chester had given her in Artz Liquor & Deli. She fired a round through the red curtain into the confessional. It was an unthinking move; perhaps she wanted just to get him to let go. Whatever her intention, there was a flash and a deafening roar, followed by silence. And the shot had the desired effect as Father Ricotto let go of her other wrist.

Kate stepped back from the confessional with a little mouse cry as the priest's body tipped over and he half-slid and half-fell to the cold tile church floor.

He sat up, eyes closed, and with his back against the wooden support at the middle of the confessional, making animal sounds, "Ahag, ag-g-g." She'd shot him in the right side of the face, and blood was pouring down his neck.

His robe was up around his waist, revealing a pair of Joe Boxer black silk underwear with bold red lips all over them. The presence of his now-deflating love stick through the opening in the Joe Boxers was more than she wanted to see.

She started to turn away when his eyes blinked wide open. He fell over on his side and grabbed her ankle. He spoke with the urgency of a doomed soul who needed a reprieve, "I forgive you, child. I forgive you."

"And who will forgive you?" she shouted, even as she tried to pull away from him."

"God is all-forgiving, child. Now go! Get Help! Hurry! I need a doctor!"

"I can't go with you holding me back!"

For his own dark reasons, she had become his life-line to all of living, breathing humanity, the last branch he clung to before he went over the eternal waterfall, and his fingers refused to give up their iron grip around her ankle. Kate's wild gaze settled on a statue of Mary, watching silently from a nearby alcove.

"He forgives me," Kate said.

Mary's lips pursed in disapproval. "You're not his first, you know."

"What? What do you mean?"

"You know what I mean. I see him do this all the time. And to the little children, too. When my

Son said *Bring the little children unto me*, this is not what he meant."

Kate reached down and grabbed the priest's hand. Desperate and grateful, his bloody finger clung to her.. She dragged him over to the alcove, leaving a fifteen foot stain on the floor behind them. Then she pointed the .38 at Father Ricotto's head.

"No! Wait! What are you doing?" he cried, throwing his hand up to protect himself.

Mary's normally placid and motherly face took on a grimly vengeful appearance, "Do it now—before you lose your nerve!"

Kate turned her head away and fired point blank at the priest's forehead. His head jerked back and he lay shuddering like a dying boar in an ancient forest clearing. But with that shot, all sense and reason seemed to flutter like birds from her mind. She looked around as if in a daze, wondering if there was some rite or procedure she was to perform next.

"Make it look like a robbery," Mary suggested.

That seemed like a good thing to do, so Kate put her gun back in her purse and ripped open the coin box. Nickels and dimes and quarters flew everywhere. She gave the priest's body a last little kick, and dusted her hands.

As she was about to leave, Mary spoke again.

"You could light a candle," she said.

Kate's hands were shaking, but she managed to strike one of the long wooden matches and light a candle. As she started to turn away, Mary spoke again. "Ahem…aren't you forgetting something?"

"Oh, right," Kate answered with a tight little smile. "Sorry." She reached in her purse, took out a dollar bill, and placed it in the coin box on the floor. As she backed away and turned to hustle out the massive wooden front doors of the church, she heard Mary's ever patient and benign voice behind her.

"Bless you, child," the statue of the mother of God said.

CHAPTER THIRTY-ONE

vengeance or something like it

Kate rushed from the church in a panic, not entirely unlike Lot leaving Sodom and Gomorrah or the Jews fleeing Egypt. She got through the doors and down the steps and nearly to the street, imagining all the while the harpies of hell swarming the air behind her, pointing boney fingers and howling, Murderess!

And as she was about to dash across the street to check whether the town drunk was still dead, a maroon pickup truck slid in front of her.

"Hey, Angel," Rod Harris said, opening the passenger door. He gave her a grin straight from the devil's card of slick tricks. "If I said you have a beautiful body, would you hold it against me?" It seemed everybody in Taft's pickup lines came from old country western lyrics.

Kate looked around for an escape route. When she tried to move to the left, Rod kicked his truck in reverse, staying with her. And when she tried the right, he did the same.

"I didn't put that filthy stuff on the internet," she said.

"I know, I know," he said in a soothing way. "I didn't say you did. Maybe we got off on the wrong foot. Us yokels aren't all bad here in Kern County. Come on, get in. I'd like to show you something."

Kate looked back at the church, thinking maybe she could run in there and go out the back.

"No, maybe some other time."

But a man and a woman were hurrying toward the main door, probably intent on confessing their sins before the priest closed shop for the night.

"No, seriously," Rod said. "Get in."

She had run out of options. She climbed in his truck and closed the door. The blast from his air conditioner slammed into her. Rod had a plastic hula girl hanging from his mirror. The girl swished her hips and her little plastic grass skirt swayed hypnotically.

"Mahalo," she said.

"What does that mean?" Kate asked.

"Huh?" Rod said, thinking he was talking to her.

"Peace. Love. Brotherhood."

"What about survival?"

"Can't help you there," the island girl said.

`Rod, eyes on the road while he was driving a bit faster than was wise, tried to keep up with the conversation.

"Survival belongs to the fittest," he said, taking a road that led out of town toward the California aqueduct.

Kate and Rod sat on the back of his pickup truck drinking beers on ice in a plastic cooler.

"You keep cold beer in the back of your pickup truck?"

"Sure," Rod grinned, "That's why they're called pickup trucks. We use them to pick up pretty women."

"This land is truly beautiful," Kate said. "I was raised on a farm, you know."

"I didn't know that. You're full of surprises."

"A big orange grove. Florida. My grandpa drained swamps, pulled up mangrove trees, planted citrus."

"We had the opposite situation," Rod said, interested in spite of himself. "Not enough water."

"Well, you did good," she said.

"Yes, we did. Hard to believe not eighty years ago it was mostly crappy desert."

"Thank you, God," she said.

"You're welcome."

"Not 'Rod', God." She shook her head and it made her whole body dip and weave.

"I feel tipsy…you…you put something in my beer."

"Just half a tab," he said agreeably. I don't like it when my women go all limp and spongy, like blow up dolls.

"But, noooooo…."

Rod turned to look at her, fallen on her back and spread out on the floor of the flatbed.

"Huh…out like a light."

He ran his hand up under her shorts, and then, losing patience, pulled them off. He got her panties down around her knees and his own pants to his ankles before his brain clouded and became mucked up with desire and he threw himself on her. She showed no resistance as he thrust deep inside her.

"Maybe a quarter tab would have been better," he muttered to nobody in particular.

Kate didn't want to be bothered or awakened. Her awareness was flooded with an endless joy as she made love to her Lord and Master. And Jesus seemed to be having the time of his life, as well. "Oh, yes, yes, yes! Rocking nights in old Jerusalem!" He cried as he went on and on, plunging into her well of pleasure as if he would and could come again and again throughout the night and on into eternity if he wished.

But then Jesus morphed into a dark knight in a black suit or armor, hammering at her with his rod of black steel, and her stomach burned and she was tumbling down, down, down into hellish flames.

She didn't return to consciousness as Rod buttoned up his jeans and walked away from his pickup truck. He texted one of his supers and had him pick up her car. The guy, who was really great at whipping crap on his workers in the field, seemed dumb as a rock about this simple assignment.

Rod switched over to vocal on his cell phone, "Look, the car is in front of the church.. Yes, I'm sure! The keys are in it. Tow it out to the storage tank on the donkey spread and leave it there."

He rolled his eyes, listening impatiently on the cell phone, and then yelled impatiently, "Yes, just leave it there! And that's it—you don't want to know nothing about nothing!"

After that, he hoisted Kate over one shoulder and headed for the big water tank. He stopped and returned to the pickup truck for her shorts and panties, which he balled up and carried with him. When he got to the base of the tank, he stood looking up at the rusty ladder. He wasn't eager to make the climb one handed up those metal rungs with Nutsy Twillinger a dead weight on his back. He sighed, knowing he was going to get all hot and sweaty. He wasn't worried that he might not make it; after all, he'd done it before.

CHAPTER THIRTY-TWO
it's all about survival of the fittest

The grey light of dawn came to Kate's battered and dusty Datsun. It was parked within twenty feet of the water tank, on a small and barren rise surrounded by several dozen donkey rigs, the pumps used to bring up oil in a proven field. The heads of half of them were rotating slowly, while the rest of them were still. These moving donkeys combined to make a rasping, ghastly repetitive sound, like ancient metal dinosaurs chewing dirt.

The front door of the Datsun was open, and the keys were still in the ignition. The back seats were packed to the roof with her boxes of books and piles of clothing. But at first glance, Kate was nowhere to be found. There was a lonely sound of the wind, and no footprints, for Rod had carefully brushed them away with a switch of dry tumbleweed.

The storage tank itself was empty. Inside, lying face up in a pool of three inches of water, Kate stirred and murmured and then opened her eyes. The first thing she saw, high and far away in the pale grey blue of a cloudless sky was the thin, rat-faced sliver of a crescent moon.

"Oh, Jesus," she groaned. She ached from head to toe. She sat up and saw that she was naked from the waist down. Her shorts and panties were nearby, soaked in the puddles at the bottom of … what? She was surrounded by a circle of rusty metal that was probably thirty feet across and thirty feet high.

She wrung out her panties and her shorts, took off her top and bra, and hung them all on a stumpy tree branch that had been tossed or fallen in her make-shift prison. She didn't remember much from the previous night. Rod Harris had drugged her, and she figured that was probably just as well.

She tilted her head back and looked at the moon, now becoming faint in the advancing dawn, and words came to her mind

Rat face edge/ A wayward moon
Could be dawn light/ Maybe June
All I know, it's late, late, late.
Late and running down.
Let's kill a hill and build a town.
Acid air and a yellow sky/ I feel so hot my skin could fry
And I, I, I, I, I...no I don't want to die.

As she walked around the base of the empty metal cylinder, she felt an inch of muddy ooze between her toes. Rod had put her here. He was trying to teach her a lesson. He'd be coming back for her. He'd let her go, probably before nightfall, and she could be on her way. But where would she go? Word would spread, and she wouldn't be able to get a teaching job. She sagged back down, back against the rough wall, and called out to her old pal, Jesus.

"Yesu, old buddy. I need my old powers back, and I need them now."

But in spite of his pledge to always be there for her through all eternity, there was no answer.

"Never, ever, ever there when I need him," she muttered in a hollow, defeated voice.

"Who?" a woman's voice answered.

"Jesus," Kate said, turning her head to see the form of a woman of about her own age, also naked, sitting next to her, back also up against the rusty wall. "Who are you?"

"I was Rod's wife. That's my head over there." She pointed to a skull half buried in the silt next to an exit pipe on the other side of the tank and then to a skeleton lying nearby. "And there's the rest of me. I believe that's part of my blue jeans skirt, still over there. She pointed to where a bit of denim fabric was sticking out of the muck.

"What was that you were singing?" Rod's wife asked.

"Nothing. Just something I made up in my head, about how we're screwing up the world and everything in it."

"Sing some more," the woman said.

"It's not a good time for singing…"

"I get so lonely here," the woman said.

"Okay, okay, okay…but don't expect much; I just make it up as I go along."

But once again, as if like magic, the words came from her broken soul and poured out in a plaintive song

Love don't bloom in a garbage dump
Call it love/ call it hump.
Bump, bump, bump/ another hump
No, love don't bloom in a garbage dump.

"That's really good!" the woman said, and she clapped her hands. "Sing some more!"

"No more, no more, no more! I can't. I don't know any more words."

"Sing just a little more. I have an idea," the woman said, the note of pathetic eagerness clear in her voice. "Sing some more and I'll tell you how to get out of here."

"Rod's going to come back and let me out."

"That's what he told me, too."

Kate's gaze wandered from the woman to her bones lying nearby, and a cold wash of realization swept over her. Nobody had been here in over a decade. Rod Harris had left her here to die!

"Promise you'll get me out of here?"

"Cross where my heart was and hope to die," the woman said.

Here's paradise/ now treat it nice.
Keep it green/ It's good advice
And I, I, I, I... / I just want to cry...

When Kate had gotten that far, she was surprised by a blast of icy cold water from overhead. It came with such heavy force that it knocked her down and she had to scramble quickly to the other side of the tank. Rod's wife sat where she was as the water swiftly rose to cover her knees.

"You'd better get over here!" Kate said.

"It doesn't matter for me. Now here, listen up. The water comes from up there, it fills the tank nearly to the brim and it takes about an hour to flow out of that low pipe over there, spreading out to irrigate some almond trees in a big orchard."

"I know how that works."

"Good. Then you know the water is already heading out. Your problem is, by the time a full tank has flowed into here, about a quarter or a fifth has already flowed out. That means you can't ever reach the top."

"I'm a good swimmer," Kate protested.

"So was I," Rod's wife said. "I lasted about a week."

The water was already up to Kate's hips. Rod's wife had remained seated, and it was nearly to her head.

'"You promised me a way out," Kate said.

"Yes, I did. Take my head, wrap it in what's left of my denim skirt, and jam it against the exit pipe."

"But I can't—"

"Now! Do it now! It's almost too late!"

Kate had to dive into the muck and feel around to come up with the skull. It took three tries, but her fingers finally closed on a ragged end of the skirt. There was another little difficulty when the suction from the water rushing out of the exit pipe trapped her fingers along with the bundled skull.

Inside of fifteen minutes, she was treading water. For nearly two hours she fought to stay above the swirling, churning water. And then the gusher stopped as abruptly as it had begun. Kate strained at one side of the pool and found the fingers of her upraised hand were about a foot short of the metal lip of the tank.

“Noooo!” she howled, beating one hand against the side of the tank. What to do? What to do? And the single word Baptism! rang in her mind as clearly as if it came from the Holy Ghost himself.

Kate took a deep breath and swam down, down, down as far as she could go. She didn’t reach the bottom, but it would have to do. Turning back, she stroked up with powerful breast strokes. She erupted from the still water like a porpoise, with enough momentum to just barely grasp the lip of the tank with one hand. And then she hooked the fingers of her second hand over the lip and, slowly, grimly began a shuffle-handed journey ten feet to where a double line of rusty bolts showed the ladder was located.

Dragging her naked body out of the water and up and over the rim of the tank sapped most of her energy, and she slipped on the rungs and nearly fell a dozen times before she felt the dusty ground under her bare feet.

To her surprise, her Datsun was there, the front door open as if waiting for her return. She found a pair of dry jeans and another of her saucy, tight tee-shirts, this one with the print out WHAT ARE YOU STARING AT? She slipped into a pair of gym shoes and got behind the wheel. Of course, the car door had been open overnight, so the battery was drained and the car wouldn’t start. But Kate had learned a few tricks watching the movies the nuns had rented. She turned the key to the on position, took off the hand brake, and, pushing with one leg with the door open, managed to get the car moving down the incline. After twenty seconds of bumpy touch and go, she let out the clutch and the Datsun coughed and sputtered to life.

As she made her way down the dusty road and turned east on the blacktop heading away from town, she found herself singing.

Laughin' like/ a crazy loon
Dance along/ and sing a tune
Isn't this/ just great, great, great
Let's kill a tree and cook a horse
Put it in a bun, of course
No, eat a cow, a burger tale
Oops, there goes the last grey whale
Oh, no, no, no, no/ not the last grey whale
Happy now, you made your bed
Look at all the dead-dead-dead
And I, I, I, I, I, I, I, I...
I just want to cry....

"I really love that song," plastic Jesus said from his position on the dashboard. "I think you're showing some real chops there."

"Hey, Jesu—showed up late again, didn't you?"

"I don't have to prove myself to anybody," the plastic figure said, stiffening up a little bit. "And who do you think gave you the complicated and entirely successful escape plan that set you free?"

"Did you ever notice how all plastic Jesus dolls face in toward the passenger compartment?"

"I don't like where this is going," Jesus said.

"That's because they have their butts to the action!" She laughed as if she was out of control.

"You're not going wacko on me, are you?" he asked

"What do you care, you've got thousands of wives, all over the earth, huddled in their lonely convent beds, craving your warm embrace."

The Savior of all humanity didn't have anything to say to that, and Kate drove on in silence, whistling the melody she'd thought up for her impromptu song. She daydreamed about getting a record deal, hooking up with one of those agent people and they scored by sending it to Willie Nelson or maybe Bob Dylan if they weren't dead already from booze and drugs.

CHAPTER THIRTY-THREE
flight across the Mojave

Kate wanted to pull off the road and camp in the trees when she got to the 166, but this was Rod Harris country, so she headed east, skirted around Bakersfield and took I-58 on east, heading for Mojave. The I-58 was an expressway, but she was taking the chance Rod wouldn't go back in the daylight hours to gloat over her trapped in the water tank. Even so, her engine was running rough, and pouring smoke out the back end. The little engine couldn't seem to make sixty miles an hour, even with the gas pedal to the floorboard. Eco-conscious California motorists, aware of the massive smog layer they created on a daily basis, honked and gave her the finger as they zoomed on past.

"Shouldn't we stick to the side roads?" Dashboard Jesus asked.

"Oh, you're a real get away man, you are."

"You look a wreck, Kate," he said.

"You're a little dusty yourself, Jesu Christi. And your plastic robe's getting a bit faded from the sun.

They drove on in silence for a while. Her heady exhilaration had faded and she was feeling tired, depressed and hopeless.

"What's wrong, Kate," Jesus finally asked. "Come on, spill the beans."

Kate's lower lip trembled, "I murdered that priest! I'm a m-m-murderess!"

"I think you could argue self-defense on that one."

"We're not talking court of law here—I'm not going to make it into heaven."

"Oh, I don't see why not," Jesus said. "Vengeance is mine, sayeth the Lord."

"You're a wuss, Jesu. I'm not worried about you. You'd let everybody slip in the pearly gates. But how about our Father, the all-avenging thunderer?

"Well, yeah," Plastic Jesus admitted with a mild Kern County shrug. "You may have a little problem there…"

"I'm going to burn forever in the unremitting fires of hell and you call that a little problem?"

"Look, I'll intercede for you. The Big Guy listens to me. And maybe you could buy a couple of those papal blessings, give some bucks to save some pagan babies, smooth the way a bit."

"That stuff works?"

"I don't know for sure, but it couldn't hurt..."

By now, the Datsun was sputtering and coughing, and so Kate took an off ramp that headed south toward the town of Mojave.

"But Red Rock Canyon is north," Jesus said, turning one of his outstretched arms back the way they'd come. It would have been a dramatic gesture, but all told his arm was barely an inch and a half long.

"We'll never make it, Jesu. How about a car engine repair miracle?"

"You should have asked somewhere around Bakersville."

"How about getting us a few miles to Mojave?"

"Let me see here. Seal the cracked block, change the charred pistons to diamond, do the old loaves and fishes act on the fuel tank…there, that should just about do it."

Of course, he was kidding, but somehow the old Datsun kept sputtering along, so she was sure he was doing something.

Lotto Binks looked up from the car he was tinkering as the smoking Datsun drove into his station. He wiped his greasy hands on his greasy mechanic's jumpsuit and eyed the fuming car with a look of appreciation. Kate jumped out of the Datsun and slammed the door, and Lotto's regard shifted from the financial opportunity her crippled car represented to the full promise of her wonderful breasts fairly bursting out of the tight confines of her tee shirt.

"Help you, Lady?"

"Fix it. Fix it. Just fix it," Kate said, jerking a thumb at her car.

Binks popped the hood, and had to back as steam and smoke boiled out.

"Hooo, holy crap!" he said.

Kate had walked twenty feet away and was angrily talking into her cell phone.

"It's Saturday, Vince! Yes, I know, the stupid ball game. Okay, but it's only a hundred miles or so. Fine! Five o'clock this afternoon. Just be here!"

She snapped her fingers at Binks, "Sir, where's a good restaurant in town?"

"There ain't no-good one, Lady," he said, grinning at his own joke."

"Any restaurant," she flared angrily at him.

"Uh, Tico's Mexican," he said, straightening up like he was back in the fifth grade.

"Tico's Mexican Restaurant, Vince. Five sharp."

Vince frowned as he put his cell phone back in his pocket. His mother had bullied his father, and he'd always hated domineering women, bitches who tried to tell him what to do. He looked around the Taft Union outdoor sports field and practically the first thing his eyes lighted on was Rod Harris's maroon pickup, which was looking a little dusty and muddy, like Rod may have spent the day driving around his fields, checking water ditches and slapping around his Mexican day workers. Vince mused that Kate would probably think Mr. Harris being there at that exact time was a sign from God…or the devil. Vince didn't believe in such things, but, what the hell, there it was. Rod was sitting in his truck while his son Randy stood outside the driver's side window. They were probably discussing making the long throw from third to first, or how best to put an affair with a teacher behind him. Vince stuck his hands in his pockets and walked across a corner of the field toward the two of them.

Meanwhile, back at the gas station in Mojave, Kate frowned at her cell phone and then gave her mechanic a stern What's up? Look.

He raised his hands to the heavens, seeming to say *God knows, it ain't my fault.*

"I tell ya, I'm sorry, but your Framboisus automatic gas regulator—or whatever the Japs call it—went kablooie."

"You're sure?" Kate looked around, but, as usual when he was needed, Jesus wasn't anywhere around.

"Yeah, yeah, I'm sure. All Datsuns use the Framboisus system cause they are greenheads, but it don't really save gas mileage, and there ain't a one of them that don't blow sooner rather than later."

"Look, just fix the cracked block and the charred pistons."

"Oh, you know about this stuff…" The mechanic gave her a calculating look.

"Nobody's going to hold your stupid lies against you except God. Now give it to me straight."

"Your engine's froze. The block is cracked. You need a new engine."

"Can you do it in an hour?"

"Nope." He gave her an appraising once-over. "Two, three days, maybe."

"Loaner?"

"Kidding, right?"

"No, I am not kidding!"

"Geez, don't take it out on me, lady. Blame the goddamn house of the rising sun."

"Who?"

"The Japs. There's one decent motel in town. Get yourself a room." He eyed her speculatively. "I'll even book one for you."

"No thanks. You can stimulate your Framboisus system on your own."

"Jee-sus, lady...okay, but I got to put out for a new engine here, how about some sort of credit card?" Kate opened the passenger side front door and pulled her backpack from the car. She counted six hundred dollars in twenties into his outstretched hand.

"Fix it," she said over her shoulder. "Just fix it."

Tico's Mexican was an old Wendy's that had been converted to South of the Border food. They still used the drive up window, but as it took five or ten minutes to stir up the food, the drive-through patrons parked and milled around in little circles, discussing dust storms and noontime temperatures.

Kate went inside and ordered an iced tea. She was on her third when Vince walked in. He glanced around nervously.

"Vince—Over here!"

He came quickly to the table and stood looking down at her

"Sorry I'm late. Homework," he said.

"I had no reason to expect you'd come at all."

"I can't stay. Got to get back. What do you want?"

"Rod Harris murdered his wife. Her bones are in that water tank out by the oil pumpers."

"So much for small talk," he said, moving back a step or two as if she was a killer bee. "Are you sure?"

"Yes."

"That's just crazyness. You're imagining things.

"He tried to kill me, too. Threw me in the same tank with the bones."

"Why aren't you dead, then."

"I'm very hard to kill, Vince."

"Yeah, yeah, yeah. Jesus is on your side." He looked around the room, worried people would hear him talking to the crazy person. "You're landlady says you stole five hundred bucks."

"She's a lying bitch."

"And that's not all, Kate."

"Katherine."

"Katherine. The sheriff wants to talk to you about having sex with a minor.

"He doesn't need my permission," she smiled.

"I'm not kidding around. Randy Harris –"

"—Is nearly 22 years of age." She gave him an exasperated look, "Never mind about Randy. I need your help. Tell me how to get to Red Rock Canyon."

That caught him off guard. "The canyon? Whatever for?"

Kate unfolded a poster/flier and set it down on the table between them.

"Vince, I heard your speech the other night. I totally agree with you. We can't let this condo abomination happen."

"There is no *we*," Vince said, leaning back and frowning at the picture of the red cliffs and barren landscape. "You blew me off, remember?"

"Vince, this has to be stopped!"

But it was a new Vince who faced her, a man determined in a new direction, and yet somehow defeated. "Hey. No. Look, Katherine, just no. I'm done with that. Done with you. Done with everything. Finished. Period."

She eyed him across the table, "You've caved in."

"I have not!" He paused. "Well, alright, seen the light of reason. Common sense. Caved, if you must."

"Did he pay you?"

Vince shook his head and gave her a bitter look. "If keeping my job is a payoff, I guess he did."

"Well, I want to go. I am going."

Vince slumped in his chair and shook his head.

"I came here to warn you. You've been run out of Dodge. They're not going to let you back."

"I'm not going back to Taft. But you said if anybody could find just one rare and endangered species—"

"I didn't say that, the commission did. And I already told you, Kate, there is no we."

"Oh, Vincent...Jesus had such great plans for you."

Vince rolled his eyes in exasperation. "Nobody calls me Vincent," he said.

"Nobody calls you at all, Vincent."

"Look, don't tell me about Jesus Christ Savior or any of his plans. I don't want to know. You have to get out of here right now. You've done your damage, and Rod's a crazy man when he's pissed...and you have flayed his patience way past anything sane.

Kate looked up as a big engine pickup truck roared into the parking lot. The heavy maroon truck slid to a dusty stop in the gravel and Rod Harris climbed out, slammed the door and leaned against it, arms folded.

"You called Rod Harris," Kate said calmly.

Vince shrugged and stood up to leave. "I have to live here. And I did come all this way to warn you."

Kate stood, picked up her backpack, and headed for the door.

"Maybe you better go out the back way," Vince suggested.

"You're a weak-dick little worm, Vincent. A limp, bendy little one-eyed monster."

Rod blinked when he saw her storming out the door and churning directly toward him. He'd spotted her in the restaurant, but figured she'd hide or run and he'd have to chase her down. But he recovered fast, giving her a superior smirk.

"Well, look-y who we got here."

"No time for small talk, asshole. Take me to Red Rock Canyon."

That took the grin off his leathery, sun-reddened face. He backhanded her, knocking her down. She got up with blood running from a corner of her lips.

"Violence isn't the answer, Mr. Harris."

He saw red then, connecting with a wild roundhouse punch to the side of her head, and she went down again. And came popping back up like a porpoise or a gopher game.

"Stay down, you stupid bitch!"

This time he connected with a right to her face, splitting her cheek with his big golden class ring. She saw flashes of dark and light and for a moment she thought she was back with Grandma Lulu again, the old lady doing her violent best to teach a young girl respect of the fist, a lesson she'd never really learned.

Vince came out of the restaurant as she was staggering to her feet again.

"Harris!" he shouted. "Rod! There's no need for that!"

He started forward as if he might move between them, but the intensity of Rod's anger stopped him in his tracks.

"You want a piece of this, you dumb-shit school teacher?!

Vince stepped back, eyeing the two of them.

"Yeah, do you?" Kate snarled at him. "Doesn't matter, you're a dead man anyway, now that Rod knows you know he killed his wife. You can count your time in days."

"What?!" Both men stared at each other, and then back at Kate, trying to catch up with this new information.

"Dead by Christmas, that's for sure Vince…unless you can get to the state police before El Hefe here gets to you."

Rod tried to backhand her, but she managed to duck, "What, Vincent—Did you think you're safe? The rat is never safe!"

"Get in the truck, you stupid whore!"

Rod fisted her on the side of the head, knocking her to her knees.

"Did you really, honestly think you were safe, Vincent?" she managed to say before Rod hammered her on the top of her head with one of his elbows, dropping her like a heart-shot deer. He managed to half-drag her to the passenger side of his truck and push her inside. Seeing her backpack in the dust, he picked it up and threw it in after her, slamming the door in her face.

Kate stared out the open window as Rod rushed around the truck and got in the driver's seat. She looked like she was in a daze, but the words came out of her mouth, almost as if she was a zombie lady

"Some sign you turned out to be, Vincent. You're worse than Perry the Pirate Parrot!"

Vincent shook his head, raising his hands as if there was nothing else he could do.

"Take the same advice you gave me, you Benedict Arnold. Get out of town before Rod gets you."

CHAPTER THIRTY-FOUR

Rod's second chance

Rod pulled out of the parking lot with his heavy truck tires spitting dust and gravel. As the sun settled behind the western hills, he drove through Mojave like he owned it, and he was still heading north as dusk settled over the empty desert landscape. After five minutes of silence, he looked over at her.

"Are you as totally crazy as I think?" he asked.

She held a wad of Kleenex tissues, already soggy red with her blood, to her swollen lip and eyed him with a look that could have meant anything from black despair to sullen fury.

"How crazy do you think, Rodney dear?

Rod's attitude hardened, taking her words like a dose of bad medicine.

He tried for a backhanded slap at her head, but she was in the far corner of the front seat, and he wasn't trying very hard, more like a fellow in control might shoo away a pesky fly.

"Nobody calls me Rodney," he said.

The plastic Hula Dancer hanging from Rod's rear view mirror swished her hips.

"Time to turn the other cheek, bitchy white girl," she said.

Kate gave her a little grimace, the best she could do through her swollen face. "The dodo birds of Mauritania turned the other cheek."

"But they're all extinct, girl," the Hula Dancer reminded her.

"My point, exactly," Kate said. "Jesus is dead, too."

"Who the crap you talking to?" Rod asked.

"You, Rodney dear. I'm talking to you. You murdered your wife. You tried to kill me the same way. Oh boy, it's going to be the trial of the century, the biggest thing ever to hit Kern County. That is, if you make it to trial."

Rod's face went red with fury. He made a quick decision, jerking the wheel to spin his pickup in a skidding U-turn, and then pulling onto a gravel road they'd just passed. By now the settling darkness forced him to snap on the truck headlights, but there was still enough of a lingering afterglow to make driving uncertain. Instead of slowing down, he drove as fast as possible, and their heads both hit the ceiling as they bumped and jounced along the rough road. After ten minutes the road straightened out, and he was able to make better time.

"This isn't the way to Red Rock Canyon," she said.

"No shit. Surprise, surprise."

"Where are you taking me?"

"The gravel quarry. My gravel quarry."

As he spoke, he reached down with his left hand and found an 18 inch length of metal pipe on the floor next to him. He raised it, switched it to his right hand, weighing the feel of the ugly, lethal weapon. Quick as a cat, he lashed out at her, connecting with a glancing blow on her shoulder.

"Lady, you're dead as that dumb dodo you're talking about!"

His try at smashing her head took his attention off the road, and the truck ditched and nearly rolled over before he managed to get it back under control.

"Okay. Okay," he said, talking to himself. "Just a little bit more. Just a little bit and we get to do it right."

Barely a minute later, they topped a low rise and came to an area pockmarked with shallow holes and pimple-hills of piled gravel. He hit the brakes hard and the maroon pickup slid to a halt near some rusty machinery.

"Good enough, good enough," he said. There was a sense of triumph in his voice and a glint of anticipation in his eyes. She wondered if that crazy look was what people saw in her when she was talking to the Lord.

She eyed him quietly. She didn't feel afraid, or even angry.

"You know, Rodney, patience is an important virtue."

He leaned toward her and raised his length of killing pipe to bash her. At these close quarters, there was no chance he would miss, and they both knew it.

"Oh, Sweet-cakes, I'm going to love pounding the crap out of you."

"I don't think so," she said.

She reached in the outside pouch on her backpack, gripped the handle of the stubby little .38 and pointed it in his face.

Rod started back, startled more than afraid, and the pipe in his hand dropped an inch or two.

But then he put on his brave face. He figured ex-nun school teachers—even crazy ones—didn't go around shooting people.

"I know one thing. You won't pull that trigger."

"And how do you know that?"

"Because you're a goddamn sheep, and little lambie-pies don't do murder!"

He reared back to crush her skull with a mighty killing blow, and as the pipe swung forward, she fired point blank into his face. The bullet entered his left cheek, taking out part of his jaw, and he screamed his surprise and agony.

"I guess you never heard of the killer sheep. They're an advanced species."

He'd been knocked back in the corner on his side of the truck, but he still held the pipe. She shifted the pistol to her left hand, and with it still pointing at him, reached behind her and opened her door. Before she could turn to get out, he let go of the pipe and grabbed the pistol. Even wounded, he was still stronger, and her only move was to pull the trigger again. This time the shot entered the right side of his face, nearly matching the one on the other side.

He screamed in his desperation, "Aggg! Noooo! Nooo!" and then lapsed into a blubbery whimper that trickled off into silence.

Kate reached in the cab for her backpack, which had slipped to the floor. Her eyes locked with Rod's, and she shuddered at the black heat of pure hate radiating from him.

She sighed, inspecting him for signs that he might be dying.

"Are you dying yet?" It didn't seem like there was much certainty of that. "Very well. This one 's for big Jesu," she said, pointing the pistol at his forehead and pulling the trigger one more time. "Just like Pachino in the Godfather."

There was a small office with a grimy restroom at the edge of the pit. . She forced ope the door and washed up, and then went back to the maroon pickup truck and wiped the door handles and the dashboard.

"You're pretty good at cleaning up the crime scene," the Hula Dancer said approvingly.

"I saw some episodes of Perry Mason in the nunnery. Very instructional."

Kate flushed the tissues down the single filthy toilet bowl in the bathroom, hiked her backpack over her shoulder and started the long trek back along the gravel road to the two lane blacktop. After a while a three-quarter moon came up, and the land was all blue-grey and shadowy.

"I wonder," she thought in sudden alarm, "If there's a worse place in hell if you murder more than one person."

"I don't know. Don't ask me," Jesus said. She looked up to see him trudging along next to her, picking his barefoot way through the gravel, robe ends trailing in the dust.

"I thought you knew everything."

"That's my Father. I don't want to know everything."

"Can I have my powers back now?"

"Not yet."

Kate and Jesus trudged along in silence for a while. She finally complained, "Why on God's Green Earth couldn't they just put the gravel pit a little closer to the highway?"

Jesus gave her his patented gentle smile of understanding.

"Bitch, bitch, bitch."

Kate was about to give him a tongue lashing, but when she looked over at him, he was gone.

A voice from a nearby yucca bush squeaked, "That's not really Jesus, you know."

Kate saw a bat hanging upside down from one of the blade-like leaves of the bush, and that made her feel angry and alone.

"What do you know? What? You saying he's some sort of holographic prayer card?

Kate found a few pebbles and flung them in the general direction of the bat. She could hear them hitting the dry yucca leaves.

"Heyyyy," the bat protested as he flitted away, "No need to get so spiky."

CHAPTER THIRTY-FIVE

going for the big time

It was after midnight with the moon full overhead by the time Kate found her way back to the two lane blacktop. She set down her backpack, took off her shoes and buried her aching feet in a small patch of still-warm sand. She felt dizzy and clumsy, as if she might fall over at any moment. At that moment she wanted to crawl into the nearby desert brush and sleep for a week, and maybe die.

Traffic was light, just a car or a truck every ten minutes or so, but she put her thumb out anyway. After a while, she took more notice of the passing motor vehicles.

“A strange parade,” she muttered as Barney Oldfield, wearing his goggles, drove by in old #99. A few minutes passed and then Thelma and Louise drove by, followed by Elvis in his pink Cadillac. Elvis waved, singing as he doppled past, “Uh-huh! Uh-huh! Oh, yeahhhh!”

Time passed and when no more cars came, Kate was sure the parade was over. But then, headlights out of the distance signaled another was on its way. A dusty pick-up truck approached and came to a screeching halt. A voice yelled through the open passenger window.

“Heyyyyyy! Miss Twillinger! Heard you were out this way!”

Kate’s eyes opened a little wider. Her vision was playing tricks on her, like she was seeing through a zoom lens that was going in and out.

But her attention finally locked on the driver. Nothing surprised her any more. She picked up her shoes and limped over to the old grey pickup truck. .

"Chester! What are you doing out this way?"

"Get in! Get in!"

He gestured in an animated and nearly comic fashion, looking back the way he'd come as if the devil or a posse was after him.

Kate pushed her backpack on the floor in front of the passenger seat, nearly falling to the ground from the effort. She struggled to climb in the truck as fast as her aching legs would allow.

"You don't look so good, Miss Twillinger."

"I'll be okay, Chester. Jesus is at my side."

"You mean 'on your side', don't you?"

"Whatever," she muttered, too tired to get into it.

Then she let out a startled, "Wooooh!" The space next to her on the bench seat was piled with boxes of ammunition, several pistols, and debris from a fast food meal. There was also a shotgun barrel resting against the seat, butt on the floor.

Chester popped the clutch, and as his pickup jerked forward, a plastic Bobble-Head Buddha wobbled his head from his cross-legged position in the center of the dashboard.

"Taft's all in an uproar!"

Chester's eyes were shining; he was a novice reporter with big news.

"I know, I really screwed things up…"

Naw, nothing to do with you!"

Chester's quick acceleration had pushed her back in the corner between the open window and the passenger seat. The afternoon desert heat was gone now, and the breeze felt good on her battered face.

Chester grinned. "Somebody else for a change. It was me, I done it!"

"You did what?"

"I shot the whole mess of them!" he said proudly. "Randy, Lucille, Joey and Judy. Taft Union High's fav four! They was at their usual outdoor table at the drive-in when I got there! Man, I was loaded for bear! And Lucille looks right at me and she don't get it! She says to me in that nasty, false voice of hers, "Hiiiii, Chester…"

Chester's happy expression faded, "But then she gives me a second look and the expression on her face turns to like something you might see in a Rocky Horror Movie. 'Chester—what?' she shouts at me as I pull out a pistol and take aim at Randy. And that ain't all. Next, I give Randy a couple lead slugs in his leg and see his knee busts into a red flower and he topples over like a busted tree. And then Joey screams something at me but he don't have his macho man tough guy look no more and I thank him for his intrusion by popping him one in his knee cap, too! There go the old sports scholarships! There is Randy and Joey holding their wounded legs and and crying and rolling around on the ground. Lucille, she tries to run away but I catch her with a quick shot right in her fat ass. She does a messy little tumble and overturns a round metal table as she crashed through it, bringing a big sun umbrella down on her head. Judy actually gets away. I took a few wild shots at her, but I guess there is no God, after all."

Kate eyed Chester, "I don't know how you can come to that conclusion."

"Just kidding, of course," he waved with a wild gesture, both hands off the wheel and punching in the air. "But that's not all, folks! There was a robbery at the church! And somebody shot that old pervert priest! Wish I'd have thought of that…makes my crackering the place look really small time."

Chester had the gas down to the floor, and the truck had to be doing over a hundred miles an hour.

"Chester, don't go so fast!"

"Don't tell me what to do!"

"Chester…ahh…I'm sorry, but I'm really not feeling well…"

"Yeah," he agreed, instantly dropping from wild rage as only a crazy person can. "I can see. Big Man Rod did that to you, huh?"

"Yes, he did," she said. She grouped for words, trying to figure a way to calm him down before he ran off the road and killed them both. "I was just thinking..." Her gaze came to rest on the small plastic figure of Bobble-Head Buddha. "Ahh, do you ever talk to Bobble-Head Buddha?"

"To who?" Chester said, shaking his head in a bewildered way. It wasn't a comforting gesture with the road flashing by on either side of them at an impressive rate.

Kate pointed to the Buddha on the dash. “Bobble-head Buddha, here.”

“That’s actually Buddha? I just thought he was a little naked plastic Chinaman.” He paused and thought about it a minute while the wind roared and the desert night raced past their open windows. “Not really,” he said.

“Not really, what?” Kate asked, the train of thought lost to her in the wild night ride.

“I never talk to him.”

Bobble-Head Buddha nodded. “That’s because he’s dumber than a brick of pressed cow pie,” he said.

“You mean ‘denser’ than a brick,” Kate corrected the small plastic fat man.

Chester had caught enough of the drift to give her an angry stare.

“You talking about me?”

“No,” she quickly corrected him. “It’s just a physics thing. When you squeeze something, it gets denser.”

“Oh, right,” Chester said with a vague nod of understanding. “Einstein stuff.” His glare softened and he turned his attention back to the road.

“Played that one nicely out of the rough,” Buddha said with a gracious bob.

“Where you headed, Miss Twillinger?” Chester asked.

“Red Rock Canyon.”

Chester nodded, his eyes on the yellow center stripe ripping away under the center of his speeding pickup. “Yeah. I heard about that.”

He fell silent, mulling some new idea while he scratched his head. "I don't rightly know how to ask this, so I'll just come right out with it: How's about you teaming up with me?"

Buddha's eyes popped wide and he shook his head violently, indicating that had to be the worst idea since he himself had helped bring down the old Persian empire and turned India into a violent turmoil of warring provinces.

"What did you have in mind?" Kate asked.

Chester excitedly shook out a small pile of money from an oil-stained white paper bag that had once held two hamburgers and a large sized order of French fries. Coins rattled and rolled around on the floorboards.

"I stuck up the McDonalds! It was easy pickings! Look, I must have nearly a hundred bucks here!"

"Chester! What are you going to do?"

"No, not 'Chester'! I ain't Chester no more. You call me 'Clyde! And you can be Bonnie, if you want!"

Bobble-head Buddha gave her a wry half-smile, showing he was capable of nuance, even in his semi-rigid state. "Cutting a path of righteous vengeance through burger joints and taco stands across the land.".

Kate frowned at Buddha, trying not to smile, which she knew would make her face hurt. "Chester…ahh, Clyde—that would be something, but I'm already on my own mission."

"Stopping Mr. Harris's fancy new condo development! I knew it! That's why he punched you out!"

"I have to fulfill my mission."

"Hey, good on you, Miss Twillinger! I ain't no fan of big daddy. Maybe later, we could team up!"

"Let's see if I can get through this one first, okay?" She held her hand up to her split lip. Her jaw was aching and her head felt like a lead balloon. "Are you going to be alright going on alone…err, Clyde?"

"Well, I do have one favor to ask."

"Sure, anything I can…"

"Seeing as you ain't going with me right away, could you loan me my pistol back? The one I put in your purse at the 7-11?

"You already have enough guns for an army!"

"I left in kind of a hurry, alright? So I got tons of .38 ammo, but all I got is this.45."

Kate took the pistol from her backpack and stared at it, knowing it was a double murder weapon.

"Maybe we should just throw it out the window?" she suggested.

Her suggestion upset Chester . He hammered the .45 against the steering wheel as he drove.

"It's my .38, and I want it! It's mine! I just loaned it to you! You have to give it back to me!"

"Okay. Here it is."

She saw a bit of blood on it, and carefully wiped it with a Kleenex tissue before handing it to him.

"Thank you," he said. He dropped the .45 to the seat and took the .38 from her, and in that same moment slammed on the brakes. At the speed he was going, the pickup skidded for two hundred yards, fishtailing all over both lanes of the road before coming to a full stop in the middle of the two lane blacktop.

Kate was thrown forward, slamming her head against the front windshield. She found herself thinking Chester was about to shoot her. There was a little impact star in the glass where her head had connected with it, but Chester didn't seem to notice.

"What? What is it?" she managed to sputter.

"Red Rock Canyon," Chester said as calmly as if he was delivering a small pepperoni pizza. "You're here."

He gestured out the window at a large sign that announced in big black letters, "NEW! Home of the Red Rock Canyon Haciendas! Get Your Own Little Piece of the Red Rock!"

Kate wrestled the door open and staggered out of the truck. She dragged her backpack after her, and slammed the door. She was weaving a little as she looked in at him.

"Good luck, Miss Twillinger!" Chester called from behind the wheel

"You too, Ches—ahh, Clyde."

He grinned and gave her a proud little salute.

"See ya later, Bonnie!"

The pickup truck pulled away, tires squealing, as Chester moved away from her, heading on down the road in a hurry.

Kate gathered her resolution and limped away from the asphalt road, moving along a dusty, unpaved side-road that cut toward a dark outcropping of cliffs that were towering grey blue under a pale yellow moon that looked like a birch tree woodcut in the starry sky.

After walking for a few minutes, she heard a whine as if a hive of bees had settled in her hair. She looked down at her feet on the dusty path. She shook her head to clear it and the buzzing sound became the distant wail of sirens. It was the police coming from the way Chester had come, and the winking red-and-blue lights approached at high speed..

Kate crouched behind a stand of desert bushes just as a Taft City police car wail by, followed swiftly by a second squad car. Kate shook her head. Things didn't look good for young Clyde. She staggered to her feet and walked on toward the dark cliffs that now loomed directly ahead of her, and as she went she prayed.

"God, he is a confused and mixed-up soul, but somewhere in your heart perhaps you could find the forgiveness to gather him to your breast…"

In the distance, a few miles past where she was, a squeal of brakes was followed by the garbled sounds of police orders barked over a bullhorn. After this, the night air was shattered by the stuttering bark of an automatic rifle, the *pam! pam! pam!* of a single shot revolver, and then a fusillade of gunshots. Chester, also known as Clyde, was making his last stand.

CHAPTER THIRTY-SIX

just another one of life's little lessons

Dawn came quietly to the Mojave desert, but Harley the desert tortoise had already been up a few hours, scrounging around for green bushes and scraps of French fries along the side of the trail. Actually, he'd found a few battered scraps from a Western Bacon Cheeseburger on the road itself, and was tracking down the last smear when something approached in the distance, traveling at high speed. There might have been some irony if Harley the tortoise had been run over by Harley the motorbike, but that is the sort of thing that only God knows, and he is generally too busy to stop for a chuckle. The biker himself, seated low on his speeding thrown, had time to huck an empty beer can in the tortoise's direction and yell, "Get off the road, turtle!"

Harley looked up as the silvery Coors can bounced off his shell. He blinked once, but did nothing else as the metal monster roared by. That is the thing about being a turtle—if anything shows up that is big and fast and dangerous, chances are you are dead anyway, so why make a fuss? He moved not a muscle, watching with waning interest out of the one eye pointed in the right direction as the biker roared off into the distance.

After that, Harley ambled back to the side of the road from which he'd come. Here, the area was littered with fast food junk, plastic containers, used condoms and other litter marking the passage of mankind. As he moved some yards further away, the roadside debris was replaced by low scrub brush and little sandy stretches. It was going to be a scorcher, but he wasn't worried. He had some hours yet to reach the cool shade of Red Rock cliffs.

He plodded along in a steady course, heading for a space in the lower cliffs where there was a little crawl space. He knew he would be able to spend the day there dreaming of a lush valley where the leaves were big as acorns and sweet as honey, and where water actually stood around in puddles, begging to be drunk. And that was when a shadow moved across his shell, blocking his sunlight, and he heard a voice exclaim, "Hello! My, my, my—what have we here?"

Harley looked up and it seemed to him as if he was beset upon by a shaggy-headed giant, probably a female of her species, judging by her mammilla. It was just Kate, but he didn't know that. He only knew when she talked he could understand her.

"Please hold it down," he grumped. "I'm trying to catch a few Z's and a few rays here."

Of course, nothing could be further from the truth. It being the time of year it was, he had all the Z's and rays he needed. In fact, any more and he might go into sunstroke.

"My gracious," Kate said, "An ice turtle!"

"Stop talking like an old maid," Harley said. "And I'm not an ice turtle. There is no such thing.

"Sure there is...you're left over from the Ice Age. You're a rare and almost extinct species!"

"Am not! Am not! AM NOT!" he cried, back-peddling a bit for fear she might have a net or some other sort of tortoise trap with her.

"This is very exciting!"

"What a mess you are! Lady, I'm a common, ordinary desert tortoise."

"When's the last time you bumped beaks with a mating partner?"

"What, a sweet-lipped girl turtle? Must have been ten years ago."

"And?"

"And nothing. Mandy was run over by a BMW 530i. Harley shook his head sadly. "Street pizza…"

"My God, what a tragedy for all of nature."

"Yeah. Sometimes life sucks."

Kate took off her backpack and sat next to the tortoise, who looked a bit dirty and dusty, like he might need a bath or two. She held her head in both hands, grimacing a bit as she looked down at the ground.

"What happened to you?" Harley asked.

"Somebody hit me a bunch of times."

"Well, that happens," the tortoise said as he started to amble off. Those cliffs weren't getting any closer with him out here in the sun jawing with a crazy person.

"Wait. You look really old."

"Well, yeah. I am old," Harley said, pausing for a moment. Talking about himself was about the only thing he really would have stopped for. "Centuries…maybe even a millennium or two. We don't show our age much."

“So you know this area, right?”

Harley eyed her backpack, “You’re not going to stick me in there, are you?

“Don’t be ridiculous. I’m just part of a survey to protest the new condos they want to build here.”

“Condos?” That got Harley’s attention and he turned in a little half-circle so he could give her the glimp one eye, the expression tortoises used over the millennium to freeze their prey.

“Yes, and I’m afraid that will not do. We build condos here, we have to rip all this up. That puts you out of a home.”

Harley thought of something and his eyes widened a bit. “Would they have swimming pools?”

“Yes, probably—but that doesn’t matter.

“And garbage cans? There’s nothing wrong with a garbage can raid, long as you don’t fall in.

“What matters is that you are an endangered species.”

“Well, I’m not. I’m Harley of the desert, as common as prairie chickens or sand lizards.”

Kate’s disappointment was hard to hide. She impatiently stood and looked around, shielding her eyes from the sun as her gaze swept over the barren landscape. “You know, mankind has been entrusted with the guardianship of the world.”

“By who? O, sorry, by whom?”

Kate took a drink from her half empty water bottle. “Don’t be silly,” she said. “Okay, granting you may not be totally endangered, are there any other endangered creatures around here.”

Harley seemed to be pondering it. He looked like he might scratch his head if only his front foot would reach.

"Well, we had some little sand fish, but I haven't seen any for a decade or so."

"Sand fish! That would be incredible! Do you think any of them survived?"

"A few of them did, but I ate them. I think I got them all."

Kate's frown deepened. This was going to be harder than she'd thought. "That's exactly what I'm talking about, you greedy little turtle."

"Tor-toise," Harley reminded her.

"You should have saved them, to preserve the natural balance."

"Come on," Harley grumped. "I was hungry. What do you expect?"

But Kate was ignoring him again, squinting off into the distance. He saw her stagger a bit, as if she might fall over and die right there on the sand. He felt sorry for her, actually. She had that St. Francis vulnerability about her, and, after all, she was the only human he'd ever talked to.

"How about the yellow stick flower plant?" he asked. "Do plants count?"

She snapped out of her reverie, "Why yes, that would be a very rare find!"

"Well, we got some of those," Harley grumped. "They're close by, too." What's the harm, he was thinking. I'll get her to run over that hill right over there and that will be the end of it.

"You must take me to them," she said.

"Well, no, that ain't going to happen."

"You must, you must!" she shrieked happily. "We will stop this project!"

He started to firm up his no, but she glanced from him to her backpack, and he could see she was calculating the odds of flipping him in there.

"Okay," he growled, "but I'm not very swift of foot…"

They must have walked for an hour, and all the time the sun climbed higher in the sky and the temperature rose until Harley started to believe he was roasting in his own shell.

"Come on, turtle—keep it moving! I don't want to die out here…how much further?'

"Aww, keep your shirt on. Not far now."

It was a beautiful, desolate area, well back from the picnic tables next to the paved roads. Harley nodded his head, indicating a brushy area.

"There it is. What do you think?"

Kate could hardly contain her disappointment. "You miserable little crooked, conniving turtle!"

"What? What did I do?"

"This is just an ordinary Screw Bean Mesquite!"

Harley bit of the tip of one of the branches and chewed thoughtfully, "Prosopis Pubescens? I don't think so. Tastes a little different to me."

Kate gave the plant a second look. "Well…It could be a sub-species."

"It's rare, alright. I never tasted another one like it. I'm going to call it Tortoisus Pubescens."

Kate gave him a scornful look, "You cannot name a plant after yourself!"

"Why not? You people do it all the time."

"You just can't, that's why…say, this plant is a little different. Huh, a rare sub-species—that would frost those stupid developers!

"Ah...lady. Lady. Well. It doesn't matter – the real yellow stick flower plant is over there."

Kate gave him a look that could kill. "You miserable—rotten—awful…" But turning in the direction Harley indicated she saw the new plant, which was indeed something wonderful, "Wonderful—incredible—magnificent!"

As Kate gazed in awe at this never before seen species of plant life, Harley reached his beak toward the strange branches of what he called his yellow stick flower plant.

"I like to eat the fresh little buds."

And to her sudden alarm, he nipped off one of the yellow flowers and began to munch.

"Nooo!! You mustn't!!"

She lunged to stop him, but in her haste tripped over a large rock and found herself tumbling to lie under a shower of rocks and boulders. When the rockslide ended, one of her legs was firmly wedged between several large sandstone boulders.

"My God, my God, the pain! Help me!"

Harley didn't move a muscle. His face was expressionless as he studied her dilemma.

"Come on," she pleaded, "I'm stuck! I can't get out of here! Say something! Do something! Oh, my God, My God, my God!

Instead of helping her, Harley turned as if he was about to leave the scene.

"Wait! Stop! Where are you going?"

Harley paused for a moment. "It's not good to hang out with the weakest in the pack."

"Pack? There's no pack here!"

Harley thought about it for a moment, mulling things over in his steady and deliberate way. "Even worse," he said. And he continued his slow exit.

"But I was going to save you! I was going to save you...you miserable, ungrateful little turtle...

"Tor-toise," Harley said over the corner of his shell as he crawled around the corner of a boulder and was gone, heading back for the sandstone cliffs of Red Rock Canyon.

Trapped as she was, Kate could examine the branches of the yellow stick flower plant, but the pain in her leg was intense and her mind drifted.

She spoke in a low chant, "Cambrian, Ordovecian, Silurian, Devonian...Triassic, Jurassic, Cretaceous..." As dusk settled, she was still alone, still trapped under the rock, and still chanting, "Australopithecus Robustus...Homo Erectus...Homo Sapiens..."

Kate was just a small dot of flesh against the backdrop of stark cliffs. Not more than a mile away, trucks and cars were rushing by on the paved asphalt road, but it was clear nobody was going to find her here.

But she was not alone. Blended into the natural cover of the brush, a wild western desert coyote raised his face to the moon and howled. He sniffed the air and then trotted across the ravine to where Kate lay.

He snarled at her, but she simply stared back at him.

"Why aren't you afraid of me?" he asked.

"You only eat dead meat.

"I could help you along in that direction."

"You won't."

"Huh." The coyote sat on his haunches and stared at her. "So you're the new, advanced species that's going to save us?"

"Doesn't look like it."

"Right. So what do you do—just give up before you've really started?"

"I—I'm trapped here!"

"You don't really want to get out."

"You're like my pal, Cheap-Trick Jesu—you know everything about everything."

"I know survival," the coyote said.

"Of course I want to get out, you stupid—animal!"

"No you don't. You think you're going to burn in hell anyway, so what's the use?"

Kate was about to shout back some retort, but instead she bit her lip and looked away. "That's not exactly it," she said in a small voice.

"Yes, it is. Look, you killed a couple of twisted creatures who were going to kill you. That's a wash, sister – no sin there.

"I'm not damned for all eternity?"

"Afraid not—No hell-fire for you! That's a bad imitation of Jerry Seinfeld's Soup Nazi, in case you don't know."

"So I've heard."

The coyote began to pace back and forth impatiently. "Alrighty now. You can do this, but it's going to hurt."

Kate braced herself and strained to pull her leg free. She tugged and pulled. The skin of her leg ripped and her blood flowed onto the sandy desert floor and still she couldn't pull herself free.

"I'm too weak."

"Of course you are. Weak human."

"I can't."

"Of course you can't. Pathetic female."

"I don't have it in me."

The coyote grinned, "Hell is knowing in the next life that you didn't try hard enough in this one."

Kate's expression darkened. She gave a mighty lunge and somehow, impossibly, came free from under the rocks. She lay panting but free, trying to collect her energy.

"Thank you."

"Better get up. You're starting to look tasty."

Kate staggered to her feet. "No meat for you!"

"That's a good topper," the coyote nodded.

In a ravine nearby, Fritz Harper hurriedly unloaded a mortar tube from the back door of his refurbished taco truck and yelled at Ollie, who was fussing around in the dim interior of the cab.

"She's trapped, man! I need backup, right now!"

Ollie poked his head out of a side window, "Fritzie-boy, give me a minute, I'm on the porta-pottie. Just go it Viet Cong style."

"What's that?"

"One man band. Wrap a dish rag around the tube, jam it in the ground by your foot and drop the round in yourself. It's easier than jacking off."

Fritz looked doubtfully at the unassembled parts of the mortar, the base and the tripod which contained the elevation meter.

"Will it work?"

"It did for Ho Chi Minh and his merry men. But you better hurry. First light's coming and we want to be out of here. I think the California conservation people are big time against blowing up the desert."

Fritz did as Ollie had instructed, but the whole procedure seemed awkward and foolish to him. He spread his legs wide and placed the bottom end of the olive colored mortar tube against the instep of one of his army boots, but he was off-balance as he dropped one of the fat shells in the opening at the top.

"Not that way, you fool!" Ollie yelled. "The fins go in first!"

But his warning came too late. The front tip of the mortar shell slid easily to the bottom of the tube where the detonation fuse hit with a little clink. Ollie realized the shell must be one of the penetration missiles with a five second delay. "Dive for cover!"

Both men rolled over a small hump in the sand as the explosion took out the taco truck. Since the truck contained enough hardware and ammo to supply a heavy squad of a dozen or so men, pre-dawn on the Mohave was treated to a fireworks spectacular.

"I was starting to like that motor vehicle," Ollie sighed.

"We'll get another one."

"Something different. I think we've blown our cover on taco wagons."

"Yeah, maybe a plumber's van."

They threw out their thumbs, hitch-hiking back toward Mojave. It was hard, with Fritz in his desert camo fatigues and skinny Ollie in briefs and a Polish t-shirt, but they finally caught a ride in a big truck carrying a load of pigs, standing in back with the oinkers, and were back at their hotel room in town by nightfall.

Heading in the other direction, the light of the new day found Kate limping north along the side of the road with the coyote following after her.

"I met one of your wild brothers out there last night."

"Yeah, I heard the yodeling."

"You don't have to tag along anymore," she said.

"Hey, you might get hit by a bus or something," the coyote grinned.

"Don't count on it, fur-boy…"

A soft and friendly voice at her side confided, "There's a Del Taco a few miles ahead. Classic Chicken Burritos to die for."

"Wondered where you were hiding, Chicken-heart Jesu."

"Don't be so nasty, Kate," Jesus said. He was wearing his halo at a jaunty angle over a pork-pie hat, and he'd traded his robe for hiking boots, shorts and a Hawaiian shirt with sprays of what might have been palm trees or maryjane leaves surrounding, of course, his precious sacred heart.

"Can I have my powers back now?

"You never lost them?"

"What? I nearly died a couple of times."

"Never let anyone trick you out of your strength. That's the lesson."

Jesus nodded, and she speeded up just a little to test if he was right.

"Where's the nearest post office?"

"Up ahead, up ahead, oh ye of little faith. I gather you're going to mail in the special twig you've found."

"Hey, give me a chew of that," the coyote said.

"Not a chance. I'm telling you, dog-face, hold out for the chicken burritos. Big Jesu here says they're worth it."

"Yeah, yeah, you advanced species, all promise but no show," the coyote grumbled, but even as he spoke he backed off.

"I got show, coyote," Kate said. "I got plenty of show."

Jesus nodded in agreement. "That you do, Kate." He placed his arm briefly on her shoulder. Her aches and pains began to diminish and the cuts, bruises and swelling to miraculously fade from her face.

As they walked on down the road, anyone might have heard Kate and Jesus singing a chunky calypso song, with the coyote howling every once in a while in the chorus.

It don't matter no how no mo'
Close out de light / an'open de do'
One thing begin / the other end
Only 'portant/ we be friend'
Cause it don't matter no how no mo'
No, it don' matter no mo'

Too soon old / an' too late smart
Dat's d' way of d' human heart.
Too soon old / an' too late smart
Dat's d' way of d' human heart.

"By the way, Kate," Jesus Jinx asked, "You have any idea what's next?"

"Actually, I think I do. Have you ever heard of Santa Barbella Island?"

"Well, yes, but…"

"We're going there to free my lawyer…if we can."

"The one who is supposed to become your lover?" Jesus asked.

"Hey, stop reading ahead."

"I thought I was supposed to be your lover," the coyote frowned.

"That was my mother, fur-boy. You should try to keep the players straight."

"It's hard when you're immortal," he grumbled.

“Is that what we are now?” Kate gave Jesus a troubled look.

“No, just us,” Jesus said, causing the hearts on his shirt to wink like LED Christmas ornaments as he pointed to himself and the coyote.

“Well, what about me?”

“That’s to be determined,” Jesus said.

“By what?”

“Well, try putting on more of a God-like attitude; that might help.”

“Like how?” Kate asked, not at all liking the sound of it.

“Well, throw back your shoulders, don’t slouch so much.”

“I do not slouch even a little bit!”

“Do, too.”

“Do not.”

And so bickering they wandered down the road toward the fast food place that served excellent but inexpensive Mexican fare while somewhere in the clouds overhead a chorus of angels might have been singing…

'Fucious, Plato / play your part
Teach me know / d' human heart
Fly the moon an' to a star
Hyper-drive an' kick dis place
So long to d' human race
Too much mass / me fallin' down
Do it over / mad fool clown.
You fail de bar/ you big disgrace.
You fail de bar / you big disgrace.

Too soon old / an' too late smart

Can't seem to find/ d' human heart
Too soo old / an' too late smart
Dat's de way of the human heart.

Buddha, Jesus / Help me please
Give me heart / some anti-freeze.
I could live a thousan' year
Find my light an lose my fear.
But I only got today
Run d' sun an dance an play
Oh, give me light to see d' way
To run d' sun / an' dance an' play
An' dance away
An' dance away
An' dance away....

www.ingramcontent.com/pod-product-compliance
Lightning Source LLC
LaVergne TN
LVHW030908080826
845145LV00010B/2807

* 9 7 8 1 7 8 6 9 5 5 9 1 3 *